T0356677

MURDER
BETWEEN
FRIENDS

MURDER

BETWEEN

FRIENDS

LIZ LAWSON

DELACORTE PRESS

Text copyright © 2025 by Liz Lawson
Cover art copyright © 2025 by Sasha Vinogradova

All rights reserved. Published in the United States by Delacorte Press, an imprint of Random House Children's Books, a division of Penguin Random House LLC, New York.

Delacorte Press is a registered trademark and the colophon is a trademark of Penguin Random House LLC.

Visit us on the Web! GetUnderlined.com

Educators and librarians, for a variety of teaching tools, visit us at RHTeachersLibrarians.com

Library of Congress Cataloging-in-Publication Data
Names: Lawson, Liz, author.
Title: Murder between friends / Liz Lawson.
Description: First edition. | New York : Delacorte Press, 2025. | Audience term: Teenagers |
Audience: Ages 14+ | Summary: Told in three voices, Grace questions her eyewitness testimony that convicted Henry's brother in a murder trial, leaving former childhood friends Henry and Ally no choice but to join forces with her to prove Jake's innocence.
Identifiers: LCCN 2024005102 (print) | LCCN 2024005103 (ebook) |
ISBN 978-0-593-30103-6 (hardcover) | ISBN 978-0-593-30106-7 (trade paperback) |
ISBN 978-0-593-30104-3 (ebook)
Subjects: CYAC: Trials (Murder)—Fiction. | Witnesses—Fiction. | Interpersonal relations—
Fiction. | Mystery and detective stories. | LCGFT: Detective and mystery fiction. | Novels.
Classification: LCC PZ7.1.G587 Mu 2025 (print) | LCC PZ7.1.G587 (ebook) | DDC [Fic]—dc23

The text of this book is set in 12-point Spectrum MT.
Interior design by Ken Crossland

Printed in the United States of America
10 9 8 7 6 5 4 3 2 1
First Edition

Random House Children's Books supports the First Amendment and celebrates the right to read.

To my Kowit boys

ALLY

OCTOBER 6

"HOW DO YOU FEEL, knowing they're letting a killer out of jail today?"

I'm getting out of my car when the question is screamed at me through the chain-link fence that runs the perimeter of school. I turn to find a reporter, young and fresh-faced, staring at me with excited eyes from the other side of the metal weave.

She must not know who I am.

I clench my keys in my fist, the sharp edges digging into the tender flesh of my palm, as I hold eye contact with her. Trying to figure out what to do. What to say. How far I want to take this.

A few beats go by, and her smile begins to droop.

"Jake Hanson?" she offers, like I might not know what she's talking about. "He's being released later today? After serving only"—a pause here, as she scrambles to remember—"thirteen months of his twenty-five-to-life sentence. He's headed back. To Brawner. How does that make you feel—"

I slam my car door shut, heart thudding against my rib cage. Walk over to her slowly. Anger vibrating off me so hard that I'm surprised she can't feel it—that she doesn't run away.

"Most people in town are very unhappy." This lady just can't quit. She's clearly misinterpreted my silence as ignorance. "The decision to vacate his sentence is enormously controversial—as you probably know," she adds hurriedly, like she's remembered that I might not be entirely stupid. "Considering it was based on a technicality, rather than evidence of Jake's innocence . . . how does it make you feel? You're a student at Brawner High. Did you know Miriam Appelbaum? Or Jake? Did *you* know *Jake*? Did you see the fight they had that day?"

I stop on my side of the chain-link fence. She leans forward expectantly. She thinks I'm about to make her day, give her a great quote she can use in her broadcast. Tell her how *terrified* I am that Jake's coming home. How violent he was.

"Listen to me," I hiss at her. "Jake Hanson is innocent. Got it? He didn't murder anyone. You can quote me."

And with that, I walk away.

The hallways inside are buzzing with energy. Bad energy. The sort that comes before a riot, before people start burning things down. Everyone on edge.

Someone crashes into me, and when they see who I am, their apology crumbles. Instead, they mutter, "Killer fucker."

I've been called worse, and it's not remotely true, yet it still takes all my willpower not to respond. But I can't. I can't give them the satisfaction—not because I don't want to, but because Henry made me promise. He knows me too well, and he said today more than any other day, I have to let things slide.

It hurts, but I do it. I let the asshole walk away, keep my head down, enter my first-period Spanish class without another incident.

I spend the period on my phone. Senora De Hoyos doesn't even notice, or at least she doesn't really care—no one's paying attention as it is—and so I'm left in peace to read awful things that people are saying about my best friend and his family on the internet.

Everyone is screaming about how horrible it is that Jake's being released, how he's a murderer, how this is a travesty of the justice system. There are a ton of articles on what are essentially tabloid news sites, full of misinformation and inflammatory rhetoric about Jake and Henry and the entire Hanson family. The sort of exploitative journalism my dad always used to rant about—it's all about the clicks.

I've been trying to keep an eye on it. Report the most violent comments. Make sure no one has posted the Hansons' address in public forums, like they did after Jake's arrest almost two years ago.

I tell myself what I'm doing matters, but I know I'm wrong. The comments are never taken down.

And everyone already knows where the Hansons live.

"Ally?" A voice cuts into my doomscrolling.

Taylor Rudloff, assistant editor of the *Boar*, the school paper, is standing in front of my desk.

"What?" Can't she see I'm busy?

"Um," she says, staring at me, hip jutted to the side, radiating judgment. "Period's over?"

I look around. Sure enough, everyone's gone, outside of Taylor and Señora De Hoyos, who's sitting behind her desk with her feet propped up on it, her own phone in front of her face.

"Oh," I say, my face heating. I grab my battered textbook and shove it into my bag.

"Are you okay?" Taylor asks, out of a sense of obligation, rather than because she actually cares, I'm sure. We're not exactly the best of friends.

My mouth puckers. "I'm fine."

"You sure? Because you were just sitting there after the bell went off like you didn't even notice . . ."

"I'm fine," I say again, with emphasis, and she rolls her eyes. What does she think—I'm going to tell her how I'm really doing? That all of a sudden I'm going to open up to her? Tell her that I'm worried about Henry, that I've texted him six times today already and haven't heard back? I'm not an idiot. If I did, she'd use it—write a story about it for the paper to try and take my editor in chief position.

"Sure, Ally. Whatever." She hikes her bag farther up her shoulder. "I'll see you later."

———

Out in the hall, I send Henry another message. Nothing long, just saying that I'm here if he needs me. He knows that, though. We've been best friends since preschool, a friendship that's outlasted most everything else. Including our ex–best friend, Grace Topham.

I watch my phone for a long moment, but it's silent. I shouldn't be surprised. Henry's dealing with a dumpster fire.

I make my way to the newspaper office, which, thankfully, is quiet. Everyone else is tucked away in second period, but I'm skipping. I can't deal with sitting through another class; I have more important things to do.

I take my notebook out of my bag and set it on the table in front of me.

It's filled with stuff about Ms. Appelbaum, a timeline of the night she was murdered, Jake, his trial, info from news articles, notes from Reddit boards that talked about the case. I started collecting all of it when it became clear Jake was the cops' prime suspect. I thought maybe I could help him, because I meant what I said to that asshole reporter.

Jake is not a killer.

I mean, this is the same guy who used to lend me books that he liked back when we were in elementary school. He used to capture spiders in his hands and put them outside rather than kill them. Even after he started working at the record store and got all caught up with Nick Marion and those assholes, I saw flickers of his old self.

Like the time a baby bird flew into one of the windows of the Hansons' house and broke its wing. Jake drove an hour each way to take it to a wildlife sanctuary. Or the time Ms. Glasgow, an English teacher, dropped two huge boxes of paperwork all over the first-floor hallway of school.

Jake was one of the only people to stop and help her clean it up.

He couldn't have killed Appelbaum. He doesn't have it in him. And it's beyond messed up that he's spent the past two years behind bars, but I guess we have Grace to thank for that.

Nothing in my notebook tells me anything new. But I reread it anyway, over and over and over again, until my eyes start to ache. Then I slam it shut.

I'm tempted to text Henry again, but I stop myself. I need to give him space.

Instead, I grab my laptop and pull up a YouTube video of the news footage from the day Appelbaum's body was found. Our neighborhood was a circus. News vans everywhere, people from school stopping by, neighbors gaping at the crime scene investigators dressed in white plastic suits going in and out of her house.

I watched it all from my bedroom window. I couldn't even cry. All my tears had been used up two months before, when my dad died.

Even though I've seen all of these videos a million times, I press Play. I know everything by heart—the news reporters' scripts, the shots of Appelbaum's house, our neighborhood, the city of Brawner.

But what I'm interested in is in the background of these shots.

It's a well-known fact that murderers like to visit the

scene of their crimes, so I examine the faces of the people watching from behind the police tape. Try to see if there's anything out of place. Anyone I haven't noticed before.

Because the thing that has been thrumming in the back of my head like a drumbeat for the past two years is this:

If Jake didn't do it, that means whoever did is still out there, walking around, free to kill again.

THE BRAWNER TIMES

Jacob Hanson murder conviction vacated on a technicality
BY KATE CHAKRAVORTY

Jacob Hanson is set to be released today from the western Virginia federal prison where he has been incarcerated since the middle of last year. In a trial that made national news, Hanson was convicted of the first-degree murder of local Brawner High School English teacher Miriam Appelbaum and was sentenced to twenty-five to life behind bars.

But a week ago, a judge approved a motion to vacate Hanson's murder conviction. To explain this controversial decision, Landon

County Circuit Court Judge Andrea Johnson cited evidence unearthed by Hanson's new attorney, Greg Kakova, that proves District Attorney Richard Attia, who prosecuted Hanson's original trial, had been having an affair with Judge Richard Walker, who presided over it.

A new district attorney, Cassie Flynn, was elected on the back of the scandal. The state has thirty days to decide whether it will pursue a new trial, but if Flynn's statement outside the courthouse is any indication, there are already plans to do just that.

DA Flynn said: "Jake Hanson's pending release only proves there were glaring ethical issues with how the original trial was conducted, not that Hanson himself is, in fact, innocent." Mr. Kakova calls his client's impending release a "triumph of the American justice system as a whole."

What to know about the case
On December 15, 2023, Brawner High English teacher Miriam Appelbaum was reported missing by her sister after failing to show up for their weekly brunch.

Two days later, Ms. Appelbaum was discovered inside the freezer in her garage, clutching a rose against her chest. The medical examiner determined blunt force trauma was the cause of death. The case shook the small community of Brawner, VA, and drew the attention of national media outlets.

Police quickly set their sights on then-eighteen-year-old Brawner High School senior Jacob Hanson, whom witnesses had seen fighting with Ms. Appelbaum in a school hallway mere days before her death. According to multiple firsthand accounts, Ms. Appelbaum caught Hanson selling drugs on school grounds and informed him he was headed for expulsion. Hanson lost his temper and, according to several sources, slammed his fist into a locker.

The case began to build against him. Police found hair with DNA matching Hanson's on the carpet in Ms. Appelbaum's living room, and his school notebook was found beneath her couch. The police also traced the IP address of a harassing message sent from an anonymous Instagram account to Ms. Appelbaum to the Hanson household.

That's when Brawner High student and neighbor of the Hansons Grace Topham came forward. She told police she saw Hanson entering Ms. Appelbaum's backyard at 6 p.m. on December 15. He was wearing his jean jacket, a distinctive item of clothing with a large bald eagle sketched on its back.

Hanson claimed innocence, saying his

jacket had been stolen from his car in an attempt to frame him. But, upon a thorough search of the vehicle, police found it under a pile of clothing in the trunk, covered with blood. Subsequent tests showed that the blood matched Ms. Appelbaum's.

This was the final nail in Jake Hanson's coffin.

On January 17, 2024, Hanson was formally charged with the murder and his bail set at $1 million. Later that year, following a two-week trial, a jury convicted Hanson after deliberating for less than three hours.

Kate Chakravorty is a senior news reporter for the Brawner Times. *She can be reached via email at katec@brawnertimes.com.*

HENRY

OCTOBER 6

ALL THE LIGHTS IN the house are off.

My mom insisted. Said it would keep the reporters away, make them think we aren't home. Apparently, our lawyer suggested it. And my mom does whatever Mr. Kakova suggests. I think she's half in love with him at this point, and who can blame her? He's the one who figured out how to spring Jake from prison.

At least for the time being.

From my bedroom window, between a small gap in the curtains, I see the reporters in the street, camped out like they have been since the news of Jake's impending release broke. They're scurrying around like a bunch of cockroaches, setting up for the main event. They don't care that the house is dark; they'll wait for days if it'll get them the money shot.

Jake, arriving home from prison.

Jake, who I haven't laid eyes on in over a year. Jake, who

I never went to visit in federal prison because of my own guilt.

I don't know what to do with myself right now, so I'm falling into old habits. Reading bad stuff about my family on the internet. There's plenty to choose from.

Interest in Jake's case died down over the past year, mostly because there wasn't anything new or noteworthy to report. He was in prison. Case closed.

But that's changed since the announcement of his vacated sentence. There've been more articles written this week alone than in the past six months combined. Which makes sense, considering.

My brother is arriving home today after thirteen months in a federal prison and, before that, eight months in the county jail.

I can hear my mom bustling around downstairs, straightening already straight things, humming under her breath. This is the culmination of nearly two years of hard work on her end. Never giving up hope that someday Jake would come home.

For months after Jake's conviction, we woke up every morning to nasty words spray-painted on the garage, toilet paper hanging in the trees, but my mom refused to move. Even though she lost all of her friends. Even though everyone in this town hates us.

Even though we can see Ms. Appelbaum's house through our back windows.

I tried to get her to leave, tried to tell her we could start over somewhere else, but she wouldn't. She was convinced

Jake would get out someday, and she wanted him to be able to come back to the home he remembered. Everyone else be damned.

I stayed, because where else was I going to go? I certainly wasn't going to go live with my dad—he's a dickhead who only cares about himself.

An arriving text distracts me from the article I was reading about my brother.

Before I can stop myself, I tap it.

It's from a blocked number, and it reads *Your murderer brother better watch his back.*

I'm actually surprised whoever sent it didn't sign it. It's not like anyone bothers to disguise the fact that they want Jake dead.

The message is a good reminder that regardless of what the courts say, regardless of the fact that the previous prosecution and judge might have conspired to convict a totally innocent person, people still believe my brother is a cold-blooded killer.

I don't, though. Never did. Jake is many things, but a murderer is not one of them.

There's a knock on my bedroom door.

"Henry?"

My mom.

I reluctantly shut my computer. "Yeah?"

"It's time to go." There are tears in her voice. Happy tears, I think. A new thing. "Greg should be here any minute. Your father is—"

I tense, waiting for the inevitable insult.

"—meeting us there." She finishes her sentence without slighting him. Another new thing.

"Coming." I slide off my bed, grab my sneakers, then follow her down the stairs.

I still haven't figured out what I'm going to say to my brother.

GRACE

OCTOBER 6

MY MOM'S IN THE kitchen, watching the live stream from the prison as she chops vegetables. On-screen, a reporter is excitedly rehashing the events of the past two years.

She snaps off the TV when she sees me.

"Grace," she says guiltily, like I caught her watching porn. "Did you just get home?"

I nod, drained. School today was a mess: reporters clogging up the entrance to the parking lot trying to get quotes, no one paying attention in class. All anyone could talk about was Jake, and every time they did, I could feel their eyes on my face. I spent most of my day pretending that I didn't notice, but it's exhausting, pretending.

"How is it out there?" my mom asks.

She's not talking about the weather. When Meghan pulled onto my street, we were greeted by news vans sitting in front of Appelbaum's place.

I drop my bag onto a stool. "Not too bad. Only a couple parked across the street getting shots of the house."

My mom shakes her head. "This is exactly why we've been pushing for her sister to sell the place. It's just sitting there, untouched. It's a total spectacle. If they'd sold it, there wouldn't be any reason for those reporters to be on our street. They'd be over on Hawthorn where they belong."

My cheeks heat up at the mention of Henry's street. I'm sure most of them *are* over there, waiting for Jake's big return.

"I recognize it's painful, but honestly, it's been *two years*," my mom grumbles as she turns back to her vegetables. "It's creepy. Better to sell. Let a developer bulldoze the place, build something new."

Yes, it's sort of creepy. Maybe more than sort of. But I think I get it.

If I were Appelbaum's sister, I wouldn't be able to confront the ghosts in that house either.

It's one of those old one-story brick houses that have mostly disappeared from Brawner by now. Appelbaum inherited it from her grandparents, who lived there for decades—way before my family moved to the neighborhood—and moved in after she started teaching at Brawner High. She only lived there for two years before she was killed.

My mom seems to remember she didn't actually ask how I'm doing. She puts down the knife again. "They left you alone?"

I nod. "They didn't see me."

"Good." She sighs. "I can't believe this is happening to

us. Again. What a mess. Everyone knows he did it. . . . This is only going to cause chaos. *Him*, back here in this neighborhood, after everything . . . it's absolutely disgusting. Your dad and I are talking about hiring a security company to watch our house. In case he tries something . . ." Her lips press together white. "God forbid."

Behind my temples, the incessant, pounding pain that started last night at the party picks back up. "I read that if they officially decide to retry him, he'll have to wear an ankle bracelet. In the meantime, I'll be fine. He's not going to do anything."

I don't know if I'm saying this to make her feel better, or myself.

"You can't be sure about that—" she starts, and I can't take it anymore. I'm going to scream if I have to say one more word about Jake Hanson.

I interrupt. "Can we please talk about something else?"

Her lips dip into a frown, but she nods. "Sorry, yes. Of course."

There's a pause while she struggles to think about what else we could *possibly* talk about other than the One Thing everyone's talked about nonstop for two years.

"Evan and your sister should be here soon. They're coming over for dinner to chat about wedding stuff."

"They're coming over *tonight*?" I sound judgmental, but, like, really? The neighborhood's a zoo and Jake's getting out of prison and . . . they want to talk about their wedding?

My mom's shoulders stiffen. "It's not ideal timing, but Lara needs to hammer out the final details. It's in a few weeks. And it's not like we're close to the Hansons."

Anymore, I think. My mom and Mrs. Hanson used to be good friends, but they haven't spoken since I told the cops what I saw that night. Another friendship destroyed by this mess.

"What's happening with Jake shouldn't overshadow the most important day in your sister's life. The show must go on, as they say. You'll be here?" She says this like it's a question, but I know it's not. Without waiting for my reply, she turns and heads to the fridge.

"Where else would I be?" I mutter at her back.

Lara is seven years older than me, and everyone's favorite. Literally everyone's—not just our parents', but teachers at our high school, old coaches. Growing up, she was the golden child and I was . . . well, sometimes I wonder if I was a mistake.

When you think about it, eight years is a long time to wait to have another kid.

When I was little, Lara was more of a second mother to me than a big sister. Our mom worked full-time, so Lara was the one who'd take care of me after school, make me dinner, even put me to bed some nights. She was my hero.

That said, she was out of the house before I got my first period, and graduating college before I had my first kiss. Sometimes it feels like she still thinks I'm eight years old. She moved back to Brawner a few years ago to go to law school down in DC, and the way she treats me really hasn't changed from when I was little, even though I'm basically an adult. She still bosses me around, and I still let her, mostly because she's usually right.

I mean, I can barely stay on top of my schoolwork and

social life, and Lara is not only a second-year law student but is also interning twenty hours a week at a local law firm. She has her life together in a way I never will.

It's annoying that we're going to have to spend dinner talking about the wedding, but at least I'll be able to ask her all the questions running through my mind. The ones I've been too afraid to talk about, for fear people will think I'm sympathizing with a murderer and start spreading rumors about me. Which they absolutely would. People have been fanatical about Jake's guilt right from the start.

Before Jake was even formally charged, someone had started a social media campaign they called *Convict Jake Hanson*. It spread like wildfire. First, local media caught wind of it, then it was picked up by the AP and got national attention. There were rallies outside the police station, and massive ones outside the courthouse during the trial. Even before the jury went into deliberations, public opinion had solidified into fact: Jake Hanson was guilty.

I have to admit, it affected me, too. Made me more certain I had seen him that night, that I had done the right thing by going to the authorities with what I knew.

But what if I was wrong?

What if, because I accepted public opinion as absolute truth, I ended up putting an innocent person behind bars?

"Just making sure." My mom starts taking food out of the fridge, setting Tupperware containers on the island in the middle of our kitchen. "I'm doing pasta; how does that sound?"

"Great," I say, distracted by a message that's just arrived on my phone from a number I don't know.

A group message to a bunch of random numbers, and it reads: *Meet in the back lot of the 7-11 tomorrow before school. Hanson is a monster and needs to be stopped*

What the hell?

The only number on the chain I have saved in my phone is Tim Martinez's, which does not bode well.

Responses immediately start to pour in:

Thx god someone said it.

IN

Yes!!! theyre letting a MURDERER out of prison and they expect us to just sit here and do nothing??

I'll be there

And then one from Tim: *Grace you're on this chain. You saw him that night!! How could they do this when you SAW him outside her house??*

I drop the phone onto the kitchen counter with a clatter, stomach turning. Why did he have to out me to everyone?

Can't they all just leave me alone?

"Everything okay?" my mom asks, concerned.

I flip my phone face down, hands shaking.

"Fine. Yes. Everything is fine."

Lara and Evan arrive a short while later. Evan, as usual, looks stressed, with deep purple circles under his eyes.

The two of them come over to the house frequently, but

usually it's for Sunday dinner. They're far too busy to stop by during the week, at least normally. Lara's either at work or school, and Evan works about seventy hours a week at his family's commercial real estate company. Right now Evan's dad runs it, but it's not exactly a secret that Evan hopes to take over one day.

Evan's family, the Millers, have lived in Brawner for generations. Back in the mid-1980s, Evan's grandpa started the company, and according to my parents they now control about half the property in town. Plus, a bunch of Evan's relatives work for the town—cousins on the police force, an uncle who's the fire chief. . . . It's a little incestuous, if you ask me.

He and Lara both went to Brawner HS, but they barely knew each other back then. He was a senior when she was a freshman. Apparently, he was *the* guy, the one people fawned over and either wanted to be like or wanted to date. One of Evan's cousins is a sophomore right now, and people treat him the same way. All because of the Miller name.

When Lara moved back home after college, she and Evan ran into each other and started dating. They got serious a few months later and the rest is history.

They're cute together, I guess, but sometimes I think he must have imprinted on her back in high school. To be honest, Evan isn't exactly who I envisioned for my sister. Sure, he's tall and handsome, but he's also a total nepo baby.

I guess I'm just not as impressed by his family legacy as everyone else. His whole life has been scripted for him from the start and as far as I can tell, he spends most of his time worrying about disappointing his dad.

My dad finally makes an appearance in the kitchen, announcing himself with a loud *"Hello!"* Evan jumps, spilling the glass of water my mom just handed him all over the floor.

"Shoot. I'm so sorry," he says. "It's been a long day."

"It's no problem, honey." My mom grabs a dish towel and squats to mop up the wet spots.

"Have things calmed down out there?" My dad pulls a bottle of wine out of the fridge. "I caught the last bit of the evening news, and it looked like a bunch of reporters are stationed outside the Hansons'. I guess Jake should be arriving home any minute."

"They're still there," Lara says.

"Ridiculous, isn't it? That they're letting him out?" my dad says, an echo of all the people at the party last night, of the people on that horrible group message. Of everyone in this stupid town.

"Dad—" I say, but stop myself. I'm too tired to argue. There's no point. If I defend Jake, he'll look at me like I've suddenly sprouted a second head.

Instead, I turn to Lara. "Can I talk to you for a sec?"

"Sure." She glances at Evan. "I'll be right back?"

He nods.

"What's up?" she asks me once we're settled on the family room couch. "How are you holding up? I was going to check in, but, you know . . ."

"Wedding stuff?" I ask.

These days, it's always wedding stuff.

"Yeah. It's in less than three weeks!" she says, voice tight with nerves, and I realize it's not just Evan who's stressed.

Lara's white button-down blouse, normally ironed within an inch of its life, is wrinkled, and there's a small stain on the upper thigh of her pin-striped pants. Even her blond hair is less shiny than usual. "But that doesn't matter right now. Are *you* okay?"

"I just . . ." I trail off. I'm not sure how to broach the subject, even with my sister, so I decide to plunge right in. "Jake getting out . . . it's messing with my head a little. I keep wondering . . . did I make a mistake? Did I not actually see him that night? Did I put someone who was innocent behind bars for two *years*?"

Confusion furrows Lara's brow. "What do you mean? You know his sentence getting vacated doesn't mean he's innocent, right? He'll be back in prison in no time."

"Yeah, but . . ." The expression on her face makes me stop.

What am I doing? I know what she's going to say—the same thing our parents would say, the same thing all my friends at school would say. The same thing the jury said.

Jake is guilty.

So, I backtrack.

"I don't know what I mean, really. I'm just worried." I don't have to fake the tears that pool in the corners of my eyes.

Lara considers me for a moment, then wraps me in a hug. "You have such a big heart, Gracie. I'm sorry this is happening. But think: My wedding is so soon, and it's going to be amazing, right? Concentrate on the good things."

I sniff a breath into her shoulder. "Okay. I will."

She pulls back, holding me by the arms. "Are you sure?

Are you nervous about him coming home? Being so close by? I'm happy to talk more."

Another reminder that soon Jake will be living only a few hundred yards from where I sleep. But as I consider my sister's question, I realize I'm not afraid, because I can't imagine him hurting me.

Which is weird, right? I'm no therapist, but if I really had seen him that night, wouldn't something in my subconscious remember? Wouldn't I be freaking out?

I force a smile before responding. "No, no, it's fine. I really am okay. I'll be in for dinner in one sec, just going to use the bathroom."

"Okay. I love you."

I get up, leaving Lara alone on the couch. I can feel her eyes on me, watching, as I head out of the room.

ALLY

OCTOBER 7

I'VE BARELY MADE IT through the front door of the school when Ari Wong runs up, breathless. Ari is news editor for the school paper and they are *extremely* fond of gossip.

"Have you seen Henry's locker?" they ask, bent in half, hands on their thighs.

"I haven't," I say, immediately on edge.

"It's *bad*," Ari replies, and I take off.

There's a huge crowd in front of the locker. People chatting excitedly, guys jumping up and down, trying to get a better view. I push through the mob, and as people spot me, they fall silent.

"It's *her*," someone whispers.

"Yup. It's *me*," I say, voice dripping with sarcasm. She blinks at me, a terrified animal caught in my headlights. I push by her without another word. It's not worth it. I stopped giving a crap what these people think of me a very long time ago. They're all such hypocrites.

Like Sam Giles, standing across the way, staring at me with dagger eyes. He used to be Henry's good friend but literally hasn't said a word to either of us in the past two years. Dick.

I arrive at the front of the crowd at the same time as Vice Principal Patout. She lets out a loud gasp.

Black-and-white photos of Appelbaum—both dead and alive—are papered all over the front of Henry's locker and the lockers nearby, and the word MURDERER is spray-painted in red across them.

I don't know where whoever did this found Appelbaum's autopsy photos, but they're horrifying.

"Who did this?" Patout shouts at the crowd, furious. You'd think the school administration would have prepared for things to get bad again once Jake was released, but Patout seems shocked. Then again, the pictures are shocking.

I storm up to Henry's locker and start pulling down handfuls of paper, ripping them in half and crumpling them into little balls. Thank God he stayed home again today; he doesn't need to see this.

Behind me, someone says, "I cannot believe they let an actual *murderer* out of jail." I whirl around to find Macey Brown and one of her dumb friends.

"What do you not understand about the criminal justice system?" I spit at them. "Jake is out of prison for a *reason*. Maybe all you idiots should concentrate on what's important. Did any of you ever think about the fact that if Jake didn't do it, that means whoever did might still be roaming around town?"

Macey snorts and nudges her friend. "We all know Jake *did* do it, though. You're the only dumbass who doesn't."

"All right, girls, that's quite enough." Patout steps between us. "Macey, it's time for you to head to class. And the rest of you too. First period starts in two minutes—get moving!"

The crowd disperses. Without all the bodies crowding around it, the vandalism of Henry's locker is even more stark.

I turn to Patout. "Are you going to figure out who did this? This is disgusting."

She sighs. "Ally, I wish I could, but I don't have the resources to question two thousand kids about their whereabouts this morning. The best I can offer is that we'll have it cleaned up before school tomorrow."

I scowl. This is harassment, plain and simple, and she should do something about it. But I don't bother wasting my breath because I know she can't.

Or won't.

The camera crews are still there, hanging out front of the school; on my way in I saw them lingering just beyond the fence, ready to take sound bites from willing students. Patout is probably trying to head them off at the pass by not making a big thing out of this, but it won't matter. Word will get out.

Most people around here are more than willing to throw Henry and his family under the bus for five minutes of fame.

The bell rings. "All right, it's time for you to get to class. Someone will be here soon to clean this up." Patout straightens the lapels of her black blazer and briskly walks away.

That's when I see her.

Grace Topham, staring at me from halfway down the

empty hall, wearing an expression I can't read. We lock eyes and my heart kicks up a beat. Her blond hair is shiny, long, perfect in a way I can never manage to get my own. She doesn't even have to try; it's naturally straight, hanging smoothly halfway down her back. I've always been so jealous of it; mine is a mess of brown frizz that I used to try and tame until I realized it was pointless.

I bet she's glad someone did this to Henry's locker. Who knows—she might have done it herself. She's friends with Macey Brown now. She turned in Jake. Anything's possible.

I'm the first to break eye contact. I can't look at her. I hate her.

I'm about to turn and leave when she speaks.

"Ally."

I'm so startled, I stop.

"Can we talk?" She says this so quietly that at first I wonder if I'm hearing things. She takes a step toward me. I immediately back up. What does she think she's doing? We might have been best friends at one point, but those days are long gone.

"Absolutely not." We're the only two people left in the hallway. The second bell rings. "I need to go to class."

But for some reason I don't move. It's like all my body remembers is Grace talking me through my first period when we were eleven; Grace and me snort-laughing until we cried after Henry found one of our tampons and got all weird about it. Grace, Grace, Grace, Grace, *Grace* . . . all my major memories from the age of eight on include her.

She closes the gap between us so quickly I swear to God she teleports. "Please, Ally. This whole thing has freaked me out and I really need to talk to someone"—her blue eyes are wet—"about that night. I think—"

The mention of that night breaks the spell. What am I doing, standing here listening to her? I must have temporarily lost my mind.

I interrupt. "No."

"But—" Her eyes plead for me to hear her out, but that is not going to happen. She put Jake behind bars.

"No," I say again through gritted teeth. "I have *nothing* to say to you." And with that, I spin on my heel and walk away.

GRACE

OCTOBER 7

I CAN'T CONCENTRATE.

My parents are out: my dad's at work, and my mom's with Lara, doing something wedding related, of course. The house is quiet.

Too quiet.

I shove my homework aside and reach for my diary, jot down a few random thoughts, then flip back through its pages, through the past two years, all the way to December 2023. The month of Ms. Appelbaum's murder.

My old entries are all so embarrassing. Full of Henry's name, hearts doodled in the margins. The writings of a silly little girl who had no idea what was coming.

I skim them until I get to that day.

December 15. A Friday.

There's a short entry about hanging out at Henry's house, about my growing feelings for him, then some stuff about my mom being mad at my sister. No mention of seeing someone in Appelbaum's backyard. I guess I didn't think it was important at the time.

The next time I wrote was on December 30, 2023. A week and a half later, after Appelbaum's body was found. The cops were everywhere during that time, at Appelbaum's house all hours of the day and night searching for evidence, conducting interviews, narrowing their attention onto Jake.

> *I don't know what to do. I think I saw Jake in Ms. Appelbaum's backyard the night she was killed. I remember catching sight of his jacket—it's so distinct, with that big stupid eagle his friend drew on the back—but . . . did I see his face? I must have. I was just so distracted by Henry that I didn't pay attention. According to Henry, the cops are treating Jake like he's their main suspect, so it fits. I need to tell someone, but if I do Ally and Henry will never forgive me. I can't sleep. I feel sick.*

The more I thought about it, the surer and surer I became that it was Jake. On New Year's Eve I confessed everything to Lara. She and I agreed I had to tell the authorities, and on January 1, I went down to the station. I thought it was the right thing to do.

But was it?

Last year in psych, we did a unit on forensic psychology, and I learned that *seventy-five percent* of DNA exoneration cases are connected to faulty eyewitness testimony. That means tons and tons of people are put behind bars because someone incorrectly identifies them. Human memory is no-toriously faulty and prone to all sorts of biases.

What if I put an innocent person behind bars?

I shut my diary. I need to get out of here. I need to think.

I walk outside. Across the street is Appelbaum's house, dark and abandoned.

I haven't gone over there since her murder, but I find myself heading toward it. I'm so caught up in thoughts of the past that I'm halfway into her backyard before I realize what I'm doing.

To my left is Ally's house. The first floor is dark, but her bedroom window is lit from within. She was so pissed to see me in the hall earlier. I can't blame her, but it still made me feel awful.

My gaze wanders across her backyard toward Hawthorn Street. To Henry's house. He lives directly behind Ally, catty-corner from Appelbaum's backyard. From where I'm standing, I can only see the windows of the second floor.

I wonder if he's in there.

If Jake is.

I shake myself. What am I doing here? What do I think, Appelbaum's ghost is going to suddenly appear and give me answers to all the questions spinning in my head?

She doesn't, of course.

Instead, all I see are overgrown hedges and tangled weeds where her beautifully manicured rose bushes once bloomed. When they found her body in the freezer chest in her garage, one of the roses from those bushes had been tucked under her cold, dead hands, a detail about the case that's always struck me as particularly creepy. Saliva fills my mouth and I turn away. Grass has sprouted through the patio stones and moss has attacked her lawn furniture, turning the brown wood greenish-yellow.

I wonder what it looks like inside her house. If her clothes are still in there, her books, her photos and papers and makeup, all sitting untouched for the past two years.

I shudder. Being here is starting to freak me out.

A branch snaps and my heart skips a beat.

What was that?

Out of the corner of my eye, I catch something moving. Something fast.

I spin around, toward the front of the property. Toward the street. My house. I almost run for it, but I force myself to stay calm. It was probably just an animal. I have to stop being such a wimp.

I turn back to face the small patch of woods behind Appelbaum's house. It's not a huge piece of land, maybe a quarter of an acre at most, but somehow it was left undeveloped when the rest of the neighborhood was built, and Grace, Henry, and I used to hang out there in the summers, playing Ghost in the Graveyard at night between the trees. Now their branches are bare, dark silhouettes against the blue-black night. They look like arms reaching up into the sky, desperate to be saved.

"Hello?" I call. "Is someone there?"

Another loud snap, and goose bumps pop up along my arms.

On second thought.

I'm about to take off running when a voice stops me.

"Grace?"

HENRY

GRACE TOPHAM IS STARING at me, her blue eyes wide with fear, frozen in place.

Crap. I wasn't trying to scare her.

"Hey," I say. The second word I've spoken to her in over a year. It sounds so silly when there are so many other things I want to say.

Jake's barely left his room since we got back from the prison yesterday. My mom's a ball of nerves. Our lawyer, Greg Kakova, keeps telling her to be patient. He says we can't expect Jake to immediately be the same as he was before. But before he was sullen, withdrawn, smoking weed constantly. Fighting with our dad. I'm not sure I want him to be the same.

"Henry?" Grace sounds confused, and rightly so. She's probably wondering what I'm doing lurking behind Appelbaum's house. I'm sure it looks bad. Then again, she's here, too.

"Yeah. Hey." I wince as the word drops from my mouth again. Shove my hands into the pockets of my hoodie. "Sorry. I was back here"—I scramble for a reason that isn't totally heavy or weird—"just taking a walk. I had to leave my house through the back and ended up here."

"Reporters still out front?"

"Yeah, a few. But most of them have taken off. Are you okay?"

Grace rubs her eyebrows with the palm of her hand, a gesture so familiar my stomach aches. Her long blond hair swings in front of her face and she tucks it back behind her ears. "Yeah, I'm fine. My fault, really. I don't know what I'm doing here." She chews her bottom lip. "I haven't been here since . . . you know."

I nod. Right after Jake's arrest, I'd see people back here sometimes—mostly kids from school doing stupid dares, and Ally's mom called the cops on them every single time. Eventually, they stopped.

"Anyway. How are things?" Now it's her turn to cringe. "That was dumb. Obviously, things are good."

I nod, even though I'm not sure *good* is the word I'd use to describe it. "Jake's home."

She goes pale when she hears my brother's name, and it's like we're right back there. That night when she told the police she'd seen him, and then came directly to my house to warn me.

In that order.

I told her I hated her.

"Your mom must be ecstatic."

"Yep. She is."

Grace probably thinks I still hate her. Nothing could be further from the truth. I didn't hate her then and I don't hate her now. But back then, I was mad—so freaking mad—because it was starting to be clear that Jake was totally screwed. And that was her fault . . . but also mine.

I clear my throat. This time when I open my mouth, words spill out.

"Well, she mostly is. We're waiting to see what the prosecution decides to do. If they're going to retry him. Our lawyer basically told us it's a given that they're going to. He says the new DA is going to make a spectacle of it. He also seems to think Jake has a chance this time around, but like, why? It's not like there's any new evidence. It's all the same—the argument he and Appelbaum had in the hallway that day. Her telling him that it was the last straw, that he was going to be expelled. His hair on her carpet, his notebook under her couch, her blood on his jacket. Your claim that you saw him—" I cut myself off a moment too late.

Shit. My mouth got ahead of my brain. I rarely let that happen these days. There's too much at stake. Too much to lose. And this is a perfect example. Grace's face slams shut. Her lips press together like she's trying not to cry. That wasn't what I meant to happen.

I'm sweating, even though the night air is cool.

"I'm sorry." Her voice wavers. "I'm so sorry. I shouldn't have told anyone that I saw him. I'm not sure *what* I saw anymore. It's—" She stops talking abruptly and backs away from me. "I have to go."

She whirls around and runs out of the yard.

"Wait!" I yell after her. "Grace! What do you mean you're not sure?"

I take off after her, but by the time I round the house, she's up her driveway, disappearing through her front door.

The house is quiet when I get back.

Jake is up in his room and our mom is in the kitchen. I slam myself down on the family room couch. Throw my arm over my eyes. Breathe.

As my brain settles, Grace's parting words start to loop through my head. What is she talking about? She's not sure what she saw anymore? What does that even mean? She told everyone it was Jake.

Is she changing her story now? Her story, aka one of the main reasons he went to prison.

I swing myself off the couch. Take the stairs up to the second floor two at a time. Stop outside Jake's door, nervous. We've barely exchanged more than a few words since leaving the prison. I've been avoiding him. Or he's been avoiding me. Maybe both.

What if he asks me why I never came to visit? I can't tell him. He'd hate me more than he already does.

I hesitate for so long that the bedroom door swings open. Jake appears, his hair sticking up haphazardly.

"What are you doing standing outside my door in the dark?" he barks.

This was a bad idea. "Nothing, sorry," I mumble. "I'll go."

"No, wait." Jake runs a hand through his hair, and it

springs back up, messier than before. "I'm a little on edge. Sorry. What's up?"

I'm thrown by his apology. I can't remember the last time Jake apologized for anything.

"I . . ." I hesitate. What I was going to tell him seems so dumb now that I'm staring him in the face.

"Yeah?" he says, impatient.

"I just saw Grace Topham," I manage.

His eyes narrow. Saying her name was clearly a mistake. "Are you serious? You still talk to her? After what she did?"

"No." I hurry to explain. "I haven't talked to her since . . . since before your trial. But I ran into her outside just now. And she said something weird."

"What."

"She said she's not sure what she saw the night Appelbaum died—"

Jake lets out a loud, bitter snort, interrupting me. "What is that supposed to mean? She told everyone she saw me— told the cops she saw me. Ruined my life by being so *sure,* actually. And now, what, she's *changing her mind*? A little late for that, if you ask me."

I swallow. "I don't know. That's all she said. But what if you were right? What if someone really did steal your jacket out of your car and wear it over to Appelbaum's that night? What if *that's* who she saw? I know the cops didn't believe you because they found it in your trunk—"

"Right," he mutters darkly. "Like someone couldn't have stolen it and put it back later. Idiots."

"Maybe you should talk to her? See what she has to say? Maybe she can help—"

He stares at me for so long I start to squirm.

Finally, he speaks. "You're kidding, right? You don't come to visit me in prison for an entire year, because—what—you're too afraid? Embarrassed? Or maybe 'cause you think I'm guilty? You barely speak to me on the ride home yesterday. And now you have the balls to try to get me to talk to your girlfriend—your girlfriend who helped *put me in prison*, might I remind you? Are you serious?"

"I'm sorry. I didn't think—"

"Yeah, no kidding you didn't think."

He storms back into his room and slams the door.

"Honey? Is everything okay?" our mom calls.

I know she's talking to Jake.

"He's in his room," I say. I walk down the stairs and push past her, heading to the back door.

"Where are you going?" she asks as I open it.

"Out," I say. The door slams shut behind me.

OCTOBER 8

BRAWNERNOW.COM

Is our community safe?

I'll start with the facts: two years ago, beloved high school English teacher Miriam Appelbaum was murdered in cold blood inside her home. A few long weeks later, Jacob Hanson was formally charged with first-degree murder and eventually received a sentence of twenty-five to life. No one in Brawner expected him to set foot in our beautiful little community again.

Except, as we all know, he's back. His sentence vacated on a *technicality*. A technicality that barely has anything to do with the case itself—who cares if the prosecuting attorney and the judge presiding over the case were having extramarital relations? Sure, it's not totally on the up-and-up, but here's the thing: Hanson is clearly guilty.

Everyone knows it. His own *father* basically admitted it. The fact that he's out of jail is a huge waste of time and taxpayer money.

DA Cassie Flynn better get the new trial underway ASAP if she knows what's good for her career. Get that killer back behind bars. And make Brawner safe again.

Thoughts? Questions? Want to tell us we suck? Write to editor@brawnernow.com.

GRACE

OCTOBER 9

I'M STANDING BY MY locker talking to Meghan Cheng, trying to pretend it's a normal day. I caught a glimpse of Henry and Ally in the hallway earlier. Ally was wearing the glare that's taken up permanent residence on her face, her brown, wavy hair pulled into a messy bun. Henry's blue eyes were ringed with dark circles, and he looked like he'd rather be anywhere else than here.

I don't blame him; I've heard what people are saying about his family. I saw what they did to his locker on Tuesday. The posts on social media about Jake, how he's a monster, how he deserves to get the death penalty this time around. They're bullying anyone who disagrees with them, who dares to question whether they might be wrong. I wonder if more people would speak out for Jake if they weren't worried about how it might affect them.

I'd call it selfish, but I can't blame them, really. Who

wants to draw the wrath of people like Macey Brown if they can otherwise avoid it?

I clearly don't.

I'm sure Henry would have preferred to stay home again, but it's senior year, first semester. How we do now affects where we'll get into college, and applications are due soon. Henry's always been really focused on his grades. We used to talk all the time about how we couldn't wait to get out of this small town and start our real lives; toward the end, Henry and I had even started talking about trying to go to the same school. I couldn't imagine my life without him.

The irony.

I wonder if he still cares as much about his grades, if he even thinks about it at all. I wonder if what happened with Jake made him even more focused on getting out of here, or if he's just given up. I could easily see things like grades and school seeming silly once your brother has been sent to prison for the rest of his life.

"So, are we going or what?" Meghan asks. She's staring at me. "You weren't listening, were you?"

"Sorry." I shake myself out of it. "I didn't sleep well. Between my sister's wedding and finals coming up and . . ."

"Jake getting out," she finishes. "Yeah. How are you doing with all that? Carmen and I have been talking about how maybe we could go on a trip or something? Get out of here for a while? Give you a break?"

"That would be fun," I say, although there's no way my mom would be cool with me doing that right now, not with Lara's wedding coming up so soon.

"Okay, great . . . So, as I was saying: Are we going to Matt's party Friday?"

It's cute that she's worrying about a party. I guess a few weeks ago, I would have been, too. Freaking about what I should wear. Talking with her about whether Matt was finally going to ask me out.

Matt Clark: captain of the track team, honor student. Heading to a good college next year. Popular. Social. Kind. Meghan knows about my half-hearted sort of crush on him, which I've played up for her benefit, because they're friends. Because he's the sort of person I *should* want to date.

But it isn't real. Because I've never gotten over Henry.

How do you get over someone you've loved practically your entire life? It took me years to admit my feelings to myself, then years of wondering whether he felt the same way. Then, just a few short months after I found out he did, it was over.

"I have to help my sister with some wedding stuff." The bell rings and I start walking. I have a free period next, and a plan to spend it in the library. I can't waste a second.

"But not on Friday *night*, right?" Meghan hurries along beside me. She can be persistent when she wants something, and it'll be faster—easier—if I just say yes.

"You're right, I don't. Let's go to the party." I try to sound excited, like I would have been before.

"Cool." She smiles. "I'll text you later."

Ms. Alderman is behind the front desk of the library working on her computer. She smiles and waves when she sees me.

Ally and I interviewed her a few times for articles we cowrote for the school paper freshman year. Back then, the two of us thought we were real investigative journalists— especially Ally. To be fair, her dad *was* a journalist, and Ally's life goal has always been to follow in his footsteps. I was more than happy to tag along. I needed some excitement in my life, plus I hoped it might help me stand out amid all of Lara's academic achievements.

I wave as I pass Alderman and head to the bank of desks on the far side of the room, where I pull my laptop out of my bag.

I type *Jacob Hanson and Miriam Appelbaum* into Google, and thousands of hits populate the page, including a bunch of links to Reddit.

Jake's release brought the case back into the national spotlight, and now true crime fanatics are back at it, speculating.

> Has anyone looked into whether Jake Hanson and Miriam were having an affair?

> I heard that Hanson said he had an alibi, but no one believed him.

> Did Miriam have a boyfriend? It's always the boyfriend.

> Anyone else remember how that college student was murdered in Arlington, Va. four months after

MA? That's only a half hour from Brawner. Maybe
we're looking at a serial killer . . .

Jake Hanson is guilty as hell. The fact he's getting
out at all is RIDICULOUS

I backtrack out of the thread and scroll down, skimming
through salacious headlines like *"Killer set free"* and more-
reasonable ones like *"Jacob Hanson murder conviction vacated
on a technicality."*

That one's from the *Brawner Times,* the paper Ally's dad
worked for. The reporter, Kate Chakravorty, has written a
bunch of articles about Jake and the trial over the past few
years.

I scan through them. They mostly contain details I already know, but there are some things I don't remember,
like how Jake's cell records showed his phone was in his
house during the time frame Appelbaum was killed.

I look up from the computer with a sigh. What am I
doing? Do I think I'm going to find something the cops
haven't? Is this just a half-hearted attempt to ease my guilt?
A way I can deal with my worries without actually having
to tell anyone about them?

A glance at my phone tells me there's only five minutes
left until the bell.

I need to figure out what I actually saw that night so I
can stop obsessing and move on with my life, but randomly
searching the internet is an exercise in futility.

At the bottom of one of the articles I notice an email

address for Kate Chakravorty. Without thinking too hard about it, I dash off a message.

> Dear Ms. Chakravorty:
>
> I'm a student at Brawner High School and was reading some of the articles you wrote about the murder of Miriam Appelbaum and the trial. You might have already realized this from my name, but I'm the person who testified that I saw Jacob Hanson the night she died. I'm wondering if we could chat?
>
> Thanks very much,
>
> Grace Topham
> BHS '25

I hit Send, log out of my email, and run out of the library to make it to class on time.

HENRY

OCTOBER 9

I HEAD STRAIGHT HOME after school. Ally has to do stuff for the newspaper and I have no other friends. Where else am I going to go?

There are only two news vans left out front, and I make it inside without incident. I'm welcomed by the sound of crying.

A second later, Jake barrels out of the kitchen and almost slams straight into me. I've avoided him since our argument yesterday.

"Wha—" I say, but he's up the stairs before the entire word is out of my mouth. A second later, the slam of his bedroom door echoes through the house.

Welcome home, Henry.

I walk into the kitchen.

My mom sits at the table, hunched over a pile of crumpled tissues. Mr. Kakova is next to her on his phone.

He holds up a finger when he sees me.

"All right. Yes. Yes. Okay, I'll see you first thing in the morning. Thanks." He ends the call.

"What's going on?" I ask.

My mom's head shoots up at the sound of my voice. She quickly wipes away her tears.

"Henry. I didn't hear you come in." Her voice is froggy.

"Hi, Henry," Mr. Kakova says. He sounds tired.

"What happened?" I repeat, even though I'm almost certain I know.

They look at each other.

"Unfortunately, they've decided—" My mom's voice breaks. She gulps a breath. "They've decided to seek a new trial against your brother. We knew it was likely, but no one expected it to happen this fast. Now that it's official, Jake's being put under house arrest. They're going to make him wear an ankle bracelet. . . . He's a prisoner in our home. Since we have Greg—ah, Mr. Kakova—on our team this time around, we're hopeful, but the DA is pressing to have the trial as soon as possible."

Even though I expected it, the news still knocks the wind out of me. There's no way Jake is going to get a fair trial anywhere near this town.

I can't believe we're going to have to go through all of this again. The media circus, the harassment, the horrible things people say online and directly to my face.

This is the worst sort of déjà vu.

"I talked to Grace Topham the other night," I blurt without thinking.

My mom grimaces. "Grace?" she says, like it's a bad word. She used to love Grace, but not anymore.

"Yeah. We ran into each other in . . . it's not important. But listen. She told me that she's been questioning things. It sounds like she might not be sure anymore, whether it was Jake who she saw. That would help, right? If she retracts her statement?"

"She's not *sure*?" my mom says bitterly. "Maybe she should have thought about that two years ago."

"I don't understand," Kakova says, frowning. "Why would she change her story now? According to both her witness statement and court testimony, she saw Jake. What's made her rethink things?"

I shake my head. "I don't know. But would it help if she tells the cops?"

Kakova considers this. "She *could* tell the prosecution, but . . . is Grace aware that she could potentially face criminal charges if she retracts her statement? She testified under oath that she saw Jake. Changing her story now could be considered perjury."

"But if she made a mistake—"

Kakova sighs. "If it was a mistake, that's different. But how would she prove that? And really, the bigger issue is, why would anyone think her memory of that night is better now than it was back then? The DA would eviscerate her— paint her as a liar, probably bring up the relationship you two had. . . . She could easily end up being charged. It really wouldn't help our case much. Unless she has new, concrete evidence, that is."

My heart sinks. I don't want Grace to be called a liar in public. And I definitely don't want her to get into trouble.

He's right. Why would anyone believe her if she changed her story now?

I switch course. "Did the cops ever look at anyone else after Ms. Appelbaum was killed?"

Kakova, who had turned back to his paperwork, looks up at me again with furrowed brows. "What?"

"Like, did the police ever look at any other suspects? Other than Jake?"

Kakova frowns. "Not seriously. I wish they had. It would make my job a hell of a lot easier if I could point the jury in the direction of someone else."

"Okay, so let's find someone else! Let's look for other suspects! Like—here's one. My friend Ally overheard Appelbaum arguing with someone inside her house about a week before she was killed. Is it in the police report? Ally told the cops, but they—"

"Yes, it's in here," Kakova interrupts. "Another fight with Jake."

"No! Ally was sure it wasn't Jake. Plus, why would he have been at Appelbaum's? It was before she busted him for drugs."

My voice is rising and my mom is growing visibly uncomfortable with me pressing Kakova like this, but I don't care. What's his plan? To sit around with his thumb up his butt and watch my brother get shipped back to prison?

"Don't you think it's at least worth exploring? Ally said the other person she heard sounded really upset. She thought it was a man, but—"

"Henry—" my mom interrupts, but Kakova holds up a hand.

"It's okay. He's just trying to help." He gives me a thin-lipped smile that doesn't reach his eyes. God, he's such a dick sometimes.

"I'll make a note of that," he says. "Now if you'll excuse us. I have a lot to go over with your mother." He motions to the piles of paperwork surrounding them.

I grit my teeth. He clearly isn't going to look into anything.

"*Fine,*" I snap. Kakova takes off his glasses and rubs the bridge of his nose.

"Henry!" my mom says. "Watch your tone."

I glare at her. "Sorry," I say, without meaning it at all.

"Henry," Kakova says my name in a way that makes me want to punch through a wall. "As I'm sure you're aware, public sentiment is strong against your brother. Although that's not supposed to matter—especially in this day and age—it's hugely important. Digging around for other people to blame would make us appear weak. Our best bet right now is to concentrate on the holes in the prosecutor's case that Jake's first lawyer didn't fully exploit. This trial is going to be an uphill battle, but I promise I know how to do my job, okay? I'm on top of it."

"Okay, so what exactly is your plan, then? Because right now, it sounds like you're just making up a bunch of excuses."

"Henry!" My mom won't stop saying my stupid name, like *I'm* the problem here.

"It's okay, Emily," Kakova says. "He's angry. I get it. The

fact that they decided to retry Jake so quickly isn't what any of us wanted."

"But it would *help* Jake if we figured out who really did it."

"I understand your concern, Henry, and I promise your brother is in good hands. I know you want to help, but trust me, this is the best course of action. For everyone." It's clear I'm being dismissed. "Now, like I said, your mother and I have a lot to go over, so if you'll excuse us?"

My mom presses her hand against my arm briefly, before turning back to the lawyer.

I'm sitting on Ally's front porch when she arrives home from school.

"What are you doing here?" she calls as she gets out of her car. She hikes her backpack up onto her shoulder as she heads across her front lawn toward me.

I stand, wiping my sweaty palms against the bottom of my T-shirt. "They're going to retry Jake."

Her face falls. "They already decided?" She joins me on the porch.

I'm silent as she unlocks the front door; then I follow her into the kitchen, where she drops her bag on the counter.

"Are you okay? We're going to handle this, Henry. I promise."

A sharp headache is growing behind my eyes, but it's really nice to hear someone say *we*, even though I have no idea what she thinks we can do.

"I don't know. I . . . have to tell you something. I ran into Grace the other night."

"*Grace?*" she says in a similar tone to my mother's.

"Just listen. She told me that she's not sure whether she actually saw Jake the night Appelbaum was killed—"

"*Excuse* me? You spoke to her? Why are you just telling me this?"

I ignore her. She knows why. Because whenever Grace's name comes up around her, Ally goes on a thirty-minute rant about what an asshole she is.

"I told my mom and Kakova. Asked whether she could, I don't know, testify saying that she's not sure anymore. But Kakova said that she could get in trouble."

"So what? If she was lying, she deserves it."

"I don't think she was lying, Al. I think—"

"Are you *defending* her?"

"God! No! I'm . . . I'm just worried." I sink down onto one of the kitchen stools. "Jake has only been home for a few days and we're already back here? And it sounds like Kakova's just going to regurgitate the same stuff from the first trial. When I asked whether he was going to investigate to see if he could figure out who else might have killed her, he basically told me to go fuck myself. Jake has no chance."

Ally unzips her backpack and pulls out a little black notebook and her computer. She sets them on the kitchen table. "Henry, I've been thinking. We knew this was coming, right? It sucks it happened so fast, but it's not a surprise. That new DA has been all over the news, talking about it. If Kakova isn't going to do it, then we need to."

"To what?"

She opens her notebook. "Figure out who actually killed Appelbaum."

"What?" I study her face to see if she's joking, but she looks very serious.

She frowns. "You were literally just saying that's what you think Kakova should do."

"Yeah, but he's an adult? With actual resources at his disposal? We aren't cops. We aren't lawyers. We're in high school. Who's going to talk to us?"

"Just listen. We can use all of those things to our advantage—no one will suspect we're looking into the case. They'll assume we're stupid teenagers. They always do."

"Okay, but how do you propose we get any information? We can't, like, call people down to the police station for interviews."

"Yeah, no. But I've been thinking. The two-year anniversary of Appelbaum's death is coming up. Remember how we did a whole special edition of the *Boar* on it last year? We can pretend we're working on a new one. It'll give us the perfect excuse to talk to the people who were close to Appelbaum. Last night, I went down a Reddit rabbit hole to see if there are any interesting theories floating around. I didn't really find much, but one post talked about how the majority of murders are committed by someone the victim knows, which means whoever killed her was probably in her life. Not to mention, if it was a random killing, why tuck a flower under her hands? Why the cleanup? Why bother unless you're trying to cover your tracks? Let Kakova deal with Jake and all the legal stuff. We can concentrate on finding new suspects. People who had motive to kill."

I can't believe I'm even considering her idea. "I don't know. . . . Do you really think we'd be able to learn enough just by asking questions?"

She shrugs. "I'm not saying that's *all* we should do. The advantage we have over the police is we don't need to, you know, totally follow the letter of the law. We can be more . . . morally flexible."

My eyebrows flick up. "Morally flexible?"

"Yeah. Like . . . God, I don't know. But think of it this way—if the cops don't follow procedure when they're doing a search, things end up being inadmissible in court. We won't have that problem."

"I guess. . . ." I'm not sure I agree. I mean, we aren't cops, but we're still not supposed to break the law. If we get caught, it might totally mess up our college chances, and I want to get the hell out of this town.

But sometimes arguing with Ally takes more energy than it's worth. So for the time being I let it be.

"Henry, like you just said—no one else is going to do it. It's up to us."

"Where would we even start?"

"I've been thinking about that, too. We need to figure out who else had a motive, right? So we need to talk to the people Appelbaum was close to. They might be able to give us leads—plus, *they* might be potential leads themselves. Like, her sister lives in town—or at least she used to. We should track her down. Also, her friends. I think she was pretty tight with Ms. Glasgow and Ms. Freeman from school. And any non-teacher friends, too. A couple of them were interviewed by the press after she was killed. Last night I cross-referenced their names with people Appelbaum follows on Instagram and found their profiles. Side note, but they really need to take her Instagram down, because it is so freaking creepy—the comments on her posts are all like *They got him, Miriam. You can rest easy now. You're in a better place.* Blah, blah, blah. People are gross."

A thought occurs to me. "Were there any suspicious ones?"

Ally shakes her head. "Not surprising, though. I'm sure the cops looked at all her socials when they were initially investigating. It's where they found those nasty DMs Jake sent her, right?"

I nod. She's right. It's where they found the DMs.

Ally taps her pen against her teeth. "Okay, so. We talk to her sister. Her friends. Who else?"

"What about the guy you heard her arguing with that day when you went over to her house? Remember that?"

"Yeah, I remember," Ally says darkly. "I told the cops about it and they completely blew me off."

"I actually mentioned it to Kakova earlier and he did the exact same thing to me. That was, what, a week before the murder? Why doesn't anyone think it's important?"

She rolls her eyes. "Because they all think she was talking to Jake, even though that explanation makes zero sense. We need to figure out who it really was."

"Okay . . . but how do we do that?"

"I don't know. Maybe her sister or one of her friends has

some idea." Ally looks at me. "Anyone else you can think of who we should talk to?"

"Um . . ." I trail off. Ms. Appelbaum was well-liked; she was young, mostly chill.

Before I can come up with any names, we're interrupted by a voice at the front door.

"Ally? I'm home!"

"My mom." Ally shuts her notebook. "You're welcome to stay. . . ."

"Thanks, but I gotta head out anyway," I say. The weight of my day is starting to catch up with me and I need to process it alone.

"Okay," Ally says. "We can talk more tomorrow. And, Henry?"

"What?" I look back at her.

"Everything is going to be fine."

"Yeah," I say. "I know it is."

Except I don't believe that at all.

GRACE

WHEN I GET HOME from school, Lara is sitting at the kitchen table with our mom talking about her wedding. As usual.

I know I need to stop being so snarky about it in my head, but honestly, I can't wait until it's over. It's been non-stop wedding talk in our house ever since Lara and Evan got engaged, and sometimes I wonder if she and my mom realize it's just one day.

When I stick my head into the room to say hello, Lara tries to recruit me to help them, but I beg off, saying I have too much homework. On my way up to my bedroom, I check my email to see if the reporter has responded.

My heart leaps; she has. I flop down onto my bed to read the email.

Hi Grace,

Would love to chat. Is this evening too soon?
If not, let's meet at Ground Zero Coffee,
downtown. 6 pm?

Let me know. You can text me—703-555-4392.

Best,
Kate Chakravorty

It's just before four. Knowing my mom and Lara, they'll be deep in wedding planning for the next few hours, so I doubt anyone will notice me slip out.

I open a new text message, copy and paste her number into it, and start typing.

> Hi this is Grace Topham.
> 6pm at Ground Zero works for me.

Her response is immediate: *Great. see you there.*

Two hours later, I'm trying to find parking in downtown Brawner.

It's not big—an eight by eight square block of mixed-use development. Retail, restaurants, a movie theater, a barber-shop and hair salon, some residential buildings.

Evan and Lara's town house is a few blocks away. They

moved in a little over a year ago, and I think they got a good deal because Evan's family's real estate company managed the renovation of the entire downtown a few years back.

It's their thing. Redevelopment. The company swoops in and all of a sudden the run-down diners and old ninety-nine-cent stores are gone, replaced by upscale chain restaurants, luxury retail, and faux-quaint brick roads.

Some people think it's nice, but in my opinion, it makes everything look bland and cookie-cutter.

Ground Zero Coffee is one of the few places down here that survived. It's a perennial favorite with pretty much everyone and there would have been riots if they'd tried to close it.

After a couple more circles around the block I finally spot an open space. I park, then sit, immobilized by anxiety.

What am I trying to accomplish by talking to this reporter? I can't tell her that I'm second-guessing what I saw that night; who knows what she'd do with that information. Run it in the paper? Call the authorities and tell them I lied under oath? What if someone from school found out? Everyone would hate me.

The thing is, I *was* sure back then, about what I saw. I wouldn't have told the cops that I saw Jake if I wasn't.

Right? I wouldn't have. I mean, I didn't just wreck his life when I told the cops that. I wrecked my own, too.

What I need right now is a little reassurance that I didn't put an innocent person behind bars.

Kate Chakravorty's picture is next to her bio on the *Tribune* website—white lady, short brown bob, perfect eyebrows, and I spot her as soon as I enter the café. She's sitting at a window table with a coffee mug in front of her, typing on her phone with the same serious expression as in her photo.

She looks up and sees me, waves, stands up, and heads over.

"Grace?" she asks, her voice kind.

I nod nervously. "Yeah. Hi, Mrs. Chakravorty."

"Oh please, call me Kate. Mrs. Chakravorty is my mother. I recognize you from the trial. Thanks for meeting me on such short notice. Would you like anything to drink? Eat? They have great pastries."

"I . . . um, I'm okay, thanks." I follow her to the table, and take the seat across from her.

Even though I'm the one who reached out, I have no idea what to say now that I'm actually here.

"So," she says, interrupting my thoughts. "I'm very curious to hear why you emailed me."

I swallow. "Right. Well, like I said, I'm a student at Brawner High School and, um, I was close to Ms. Appelbaum before she died? But I was also really close to Henry . . . Hanson. Who's Jake's brother?"

"I remember Henry," Kate says with a sympathetic smile.

"Yeah . . . well, as you know, Jake was just released from prison. . . ." I trail off, unsure where I'm going with this.

"Yes?" she prompts.

I pick one of the paper napkins up off the table and start shredding it. "Well. Ever since his release was announced, I've been thinking a lot. About everything. And . . . I guess

I've started wondering . . . did you talk to anyone back then who thought maybe it *wasn't* Jake? Like, that maybe he wasn't the one who killed her?"

Her eyebrows arch in surprise. "You mean, did I talk to anyone who thought he was innocent?"

I nod.

Her brow furrows. "No, not really. Not outside of his family. His mom. As I'm sure you're aware, there was evidence that pointed to him right from the beginning, even before you came forward. And, of course, his track record didn't help: failing a bunch of classes, about to be kicked out of school for dealing drugs—and reported to the school administration for it by Miriam Appelbaum, no less. Plus, he initially lied to the cops about having an alibi. And as I'm sure you're aware, lying to the cops is *never* a good idea. But that said, I'm curious—what are you really asking here? Whether Jake did it? You're the one who saw him that night, heading toward her house. . . . You testi-fied against him. Has something made you question what you saw?"

I'm tempted for a brief moment to tell her everything.

But I can't. I can't tell her. Or anyone. I Googled what they do to people—including minors—who lie under oath, even when the lie was a mistake. It's not pretty.

"Of course not," I say. I hurry to find safer ground. "I saw him. It's more . . . it's more him getting out of prison. It's messing with my mind a little. . . ."

Kate cups her mug between her hands. "That's under-standable. His release was a surprise to everyone. Speak-ing of surprises—I was *quite* surprised when I got your message. I'd tried to reach out to you when news about Jake's release first broke, but the person I spoke with said that you weren't available. A woman—maybe your mom?"

"You did?" My mom never gave me that message. I'm sure she was trying to protect me, but I would have appreciated a heads-up. I'm not a child.

She nods. "I was hoping to include your reaction to Jake's release in one of my articles. People are extremely unhappy about it, but, as tends to happen with things like this, most of the loudest voices don't have any direct relationship to the case. I'm trying to speak with people who do: you, Miriam Appelbaum's sister, people like that."

"Her sister? She still lives in Brawner?"

"Yep. She does."

"Oh wow." I'm surprised. If I were her, I would have moved immediately. Put as much distance between me and those horrible memories as possible.

Then again, Henry's family is still here. I suppose everyone has their own reasons for staying.

"I think it helped that she got married last year and changed her name. That gave her some separation from the case and what happened to Miriam. Needless to say, she's a very private person, particularly about her sister, and unfortunately I haven't been able to get ahold of her this time around. So, I was happy to get your email."

She leans forward eagerly. "Your eyewitness testimony helped put Jake behind bars. Now he's living at his parents' house, practically in your backyard, at least until they retry him and send him back to prison. Are you concerned at all for your safety?"

I shake my head. I've known Jake since I was six years old and he was eight. There's no way he'd hurt me. "Jake won't do anything."

"You don't think he's angry about what you did?"

My stomach clenches. Is she trying to scare me? "I don't know if he's angry. Probably, I guess. But Jake isn't . . ." I trail off when I realize what I was about to say.

"Isn't what? Isn't violent? He was sent to prison for *murder*, Grace. He clearly has the capability to be." Kate says this gently, but like she's sure it proves her point. Jake is violent. I should be scared.

But it only serves to add to my confusion.

I thought I saw Jake that night. I turned him in to the cops. But why didn't I stop and consider the fact that he'd never been physically aggressive with anyone? That I'd known him for *years*, and I'd never seen him do anything remotely violent?

His dumb friends, sure—his best friend, Nick Marion, was always getting in people's faces and had been suspended from school multiple times for fighting.

But Jake? Never.

I didn't think about that back then, but I should have.

Maybe it, coupled with the fact that I'm not scared to have Jake back home, living a few hundred feet from where I sleep, should tell me something.

When I don't respond, Kate keeps talking. "I hope you're taking measures to protect yourself. As you probably know, the DA has already decided to retry, which I'm sure he's not happy about. You take care of yourself, okay?"

"Okay."

"Good. Now, while I have you here, would you be willing to comment about his release, on the record? The article will be posted tonight."

"I don't think so."

She frowns. "Are you sure? You need to get ahead of all of this, Grace. I assume you know that you might be called to testify again."

My breath catches in my throat. I hadn't even thought about that, but it makes sense. My testimony in the first trial was a huge win for the prosecution.

But I can't do it again.

"What if I don't?" I ask.

"Don't what?"

I swallow. "Don't testify."

Her head pulls back in surprise. "Why wouldn't you? I'd think you, more than almost anyone, would want him back behind bars."

"I . . . I'm just wondering. It was a lot the first time around."

She makes a sympathetic face. "Ah, I understand. Well, even if you decide not to testify, they can still use your testimony from the first trial as evidence, so you don't have to worry about that."

Kate pulls a business card out of her jacket pocket and slides it across the table.

"Look, I have to run. It was nice chatting with you. You already have my info, but here it is again. If you change your mind about that quote or want to chat again, reach out."

She stands, gathering her things. "Take care, Grace."

And with that, she's gone.

I walk to my car, her words haunting me. How she said that they can reuse my testimony from the first trial, even if I don't testify myself.

Her questions about my safety. If I'm scared.

The fact that I'm not.

When I get to my car I settle into the driver's seat and squeeze my eyes shut, trying desperately to pull up a clear memory of that night. Of the person I saw walking into Ms. Appelbaum's backyard.

I remember how big they were.

I remember the baseball cap, pulled low over their face.

I remember that stupid jacket.

But no matter how hard I try, I don't remember seeing Jake's face.

HENRY

OCTOBER 10

I WAKE TO THE sound of yelling downstairs.

What is going on now? Late last night, Jake's parole officer showed up with a GPS monitor and slapped it on my brother's ankle. Needless to say, he was not happy, and after the officer left, he and my mom got into a huge fight.

Tensions are running high in the Hanson household—unsurprising, given everything—but honestly, it's barely seven a.m. Way too early for this.

I heave myself out of bed, slip on a pair of sweats, and hurry into the hallway.

Halfway down the stairs, I see the source of the commotion.

My mother, at the front door, shouting at two cops.

"—on our front *lawn*! Again! How many more times is this going to happen before you finally do your jobs?" Anger flushes my mom's cheeks red. "Isn't that your sworn duty—to serve and protect?"

"Mrs. Hanson," one of the officers says like he's talking to a small child. "Like we already said, we're going to do our best to track down whoever did this. Unfortunately, the Ring cam footage you showed us isn't helpful. The people in it have on black hoodies and face coverings, so there's not much we can do—"

"You *could* have a cop car stationed out front of my house. You *could* be patrolling the neighborhood to make sure this doesn't continue to happen. But wait. Hold on, let me guess. You don't have the man power."

"We don't have the man power," the cop says at the same time as my mom.

"Yeah," my mom scoffs. "Sure. Not enough cops. Strange, how there haven't been enough cops to help us out for the last *two years.* Convenient. I'm sure none of this has anything to do with my son upstairs."

The cops exchange a glance. The younger one hikes up his pants and barks a cough into his fist.

"If there's nothing else?" says the older one. My mom's face turns an even brighter shade of red like she's about to lose it. The last thing this family needs is for another person to end up in jail.

I hurry down the rest of the stairs. Step between her and the cops.

"Everything okay?" I ask.

"Someone egged our house last night." My mom shoves an outstretched finger into the older cop's face. "And these motherfu—"

"Who?" I interrupt.

She scowls. "I don't know. Their faces were covered."

I never thought I'd miss the reporters out front, but they would have been useful right now. Unfortunately, the last one left yesterday. Not much to report now that Jake is officially trapped inside.

I sigh. After Jake's arrest, things got really dark around here for a while. Nasty words graffitied on our house and driveway, toilet paper in our trees, smashed mailboxes, shaving cream all over our cars. The whole nine yards.

The worst of it was right after the guilty verdict, when someone had the nerve to throw a brick through our front window. Luckily, we weren't home, but it was still terrifying.

It took a few months, but eventually things settled down. Now that Jake's out, though . . . here we go again.

The cops did absolutely nothing to help us back then, so it's no surprise they're totally useless now, too.

After all, they're the ones who arrested my brother for murder.

I put a hand on my mom's arm, trying to calm her down. "It was probably some idiots from school. You know they've done this before. They're idiots, but mostly harmless."

The older officer clears his throat. "If there's nothing else we can do—"

My mom swings around, glaring at him. "There are sure as *shit* other things you can do. But—"

The cop opens his mouth. My mom rolls her eyes.

"Right. You don't have the man power. Forget it."

"If there's nothing else?" he repeats, and he and the younger officer edge out the door.

"Nope." My mom's voice is sharp. "Nothing that *you* can help with, at least."

The two officers leave without so much as a glance back. Through the open door, I see yellow and white streaked up and down our front porch and driveway. Whoever did this must have used several cartons of eggs. In this economy?

Clearly, they're dumber than I thought.

"Dicks," my mom says under her breath as the cops pick their way through yolks and shells. "You didn't hear anything last night, did you?"

I shake my head. "No. Maybe Jake did?"

My mom sighs tiredly and shuts the door. "Even if he had, I don't want to get him involved. I knew it was pointless to call the police. Will I ever learn?"

She heads to the bottom of the stairs and picks up a stack of folded dish towels. "Anyway. Let's move on. You need to get going so you're not late to school. I'll clean up the mess later," she says, and disappears into the dining room.

Back upstairs, it's still quiet. Jake is probably hiding out in his room.

I wonder what he's thinking. If the cops showing up this morning scared him. I imagine it did. The last time they came here was under very different circumstances.

The night they came to formally arrest him for murder.

ALLY

OCTOBER 10

HENRY AND I FIND each other at lunch where we always do, at the back doors of the school.

Most people in our class head into the cafeteria or go off campus for lunch, but Henry and I learned a long time ago that when the weather is nice, eating out back is a much better option for us. Fewer people. Fewer opportunities for them to be assholes.

"Hey," Henry says as I walk up, impatience written on his face. "There you are."

"I'm not even late." I raise an eyebrow. "Are you okay?"

He gestures to the doors. "Let's talk outside."

Outside, the fall air is unseasonably warm. We head to our usual bench over by the sports fields.

Once we're settled, I ask, "What's going on?"

"I was woken up by the cops this morning is what's going on."

"Oh God. What happened?"

"Someone egged our house." He laughs with bitterness. "Just like the old days. As usual, the cops weren't willing to do anything to help. My mom's super pissed. Not a great way to start the morning."

"That sucks. I'm sorry." His demeanor makes a lot more sense now.

He lays his forehead on the table. "This isn't going to stop, is it, Al? Not unless Jake is proven innocent."

I pat the back of his hair. "Probably not. Look, at least this time we're doing something to help him. We just need to decide where to start. Maybe with Appelbaum's sister?"

He straightens up and nods. "But do we have a way to get in touch with her?"

"Well . . . no," I admit. "At least, not yet. I tried to look her up last night, and basically found nothing. I think she might have hired one of those firms to purge her personal information from the internet, because it's like she doesn't exist."

"Wouldn't surprise me," Henry says. "Remember all those freaks who tried to contact me and my mom after the news about Jake became public? I bet she got some of that, too. I wish my mom had been smart enough to think about getting our info off the web when there was still time."

"Yeah. So that was a dead end, but maybe Appelbaum's old friends know how to get in touch with her? Last night I DMed a couple of them—Lucy Phillips and Rachael Wu. They were quoted in a bunch of newspaper articles after Appelbaum was killed. I told them I'm a reporter for the school paper she used to advise, so hopefully they message back soon. . . . What?"

Henry's expression has shifted.

"Um," he says quietly. "Ally . . ." He's staring at something over my shoulder.

"What?" I twist around and immediately see what—*who*—he's staring at.

Grace Topham.

Heading our way.

"What is *she* doing here?" I hiss.

"I don't know," he says. I glare at him, suspicious.

"I don't!"

Before I can say anything else, she's standing a foot from us. At least she has the decency to look nervous.

"Hey," she says, mostly to Henry. She quickly glances at me and looks away.

"Hey," he says, not unkindly. He's such a sucker. "What's up?"

Grace clears her throat. "Uh, well, I thought I might find you out here . . . and I was hoping we could talk—"

"*Talk?* Are you serious?" I say, voice sharp. "Don't you think you've done enough?"

"Ally," Henry says, like *I'm* the unreasonable one.

"*What?*" I snap at him.

"Let her speak."

I cannot believe him. But I guess some things never change. Here I am, doing everything in my power to help his brother, and even now he's on her side. He can't be serious. I know he and Grace were all lovey-dovey before the murder, but it's been two years and she sent his brother to *prison.*

"I gotta go." I start scooping up my things and stuffing them into my bag.

"Ally," Henry sighs. "C'mon. Don't be like that."

I ignore him. Stand.

Grace finally speaks. "I think you'll want to hear this, too, Ally."

"Doubt it," I say.

"Yesterday, I talked to someone from the *Brawner Times*."

The name sends a little shock through me. That's the newspaper my dad wrote for.

But I'm not about to admit I'm interested. I scowl. "Thrilling. What did you tell them? That you knew Jake way back when? Did you sell them juicy little tidbits about his past? Make some money off his pain?"

She rolls her eyes. "No, obviously not."

"*I* don't think it's that obvious."

She lets out a frustrated huff. "I'm trying to help."

"Don't you think it's a little late for that?"

"Look, I know I messed up"—her voice cracks—"that's why I'm here. I thought I was doing the right thing—"

"By turning Jake in for *murder*?" I'm almost yelling now.

"What would you have done if you were me, Ally? I saw someone that night. I cared about Appelbaum—"

"I would have talked to Jake first. I wouldn't have said anything unless I was one million percent sure about who I saw. Didn't you tell Henry that you're not sure anymore? How do you go from literally testifying that it was Jake to . . . *that*? Unless you were lying."

Her jaw juts. "I wasn't lying. Can I—"

"You're changing your story now. What else would you call it?"

"Back then, I thought I *was* sure. I saw his jacket—I know

I saw that jacket—but . . ." She bites her bottom lip and crosses her arms tight across her chest.

"But what?" I can't help but ask. My stupid curiosity getting the better of me, as always.

"But now . . . I don't know. I started wondering about it during his trial, a little, but I sort of shoved it out of my head, because everyone—because it seemed clear he was guilty. But, since the news broke about him getting out, I've realized I can't remember if I actually saw a face that night. I read something the other day about memory. Apparently when you see an object, your brain fills in the blanks of what's missing from the picture . . . and now I'm wondering whether mine did that. If maybe I saw Jake's jacket, but not his face and just assumed I did?"

Her mouth quivers. "I really did think I was doing the right thing when I went to the cops," she says. "I wanted to help Ms. Appelbaum. But . . . if I made a mistake, I want to help fix it."

The knot in my chest is growing bigger with every word she says. She must be kidding. What she did—what she said—cost Jake two years of his life. I would hardly call that a mistake. I'd call it a huge, massive, life-ruining fuckup.

"You're trying to fix it?" Henry asks Grace in a far nicer tone than I would have used. I roll my eyes.

She nods. "That's why I'm here. Like I said, I went to talk to this reporter. She's been writing about the case since the murder. . . ." She trails off. "I wanted to get clarity on things, but she kept asking whether I'm afraid, you know, now that Jake is back. And . . . I realized that I'm not."

I'm about to sarcastically congratulate her for being so brave when Henry pipes up.

"Do you want to sit?" He motions to the empty space beside him. I shoot him a pointed look.

Grace's eyes dart to my face, but she slowly sits down on the bench, leaving a few feet between herself and Henry.

"So, what did the reporter say?" he asks.

"Nothing new, really. But she reminded me about Jake lying about his alibi to the cops. Remember how he originally said he was with Mr. Berkeley? You told me about that right before—" Grace cuts off, face flushing, but I know what she was about to say and I'm sure Henry does too. Right before she went to the cops. Right before she told them what—*who*—she'd allegedly seen.

Right before she screwed everything up.

Henry nods. "Yeah. I remember."

"I've just been thinking . . . why would Jake lie about that? It's so random."

Henry shakes his head. "Not that random. Berkeley was Jake's advisor his junior and senior year. He helped Jake out of trouble a bunch of times, like when Jake got caught cheating on his bio exam toward the end of his junior year? I never told you guys this, but Mr. Patrizio tried to get him expelled. Berkeley stepped in and managed to convince the administration to give Jake another chance. I'm pretty sure Jake told the cops that because he assumed Berkeley would back him up. Jake was probably freaked out, grasping at straws, you know?"

"Wait, hang on." I grab a folder out of my bag. It's

stuffed with pages from the police report that the lady at the Brawner Police Department's media relations team gave me last year while muttering to herself about armchair detectives and nosy kids and parental supervision.

She was a real joy to deal with.

"Look at this." I flip through the pages until I find the interview between Berkeley and the detectives handling the case. "When they asked Berkeley about it, he told them that he was tutoring a kid from school that evening—Nick Marion. Jake's friend. Then Jake retracted his alibi the next day, probably because he realized Berkeley wasn't going to help him out of trouble this time."

Grace sits back, wearing a defeated expression. "Yeah. True. Well, what about this? I was thinking—the strands of hair they found in Appelbaum's house that matched Jake's DNA? He said someone stole his jacket from his car, right? Which, if you think about it, is totally possible. That person could have found strands of his hair on it and planted them on her living room rug. Did you guys consider that?"

A flash of anger runs through me.

"Yes," I say, digging my nails into the soft flesh of my palm in frustration. "Of course we considered it, Grace. Jake told everyone that probably *was* how his hair got there. But it didn't matter. Once you came forward saying you literally saw him going into Appelbaum's house that night, no one believed a word he said anymore."

Grace's face flushes. "I'm sorry," she says again quietly. "I know I screwed everything up. Please believe me, I know. I'm trying, though. I want to help."

Henry scoots a few inches closer to her and then kicks me under the table. What is his problem? Actually, scratch that. I know what it is. He's not thinking with his head.

"During the trial, Ally and I talked a lot about how, if you were going to frame someone, Jake was the obvious choice. He didn't exactly have a good reputation. Plus, he had a clear motive. I mean, everyone knew about Appelbaum catching him with drugs and the fight they got into."

If I remember correctly, Grace was there in the hallway when it happened. She texted us after, all shaken up. "But wait, Grace, you saw it happen. He never touched her, did he?"

She shakes her head. "No. He yelled a bunch, but that's it. The only time it got physical was when he punched that locker. But still, I see what you're saying. If that's the case, it means whoever killed Appelbaum knew about all of that. I wonder if they go to Brawner." Grace turns a little to stare at the building. She rubs her arms. "Do you think it's one of our classmates?"

I shake my head. "I don't think we can assume that. A bunch of people put that fight on socials, so really anyone could have seen it and decided Jake was a good fall guy. This line of thinking isn't going to get us anywhere, but thanks. We'll see you later?"

I stare at Grace, waiting for her to leave, but she doesn't budge.

"Ally—" Henry says.

"What? Did I miss the conversation where we agreed to forgive Grace and let her join us?"

Henry stares at me.

"I can go," Grace says, rising to stand, but Henry pulls her back down.

"No. Stay. Ally is going to stop. *Right*, Ally?"

I let out a sigh. Henry rarely digs in his heels about things—that's usually my MO—but when he does, I have learned it's pointless to argue.

"Fine. Stay. Whatever." I really don't want to talk about the Jake stuff in front of Grace, but I guess I have no choice. I turn my body so it's clear I'm speaking only to Henry. "To get back to what we were talking about before we were interrupted: The two of us need to track down Appelbaum's sister ASAP. And her friends. That's where we're going to find what we need."

Grace leans forward. "Her sister still lives in Brawner, did you know that?"

I frown. "How do *you* know that?"

"I have my sources." At my glare, she rolls her eyes. "The reporter I talked to mentioned it. I don't get it, though. Why stay? All those bad memories . . . It has to be hard to keep under the radar, even though she got married and changed her last name."

"She did?" I say before I can stop myself. I turn to Henry. "Maybe that's why I couldn't find anything on her last night. Her first name is Gabrielle. I wonder what her married name is. . . ." I grab my phone from my bag and type *Gabrielle Appelbaum* into Google, just like I did last night, and add the word *wedding*.

Google unhelpfully informs me that there aren't any good matches.

"Ally DMed some people to try and get her info," Henry overshares to Grace.

"Maybe I can help. Let me see . . ." Grace types something on her phone. "I just texted the reporter to see if she knows anything—hang on, she's already responding! She says Gabrielle's last name is Flowers now."

My heart leaps. "Can you ask for an email? Phone number?"

Grace scrunches up her nose. "Why would she give that to me?"

"Just try!"

"Fine." She refocuses on her phone, typing, then looks back up at me. "She's asking why I need it."

"Tell her that you're writing a piece for the school paper about Ms. Appelbaum and you're hoping to talk to her sister."

Grace gives me a skeptical look.

"Just do it."

"Fine," she snaps, and turns back to her phone. "She says she has an old email address, but she's not sure if it's still active." Her lips tighten as she continues to read from her phone. "Now she's wondering if I'll reconsider giving her a quote for her next article about Jake. She still hasn't sent the sister's info. I feel like she's holding it hostage unless I agree to talk."

"Tell her you'll strongly consider it," I say.

"Ally!" Henry says.

"What? It's not like she actually has to. There's no harm in letting her think you might."

"I—" Grace glances at Henry.

"This is a bad idea," he says.

"How else are we going to get what we need?" I ask.

"Ugh, fine. *Possibly, but I have to talk to my mom first. That email address might persuade me,*" Grace says as she types into her phone. "Okay . . . she's excited. She . . . she sent it! I have the address!"

"Let me see." I reach over the table and grab at her phone, but she holds it out of my reach.

"No!"

"What is your problem?" I glare at her. "Show me!"

"No. Not unless you agree to let me help."

"Help with *what*?"

"Whatever it is you two are doing."

God, she's annoying. "You're kidding, right?"

"No. I'm not. We all want the same thing. To figure out what really happened that night. I'm going to do it whether you guys let me join you or not, so we might as well work together. Plus," she says smugly, "I have the info you want."

My nostrils flare. Who does she think she is? "I'm sure I can find her on my own."

Henry kicks me under the table.

A few beats of silence. Something inside me—something rude and traitorous that sounds suspiciously like Henry—is whispering that I should agree.

At least, I rationalize, this way I can keep an eye on Grace. I don't know what game she's playing at, but I highly doubt it's going to help Jake.

Finally, I nod. "Fine. You can help. But, Grace?"

"What?"

"Don't screw this up."

GRACE

OCTOBER 10

I'VE BEEN SURREPTITIOUSLY CHECKING my phone under my desk all afternoon, waiting for Mrs. Flowers to reply, and when the email finally lands in my inbox during last period, I let out a little gasp.

"Can we help you with something, Grace?" Mr. Porter asks from the front of the room. He glares at me from behind the wire-rimmed glasses he started wearing earlier this year in a vain attempt to be fashionable. "Care to share your thoughts on this passage from *Frankenstein*?"

I freeze. If I were Ally, or someone braver than myself, this is where I'd give some snarky reply and the class would laugh with me instead of at me. Instead, I wither under everyone's stares. My cheeks redden. I shake my head.

"No?" Porter gives me a look that clearly says, *Put your phone away.* I slide it into the outer pocket of my bag as soon as he turns back to the board.

I struggle to pay attention for the rest of class, mostly

because I'm dying to read the email but also because *Frankenstein* is incredibly boring. Why the school forces us to read books that are like two hundred years old and completely irrelevant to our lives in the year of our Lord 2025 is beyond me.

As soon as Porter ends class, I grab my phone from my bag.

The response is short.

Grace,

Thank you for reaching out. I remember Miriam mentioning you. Yes, I am still in Brawner and open to chatting. Miriam always loved working with you all on the Boar. You can text me at 703-555-0805 and we can figure out a good time to meet this weekend.

Best,
Gabrielle Flowers

With shaking fingers, I pull up a text, plug in her number, and type.

Hi Mrs. Flowers, this is Grace (from Brawner High). I'm free most of the day Saturday, so let me know what works on your end. As I said in my email, I will be bringing along a couple of my colleagues from the paper, if that's okay?

Three bubbles pop up almost immediately and her reply follows shortly after.

Yes that's fine. Saturday @ 11 a.m.
311 Lincoln Rd

OK thank you. See you then.

I have to tell Ally and Henry.

I close the message, stuff my books into my bag, and make my way out of the now-empty classroom into the busy hallway. I'm about to compose a text to Henry and Ally when a hand grabs my arm.

Meghan.

"So apparently Matt's been asking about you again," she launches in, a giant smile on her face. "He's excited you're coming tonight."

It takes me a second to remember what she's talking about.

Oh. Right.

I told her I'd go to Matt's party tonight.

Yay.

My thoughts must be written on my face, because Meghan's smile drops away. "Grace, *nonononono*. You cannot ditch me. You are coming."

"I—" I'm scrambling to come up with an excuse she'll accept, but my brain is blank.

"You're coming. Everyone is expecting you—I need you there. Please, Grace. You have to." We're almost to the front of the school and she stops in her tracks, holding up her hands in prayer. "Pleeeease?"

I sigh. I wish I were someone who could say no. Someone like Lara or Ally.

But, of course, I'm not.

"Yes, sure. Fine. I'm going."

She bounces up and down, clapping her hands. "Good!
You won't regret it."

Unlikely, but sure.

"I'll pick you up at eight."

"Great," I mumble, mostly to myself, because Meghan is
already hurrying away.

We're forced to park halfway down Matt's driveway because
there are already so many cars here. As we walk up to the
house, I hear the loud thump of bass coming from inside.

Matt lives fifteen minutes from my neighborhood, farther out from downtown, where both the houses and plots
of land are bigger. His property has to be at least a few acres;
it's impossible to see the neighbors from here, even though
the trees lining the driveway are almost bare of leaves.

He's here alone a lot because his parents are always trav-
eling for work. I don't know how he does it.

It's creepy.

Then again, from my front yard I can see all my neighbors' houses, and that didn't stop Ms. Appelbaum's murder.

"It's packed," Meghan says enthusiastically as we reach
the front door.

"Yeah," I say, wishing I had just stayed home.

"Are you excited to see Matt?"

Not really.

I nod.

"Hey." She stops with her hand on the doorknob. "Are you okay? You know you can talk to me, right? About Jake and all of that . . . or anything. I'm here."

Meghan's so great. She doesn't deserve to deal with my grumpy ass all night. I have to pull it together.

"I know. I'm okay. Sorry." I take a deep breath, forcing my thoughts away from Jake and Henry and Ally. I can deal with all of that tomorrow.

Tonight, I have to pretend to be a normal person, with normal issues. I have to be a good friend to Meghan.

The first hour goes by in a whirlwind of drinks and random chatter. It's fine—fun, even—but no matter how hard I try to concentrate on what people are saying, my mind keeps wandering to Ally and Henry.

I'm sure they're together right now, discussing tomorrow, what we're going to say to Ms. Appelbaum's sister, and I'm missing it. Not that I was invited in the first place.

After a while, Matt and his friends head out to the backyard. Meghan insists we go with them.

I know she's doing it for me, because she thinks I like Matt, and for a second I wish I had trusted her with what's going on in my head. The fact that now that I've spoken to Henry, I can't stop thinking about him.

Maybe she would actually understand.

But it's too late, so I trail after the group past the pool to the gazebo. I perch on the edge of a bench and listen as everyone starts to talk about Jake. They managed to wait until now to bring him up, shockingly, but after a few drinks it's like they can't help themselves. Tim Martinez, particularly, is on a real tear, which draws the attention of Macey Brown, who loves nothing more than drama.

She immediately starts in on how Jake's release is a travesty of our judicial system.

Apparently, she graduated from law school while no one was watching.

I sit listening to them for a few very, *very* long minutes before excusing myself with a muttered explanation about having to go to the bathroom. Not that anyone other than Meghan notices. They're too focused on ripping Jake and his family to shreds.

The last thing I hear before I walk away is Macey saying, "You'd think he'd just transfer."

She's talking about Henry.

It's funny—not funny *haha,* but funny like being a total hypocrite is funny—that she's so anti-Henry these days. Given the fact that when we were all sophomores, before the murder, before I was "friends" with her, it was well-known that she had a huge crush on him.

Henry never cared—to be perfectly honest, a lot of girls had huge crushes on him back then, because he was smart and funny and didn't care about being friends with the people I'm surrounded by now. He always seemed above it all, above the stupid high school drama, particularly after Jake started getting into trouble. He had too much to deal with at home to care, and it was hot.

But none of them knew the real Henry. He only showed that to a few people. Jake. Ally.

Me.

Once I'm out of their sight, I slide into an empty chair at

the far end of the pool, where it's dark and quiet. I plan to stay here until Meghan's ready to leave.

The only people nearby are talking quietly, and it takes me a minute to register that one of them is Jake's old friend Nick Marion. He graduated—barely—from Brawner two years ago, the summer Jake was supposed to.

I've seen him at these parties before—from what I've heard he hasn't moved on from his high school days of dealing drugs.

It takes a minute for my eyes to adjust to the dark, but once they do, I see he's talking to Bryce Brody, one of the biggest burnouts in my grade.

As I watch, Nick hands something to Bryce, who takes out his wallet and pulls out some bills. Nick counts the money and nods, then Bryce stands and slinks away. All of it is *super* casual and not at all obvious . . . not that anyone else here seems to care.

After Bryce takes off, Nick stays, looking around the backyard. His gaze falls on me. I avert my eyes.

I've never been sure if he recognizes me at these things or not—I met him a few times in passing at the Hansons', and I'm pretty sure he was stoned out of his mind. Regardless, I usually try to avoid him.

Tonight, though, I hesitate. He and Jake were really tight, back before Jake's arrest. I wonder if anyone ever talked to him about all of it. I wonder if he knows anything that might be useful. That I can bring to Ally and Henry as proof of my usefulness.

I take a big swig of my drink, then swing my legs off the chair, suddenly nervous. Am I really going to go talk to him? Nick always intimidated me; there were a ton of rumors about him floating around school: he'd gotten the jagged scar that runs across his chin in a bar fight; he'd been kicked out of his dad's house for doing drugs; he had his own apartment downtown.

Things that made him seem much, much older than the rest of us.

He stands at the same moment I do. I have to stop him.

"Hey," I call softly, trying to keep my voice steady.

Nick pauses, eyes landing on me again. I wave, then quickly walk over to him, doing my best to stay hidden in the dark shadows of the trees, worried as usual about being seen doing something people might judge me for.

"Yeah?" Nick asks sharply. Up close, his face is pockmarked and pale. His shirt hangs off his body like a rag, his voice a low growl.

It takes everything in me not to walk away. Ally would talk to him. Even the old me, the one who wrote for the newspaper and wasn't so worried about other people's opinions, would have managed to eke out a few sentences.

"*Hello?* What do you want?" Nick's growing impatient.

"Are you Nick Marion?" I ask, like I don't already know.

"Yeah?" His eyes narrow. "Why?"

"I'm friends with—" I stop, then start again. "I used to be friends with Jake and Henry Hanson."

An emotion skitters across his face, gone before I can identify it. "The Hansons, huh? I heard Jake got out. What's he up to?"

I stuff my hands into my armpits to hide their shaking. "You guys don't talk anymore?" I ask.

"Haven't talked to him in years. If I had, why would I have asked you what he's up to?" he says, like I'm a total idiot. He pulls a pack of cigarettes from his pocket and starts hitting the bottom against his palm. "You mind?"

I very much do, but shake my head no. The one time I smoked a cigarette, freshman year with Ally and Henry, after Ally dared me to, I threw up all over the sidewalk. I've avoided them since.

"Cool." Nick lights a cigarette and I step back.

"But you and Jake were friends, right?" I ask him. "Before . . . ?"

He squints out into the night, exhaling a cloud of smoke as he says, "Yeah. So?"

I try to hold my breath but end up gagging on a mouthful of cigarette haze. I start coughing uncontrollably, and it takes me a minute to recover. Nick smirks.

When I can speak, I say, "So . . . you know they're going to try Jake again?"

He shoves his free hand deep into the pocket of his jeans. "Yeah, I heard something about that."

"Do you really think he could have done it? *Killed* someone? Jake was a lot of things, but he wasn't violent."

"People can surprise you." Nick's eyes narrow as he stares at my face.

"Yeah, but—"

Nick interrupts. "What'd you say your name was?" He throws his cigarette down and stomps on it. He's looking at me like he's just figured something out.

I hesitate.

"When you first walked up, I thought, *Man, she looks familiar,* but I thought it was just 'cause we'd run into each other at Jake's place. But it isn't, is it?" Nick's lip has curled into a sneer. "You're that girl."

"What girl?" I ask, even though I know exactly what girl he means. I have to get out of here. Now.

"I actually gotta go—" I start, but he talks over me.

"You're the girl who told everyone you saw Jake that night, aren't you? What are you doing here, asking me questions? Who sent you?"

Nick moves toward me and I stumble back, stopping only when my calves press up against a lounge chair. I'm trapped.

"No one sent me—"

"Then what the hell are you doing?" His voice is low. He leans in toward my face, his breath like a trash can. Saliva pools in my mouth.

"Nothing. I just . . . I'm worried that I might have made a mistake?" Tears spring into the corners of my eyes. "And you guys were friends—I thought maybe . . . maybe he told you something about that night. Maybe you know something that could help him, and you don't even realize it."

Nick stares at me for a long moment, then straightens. He steps back, putting a few feet between us. His aggression has disappeared as suddenly as it arrived, and something different has settled on his face. If I didn't know better, I'd say he's afraid.

"You're dead wrong. I don't know anything," he says. "I didn't even see Jake again, after that bitch was killed.

You got it? Jake's a lost cause. He dug his own grave and I suggest you stop asking stupid questions. Stay away from trouble and it'll stay away from you."

With that, he stalks off into the night, leaving me with a sick feeling in the pit of my stomach.

ALLY

HENRY AND I ARE in his car waiting for Grace, who has yet to make an appearance.

We arranged to meet her midmorning at Grant Park, a few blocks from our houses, to avoid the prying eyes of parents. I would have happily left for Mrs. Flowers's house without her, but she's still holding the address hostage—probably for that exact reason.

Henry is here at my insistence. It took some persuading; he kept saying that it could turn out really, really badly if he showed up at the house of Ms. Appelbaum's sister. He thinks—and it's possible he has a point—that if she recognizes him, there's no way she'll talk to us. I told him I'd bring him a disguise, which I did. Black-rimmed fake glasses and a baseball cap. It probably sounds silly, but also I have just about zero desire to be alone with Grace Topham ever again.

"Where is she?" I ask Henry grumpily. I'm in a sour

mood. Sunday is the second anniversary of my dad's death and I haven't been sleeping well. Plus, when we pulled into the parking lot, we almost ran headfirst into Mr. Berkeley, Jake's old advisor from Brawner High, who was exiting and deep in an argument with a bald, angry-looking man in the passenger seat. I hate driving to begin with, and I'm extra sensitive about it around this time of year. Henry knows this, but was clearly too excited about seeing stupid Grace to slow down or care.

Henry sighs. "She isn't even late, Al."

I hold up my phone. "She will be in two minutes."

"Seriously? Can you please chill? It's been a long few days; I'm too tired to deal with this right now."

I make a face. Rude, but I managed to bite back my retort. To be fair, he's had a pretty awful week. "Fine."

"Thank you."

A moment later, I spot Grace hurrying up the street, her long blond hair swinging behind her.

"She's here," I say, displeased.

Henry rolls down his window and waves. I roll my eyes.

Grace reaches the car and slips into the back seat, greeting us with a question. "Okay, so. What's the plan?"

I scowl. "Good morning to you, too. Why is it *our* responsibility to come up with the plan?"

Grace rolls her eyes. "Good morning, Ally. I just assumed you guys talked about it last night?"

Henry elbows me a little harder than seems necessary. "We did. I'm posing as your photographer—Ally borrowed a camera from the newspaper for me to use. And she wrote up some questions you guys can ask her that might help us figure out who else had a motive. Also, if *she* had a motive. She is the one who found Appelbaum, after all."

Henry and I argued about that one last night. Appelbaum always seemed close to her sister . . . but as he pointed out, sometimes it's the people you least suspect.

We lapse into silence as Henry drives. Mrs. Flowers lives on the south side of Brawner, where it's hilly and more wooded, with lots of big parks and man-made lakes. It's also home to a ton of new developments filled with McMansions.

Finally, we turn onto Mrs. Flowers's street, a quiet, tree-lined block with big, two-story houses. On this side of town, you won't find any older brick homes like Henry's or the one-story house Appelbaum inherited from her grandparents. It's all new builds and expansive, carefully landscaped lawns. Here, Henry's old Mazda sticks out like a sore thumb in a sea of Teslas, BMWs, and Land Rovers.

Henry parks halfway down the block. "It's that one." He points to a large, attractive house.

"All right. So. I'll take the lead," I say immediately. Henry can't do it—he needs to stay in the background, and there's no way I'm letting Grace do it. This is *our* investigation. Not hers.

"We don't want to give her any reason to be suspicious of us. Which means we can't ask anything too personal or anything that hints we're here trying to help Jake. I think we can all agree she would not like that. You guys ready?"

"Yes, ready," Grace says. Henry nods in agreement and slips on his glasses and hat.

———

"It's so nice to meet some former students of Miriam's," Mrs. Flowers says as she leads us into her living room, a steaming mug of tea clutched in one hand. "Please, take a seat. My husband took our baby out, so we won't be interrupted."

She sets the mug down on a coaster on the coffee table and settles into a chair. Grace and Henry sit on the couch opposite Mrs. Flowers and I carefully arrange myself on the chair closest to her. Her home looks like it's straight out of an interior design magazine, and I'm a little afraid I'm going to break something.

"Thanks so much for taking the time to speak with us, Mrs. Flowers," I say.

"Please, call me Gabrielle. I actually recognized Grace's name when her email landed in my inbox. I was one grade ahead of Lara at BHS. From what I remember, she was quite the star student."

"Yeah. She was," Grace says, and smiles, but it doesn't quite reach her eyes. She's lived in Lara's academic shadow for a long time now, and I remember how much it used to annoy her. I guess that hasn't changed.

"How's she doing?" Gabrielle asks. "I've lost track of a lot of my old classmates since I don't have social media, but I always assumed Lara would do big things."

"She's in law school," Grace says. "And getting married soon. To Evan Miller. He went to Brawner, too. Their wedding is in a few weeks."

"Evan Miller?" Gabrielle leans forward to put down her cup but misjudges the distance to the table. It hits the surface with a *bang* and tea sloshes over the cup's edge onto the wood.

"Oh *shit*—shoot," she corrects herself, flustered. "I'll be right back." She jumps up and hurries out of the room.

I lean over toward Grace. "I totally forgot Lara was only a few years younger than Appelbaum. Did they know each other?"

Grace shakes her head. "Appelbaum was a senior when Lara was a freshman. They never crossed paths."

"What about Evan? He's older, right? Did he know her?"

"I don't think so. He was shaken up when she was killed, but I remember him saying that they never really crossed paths back then."

Mrs. Flowers returns to the room with a cloth and carefully blots the wet spot as she talks. "Sorry about that. Now, Ally, I remember Miriam talking about you often. You live next door to her old place?"

"I do."

Gabrielle nods. "It's been a difficult few years, and I have to admit I've been putting off some things. Like dealing with that house. I want to assure you that I do have plans to . . . to clean it out. At some point soon. It's just . . . it was my grandparents' place, which is how Miriam came to live there. They'd paid off the mortgage in full years before they passed away, and they left it to her—she was really close with our grandmother. Best friends, really. Plus, it's"—her voice breaks—"it's where I found her that day. I haven't been able to bring myself to go back in there and sort through her things. Or put it on the market."

"I understand," I say quietly, trying to ignore the heaviness in my chest. My dad's office is the same—still intact, like he just stepped out for a moment, even though it's been almost two years since he died. My mom tried to clean it out right after his accident, which caused one of our biggest fights ever. It felt like she was trying to erase him. I totally freaked out—said some awful things that I wish I could take back. Once I'd calmed down enough to be rational, I convinced her to wait, that I needed more time, and we haven't talked about it or touched it since. I think she's waiting for me to bring it up, tell her I'm ready, but I don't know if I'll ever be.

I can't think about that right now.

I change the subject, launching into our cover story.

"So, as you know, we're here because we're putting together a special edition on your sister for the BHS newspaper, but we're doing it a little differently than last year. We want to focus on her life, on who she was. We want the student body to remember her as more than a . . ." I trail off. I'm not sure how to finish that sentence. I was about to say *victim*, which sounds all sorts of wrong.

"I understand," Gabrielle says. "That sounds like a great idea to me. What kind of things are you looking for?"

I clear my throat. We need to tread carefully. She might be cool with talking to us about Appelbaum's personal life, but at the end of the day, we're still a bunch of high school students she's never met. I don't want to scare her off.

"I guess . . . stories from when you guys were little? Funny anecdotes. Things like that. Were you close?"

Gabrielle leans forward and straightens the stack of books sitting on the coffee table. "We were. I am—*was*—only two years younger than Miriam. Growing up we had our fair share of arguments, but by the time she moved back to

Brawner in her early twenties, we'd both grown up a lot. It was a surprise when she came back, actually—I don't know if you knew this, but she landed a great job right out of college writing for the *Philadelphia Querier*. We all expected her to stay up in Philly for a while; it was her dream to write for a big newspaper. But she only worked there for about a year and then . . . well. You know the rest."

She sits back and wipes away tears.

"Excuse me. The past two years have been awful, and just when things were starting to settle, they let that . . . that *monster* out of prison."

Henry's face reddens, and I hurry to steer the conversation away from Jake.

"Well, we appreciate your willingness to talk to us."

"I'm happy to. Before we get into it, can I ask who else you plan to interview for the piece?"

Grace jumps in. "The other English teachers at BHS. Some of your sister's advisees, her former students. We're also interested in speaking with her friends, if you have any suggestions."

"Let me think. She was still close to a couple of friends from high school—Lucy Phillips and Rachael Wu. I haven't spoken to them in a while, but let me see if I can find their contact info. . . ."

"I actually DMed both of them," I tell her. "But I haven't heard back."

"I'll reach out and tell them I spoke with you. Hopefully that motivates them to respond."

My heart lifts. "That would be amazing. Thank you."

Gabrielle nods. "In terms of the other people you

mentioned . . . I'm not sure how to say this, but . . . you might want to be careful about who you talk to. A lot of people loved my sister, but one thing about being a teacher is there are always going to be people who aren't happy with the job you're doing."

I think back, trying to figure out who she's talking about, but nothing sticks out. I guess it's possible that whatever happened was never made public. Last year when we actually did a big piece in the paper about Appelbaum, we didn't interview anyone other than the principal and some other school admins.

"Anyone in particular?" Grace asks.

Gabrielle hesitates. "Well. Please understand that I'm only saying this because I don't want you all to get into an uncomfortable situation. . . ."

"Of course," Grace prompts.

"I'd appreciate it if you kept this between us, but there was one student who she had some issues with in those last few months. Matt Clark was—"

"Matt *Clark*?" Grace's voice is sharp. Her cheeks grow red. Interesting. I wonder if there's more between Grace and Matt than friendship.

Everyone thinks Matt is this great guy—he's captain of the lacrosse team, always on honor roll, and throws these parties that are supposed to be amazing, if you like that sort of thing. I've never been, of course, because everyone hates Henry and, by extension, me, but that's what I've heard. His dad is a big-time lawyer and his mom is a lobbyist down in DC and Matt walks around school like he thinks he's God's gift to humankind.

This is all to say: Matt's a douche.

Back when we were friends, Grace never would have been interested in someone like that. Honestly, she can do better.

"A month before she died, Miriam gave him a bad mark on a paper. He was . . . Let's just say he and his parents thought he deserved better. His father wrote a nasty email to the school board, claiming that Miriam's grading was unreasonable. He literally tried to get her fired. It was a whole mess; Miriam had to testify in front of the board, and when nothing came of it, Mr. Clark was *extremely upset*. Parents really are the bane of a teacher's existence. Anyway. I've said too much, but just do me a favor and skip Matt Clark. There's no point in dredging all that up."

I'm struggling to keep my face impassive. I've long heard that Matt is a shoo-in at an Ivy League school, and from what Mrs. Flowers just said, it sounds like his parents don't care *how* it happens, only that it does. I wonder how important it really is to them—important enough to kill?

"Thanks for letting us know. We'll definitely avoid him," I tell her, lying through my teeth.

HENRY

OCTOBER 11

TWENTY MINUTES AND SEVERAL poorly shot photographs later, we're back in my car.

"We need to talk to Matt," Ally says. She twists in her seat. "Grace, did *you* know he tried to get Appelbaum *fired*? What a dick."

In the rearview mirror, I see Grace chewing on her lower lip. I can't help but wonder what exactly her relationship with Matt Clark is. I've seen them together in the halls, but I've tried not to think about it. Right now, though, I don't have a choice.

"No," she finally says. "I didn't. But Matt really isn't like that—it's his dad who's obsessed with that stuff. Matt was probably embarrassed by the whole thing."

Ally frowns. "His dad is a really successful attorney, right? Guys like that hate losing. Mrs. Flowers said he was pissed when the school board sided with Appelbaum. It made me wonder . . . was he pissed enough to murder her?"

"*What?* Oh my god, *no*, Ally. His parents are intense, sure, but they're not going to *murder* someone over a grade," Grace says.

"Are you serious? People do stuff like that all the time. There was a news story a few years ago about a couple of high schoolers in the Midwest who killed their Spanish teacher over a bad grade. If it was going to affect Matt's chance to get into an Ivy, who knows what he and his dad would do?"

"It's worth considering," I agree, pretending that I'm being driven purely by rational thought and not by anything silly like jealousy. "We should add them to our suspect list."

"You have a suspect list?" Grace asks. "When was someone going to tell me about this? Who else is on it?"

Ally's lips tighten, but I ignore her. She needs to get over her unwillingness to share with Grace.

"It's not really, like, a list, per se," I tell Grace. "More just people we started talking about who might have motive. And, honestly, before today we only had one name. . . ."

"Who?"

I look at Ally. "A week before the murder, Ally went over to Appelbaum's to talk to her about her next cat-sitting job—"

"Yeah," Ally interrupts, suddenly over her hesitancy to share. I figured bringing this up would help; she loves telling the story to anyone who will listen, mainly, I think, because most people won't. "I was almost to her front door when I heard voices. Loud, angry voices coming from inside the house. I recognized Appelbaum's, but I couldn't place the other. . . . It was deep. A man, I think. The argument sounded pretty intense, so I left. I figured I'd talk to her another time. I didn't see who it was—I wish I had, but how was I supposed to know what was going to happen?"

"Did you tell the cops?" Grace asks.

"Yeah. They blew me off. Told me it was probably Jake. But I swear to you, it wasn't. It didn't sound anything like him. Plus, what do they think he was doing there? It was before Appelbaum found the drugs in his locker."

"Did you guys ever ask him about it?"

Ally and I exchange a glance. "I tried," I say. "He said it wasn't him."

"I *know* it wasn't him!" Ally says. "The voice was way deeper than his. It was someone else. Someone no one ever investigated. And we need to find them."

"How?" Grace asks, echoing what I say to Ally whenever this subject comes up.

She scowls. "I don't *know*. Why is that my job—"

"But now we have three suspects: Matt and his dad and that guy," I say, interrupting Ally. I cannot deal with listening to her bitch at Grace again. "Can you guys think of anyone else?"

"Well," Grace says after a moment's silence, "I ran into Nick Marion last night at Matt's house."

"Nick Marion?" My fingers tighten around the steering wheel. Nick Marion is the devil. He helped ruin Jake's life. "Why was he at a high school party?"

"He's always there. Mostly dealing drugs."

I shouldn't be surprised to hear that he's still doing that after everything with Jake. But somehow, I am. "Jesus. What a loser."

"Yeah, no kidding," Grace says. "I usually avoid him,

but last night I decided to try and talk to him to see if he remembered anything from around the time of the murder. Thought maybe he'd know something that could help us."

"You *talked* to him?" It comes out more judgmental than I mean it to, but I'm not kidding when I say Nick is one of my least favorite people on the planet.

"Yeah, but think about it. I bet you no one ever asked him if he knew anything, and he and Jake hung out all the time. I thought maybe . . . I don't know. Maybe he knew something. But he told me he didn't see Jake again after the murder, and when I pressed him on it, he got super pissed. Then he recognized me as the person who testified against Jake, which ruined any chance of him telling me anything at all. He actually asked if someone had sent me, like he thought maybe the cops had."

"Oh," I say. We fall into an uncomfortable silence. I'm trying not to picture her up there on the stand that day, sealing my brother's fate, when something she said about Nick wriggles its way to the front of my mind.

I slam on the brakes and the car behind us lets out a loud honk.

"Henry, what the hell?" Ally cries.

"Sorry, sorry." I wave an apologetic hand to the old, white-haired driver of the car, and get a middle finger in response. "Wait, Grace. Nick told you he didn't see Jake again after the murder?"

"Yeah? Why?"

"Because I swear Nick came over to our house the day after Jake was brought in for questioning. Which was after Appelbaum was killed, obviously."

"Did they talk?" Grace asks.

"I think so. Not for long, because as soon as my dad figured out Nick was there, he kicked him out—he's always hated him—but I'm like ninety-nine percent sure Jake and Nick at least saw each other."

"Maybe Nick forgot?" Grace suggests.

"Yeah, maybe . . . but the thing is, from what I remember, Jake was really upset after he left. It didn't seem like the type of conversation someone would forget. But why would Nick say they hadn't seen each other?"

"Maybe he's lying," Ally says.

"Yeah, but why? Seems random," I say.

"Maybe not. Maybe . . . maybe they talked about something that night," Ally says. "Something important that Nick doesn't want anyone knowing about. What if . . . I don't know, what if *Nick* had something to do with Appelbaum's death? He hated her, didn't he?"

"Didn't she fail him junior year?" I say.

"Exactly," Ally says. "I remember him talking about her that summer at your house, stuff about how she better watch her back. You have to ask Jake about it, Henry. Maybe he'll remember what they talked about."

The last thing I want to do is talk to my brother. Outside of a few awkward run-ins, we've barely interacted since I pissed him off by mentioning Grace.

"Okay, but if Nick had something to do with the murder and he told that to Jake, why wouldn't Jake tell someone? That makes no sense," I argue. "Plus, he was with Berkeley that night. Remember? That was in the police files you got last year."

"Okay, fine, true, but I still think this is important. Maybe he didn't do it, but he knows something about who did," Ally says. "Just ask Jake about it, Henry. He's literally in the room next to yours. How hard could it be?"

I almost laugh. How hard is it to talk to Jake? Nearly impossible.

"I'll try," I say, but I'm not sure I mean it.

After I drop off Ally and Grace, I head home. Kakova's car is in the driveway, where it's taken up semipermanent residence lately. This time around, my mom's insisted on being as involved as possible in everything Jake's attorneys are doing, so Kakova is here all the time, updating her on what he's doing. Which, if you ask me, isn't much.

All I want to do is head to my room and shut myself inside. Not see anyone else until tomorrow. But then tomorrow's going to come and Ally's going to ask me whether I talked to Jake. . . . I might as well get it over with. Plus, she's not wrong. It is weird that Nick would lie about that, although it's also entirely possible that he's just burned too many brain cells at this point to remember much of anything.

As usual, Jake's bedroom door is closed. I knock gently, part of me hoping that he won't hear, which is unlikely. He's definitely inside.

Sure enough, a few moments later I hear shuffling sounds and the door swings open, Jake's tired face emerging into the light. He scowls when he sees me.

"What?" he snaps.

I hate that we're on such bad terms. Especially because it's partly my fault.

I don't know what to say. This is the perfect moment to confess. Why I didn't come to visit, what Ally and Grace and I are doing. But the longer I stand here silent, the less my mouth seems able to form words.

"What do you want, Henry?" he asks, his voice less angry and more tired this time.

"I . . . I don't think you did it." He needs to know that, above anything else. "That's not why I didn't come to see you."

"Oh yeah? Then why?"

"I . . . I can't explain."

He rolls his eyes. "Cool. Great talk." He moves like he's about to shut the door and I rush to speak.

"Did you talk to Nick?"

Something flashes across his face, dark and angry. *"Nick?"*

I suck a breath. "Yeah. Nick Marion? The first time the cops dragged you to the station—later that night, I remember Nick coming by the house. Did he?"

Jake stares at me silently. For a moment I wonder if he's going to respond.

"What are you talking about?" he finally says.

"I . . . well, someone I know ran into Nick"—I'm not going to make the mistake of mentioning Grace again—"and he told me that you guys haven't spoken since before Appelbaum died, and I was confused. I remember him coming over that night when you got back from the station. Why's he lying about it? That's weird, right?"

I fall silent. Jake is staring at me, expressionless.

"He didn't come over," he says.

That is not the answer I was expecting. I pull my head back in confusion. "But I saw him."

"He didn't come over," Jake repeats slowly. "Okay? He wasn't here. I don't know what you and Ally are up to, Henry, but if it involves *anything* with Nick Marion, it has to stop. Immediately."

"But—" Why is he being so intense about this? About Nick? They were friends before Jake went to jail. At least, I thought they were. "But I remember him coming over—"

"You need to stop." The way he's staring at me makes my stomach flip.

"We're just trying to—"

"I don't care what you're trying to do. Stop. Do not speak to Nick. Leave it to Kakova. Okay?"

When I don't reply, he says it again. "*Okay?*"

I want to argue, but I can tell there's no point. I also don't believe him. I remember Nick being here. Jake is lying to me right now, and I don't know why.

"Okay."

"Good." He steps back into the darkness of his room, about to shut the door, when he pauses. "And, Henry?"

I meet his eyes. "Yeah?"

"Thanks for caring enough to ask me about this. It's more than most people have done."

His door shuts between us.

ALLY

A GIANT KNOT IN my stomach greets me upon waking this morning. Today is the day I've been trying to avoid thinking about for weeks.

The two-year anniversary of my dad's death.

When he died, everyone told me that it would get easier with time, like that was a good thing—like forgetting him was what I wanted. What I wanted was for him to come back.

They weren't wrong, fortunately or unfortunately. Two years later, the realization that he's gone still whams me in the gut, but it's not as bad as last year or the year before . . . which makes me feel both better and worse.

Grief sucks.

Maybe it would be different if he hadn't died like he did—totally unexpectedly, in a car wreck late in the evening in a random area of town when we thought he was still at work. His office said it wasn't unusual, that sometimes he'd leave without explanation to chase a lead. They said that's probably what he was doing, even though no one seemed to know what story he was working on or why it took him to the far edge of Brawner. All I could think is, if he had been where he said he was going to be, he would still be alive.

I drag myself out of bed and through my morning routine, forcing myself to focus on that and not on memories of my dad.

My mom's already in the kitchen when I get downstairs, her eyes rimmed with dark shadows.

"Hey," she greets me, holding up her mug. "Coffee's ready."

"Thanks." I pour myself a cup.

"How are you? It's the twelfth," she says, like she thinks I might not be aware. I bristle even though I know she didn't mean it like that.

My mom and I went through a rough patch after my dad died. I was always closer to him, and in the wake of his death, there was so much empty space left behind. I was angry at everything and everyone—my mom, him, the world. And then two months later, Appelbaum died, and things got even worse.

It took a while, but we're back in a good spot where we coexist mostly peacefully. Even so, I still have to remind myself her intentions are pure. She's checking in. Being a good mom.

"I know."

"If you need anything . . . or want to talk . . . ," she says.

"I'm good," I say. Her face falls. I feel bad for a second, but I can't. I can't have another long, drawn-out conversation about my dad.

I set my mug of half-drunk coffee in the sink. "I need to do some homework."

"Okay," she says. I can feel her eyes on me. "I'm heading to the gym, but I won't be long. I'll be around later if you change your mind. . . ."

"Will do," I say, even though I absolutely won't.

Once upstairs, I sprawl out on my bed and check my phone. There's still no response from any of Appelbaum's high school friends, which is so frustrating. I wonder if Mrs. Flowers bugged them like she promised.

Matt Clark is next on my list. Grace might think it's a stretch to investigate him and his dad, but she's clearly biased. Plus, am I supposed to trust *her* instincts? I think not.

I start Googling to see if I can find anything online about Mr. Clark's school board fight, but there's nothing. I guess they keep things like that quiet unless a teacher is actually found guilty, which makes sense if you think about it.

Matt's social media is set on private and we're not friends—in real life or on the internet. Unlike *some* people I could mention, I choose to spend my time with people who aren't total dickheads.

All I can see of his profile is his tiny thumbnail photo. I screenshot it and zoom in. He's grinning, holding a lacrosse stick. He really thinks he's God's gift; I can't believe Grace fell for his act.

Grace.

The name snags in my brain and my heart sinks.

I know how I can see Matt's page. Ughhhh.

I text Grace, but after five minutes and no reply, I decide to take matters into my own hands.

I slide off the bed and head out of my room.

Mrs. Topham answers the door, her smile falling off her face when she sees me standing on her porch.

"Oh. Ally. What are . . . you doing here?" She turns and looks back into the house like the answer to her question is somewhere in her foyer.

"Hi, Mrs. Topham," I say, ignoring her obvious displeasure. Like I care what she thinks about me. Like I don't already know.

She and my mom used to be good friends—she and Henry's mom, too. But after the murder and Jake's arrest, Mrs. Topham stopped taking Ms. Hanson's calls. She was still friendly with my mom until it became clear that I wasn't about to turn my back on Henry's family, and then she stopped talking to us, too.

I felt bad at first—I didn't want my decisions to mess up my mom's life—but to her credit, she told me she didn't care. She said that if I wanted to keep my friendship with Henry, she supported me.

It was right around then that our relationship started to get better.

"Can I help you?" Mrs. Topham asks, just this side of full-on rude. Clearly, Grace hasn't told her that she's been hanging around with me and Henry again.

How shocking.

"I was looking for . . . Is Grace here?"

Her eyebrows jump. "Grace?"

"Yes. Grace." I'm tempted to add *You know, your younger daughter?* but bite my tongue.

"Let me see . . . ," she says. Then, instead of inviting me inside, she shuts the door in my face and leaves me standing on the porch, wondering if she's going to come back.

A few long moments later, the door opens. But instead of Grace, it's Lara.

It's been over a year since I last saw her. She looks older. Thin. Stressed. Grace mentioned that Lara's wedding is coming up soon and that she's been feeling the pressure, which would explain it, I guess, although why people care so much about weddings is completely beyond me.

"Ally Copeland." Lara's voice is flat. "What are you doing here?"

"I'm here to see Grace, obviously," I say, trying to peek around her to the inside of the house. She blocks my view with her body.

"I didn't think you two talked anymore."

"We're working on an article together. For the paper."

"Grace quit writing for the paper two years ago," she says as if I'm not fully aware of that fact. Who does she think she is, Grace's bodyguard? She needs to chill.

"Well, she's writing again. Maybe you missed the memo," I say snippily.

"Why didn't she tell me?"

"I don't know. You'd have to ask her that, I guess? Can I talk to her now?"

Lara's mouth dips down, but before she can respond, the door is pulled open farther and Grace finally appears.

"Ally, hey." She's wearing the Baby Yoda T-shirt I gave her freshman year. It's fraying at the hem.

"What's up?" she asks nervously. Her eyes dart between me and Lara.

"I texted you," I say.

"Oh, sorry. I've been helping with some wedding stuff and left my phone on the kitchen counter. Do you need something?"

Lara's still standing in the doorway with her hands on her hips, staring at me.

"Yeah, I just need to talk to you about that article we're working on. . . ." I widen my eyes, trying to silently get across the message that I need to talk to her in private, i.e., not in front of her nosy sister.

"Oh. Right. Gotcha. Let's go out back." Grace waves me into the house.

"I can't believe you didn't tell me you'd started writing for the newspaper again," Lara tells Grace as we pass her.

Grace's face tightens. "It only happened recently."

"Still. I would have been excited for you." Lara sounds anything but excited right now, but okay.

"We're heading out back," Grace says as she guides me through the familiar living room to the sliding back door.

"Well, don't be long," Lara calls as we step outside. "We still have things to discuss for my wedding."

"Isn't that something she should be doing with Evan?" I ask Grace in a low voice as I follow her to the patio chairs.

Grace shrugs. "Evan's busy at work."

Her yard is the same as I remember it. It's weird, being here; it feels simultaneously like no time has passed and one hundred years have gone by since the last time I was here.

"Sorry if Lara and my mom were . . . you know . . ." Grace makes a face. A cool breeze blows, and I zip up my hoodie.

"Less than pleased to see me?" I finish her sentence.

"Yeah, sorry about that. They're just protective. I was actually going to text you. I wanted to say . . . you know, it's October twelfth. I haven't forgotten. How are you doing?"

Grace was sleeping over at my house when we learned about my dad's accident. She helped hold me together—both that night and so many after. I hate to admit it now, but I don't know if I would have survived if it hadn't been for her.

But that was a long time ago.

"I'm fine," I tell her, ignoring her skeptical expression. "I'm not here to talk about that. I'm here on business. You're friends with Matt on social media, right?"

"Yes . . . but, Ally, I swear to God, he's not a killer."

"Don't you think you might be a little biased? You guys are dating."

"We are not!" she exclaims.

"Well, whatever you are, it's clearly clouding your judgment. Can I just see his social media, please? If he has nothing to hide, it won't matter either way, will it?"

"I suppose." She unlocks her phone and hands it to me. "Here. His Insta. He barely posts, though. He mostly sends stuff through Snap, but that's not exactly going to be helpful, considering Appelbaum died two years ago. If he sent anything about her back then, it's long gone."

"I'm aware of how Snap works, Grace." I examine Matt's profile. He only has nine grid posts, which is really quite unhelpful of him. "I'm trying to figure out where he was the night of the murder. Whether he has an alibi. We might need to talk to some of the English teachers. See if they remember the drama; I'm sure they heard about it."

"Wait. Hang on, lemme see that." Grace snatches her phone back. "In the winter, Matt plays basketball. Lemme pull up . . . Here's the schedule from 2023. Appelbaum died on—"

"December fifteenth," I supply. "A Friday."

"Hmm. No game that night." She looks up at me. "But if it was Friday, I'd bet he was at some party. Though I could be wrong; it was back before I started going to them, so—"

The way she says it pisses me off. "I'm *so* sorry Henry and I held you back from having such an amazing and active social life for so long."

Grace is quiet for a long moment. "That's not at all what I was trying to say. It's not like I had much of a choice. You guys wouldn't give me the time of day, and Meghan Cheng and I were lab partners and she started inviting me to do things. . . . It was either that or be all alone."

"You mean all alone, like Henry and I were? Everyone at school *hated* us, and there you were all of a sudden, hanging with people we never liked, people who were total assholes to Henry and his family—" I cut myself off. I can't do this right now. Not today. Not ever, maybe. It's not worth it.

"Whatever. Coming over here was a mistake. I gotta go." I stand. "I'll leave through the side gate so my presence doesn't upset your mom or sister more than it already has."

Grace stands up too, her chair scraping loudly against the patio stones. "Ally, c'mon. Stay. I'm sorry, okay? I'm sorry about everything. We need to figure out how we're going to track down Matt's alibi, right? What are our next steps? Maybe we should text Henry?"

I shake my head. Of course she wants to text Henry. He's the one she really cares about.

I'm afraid to speak; the lump in my throat is growing larger with every passing second, tears springing to the corners of my eyes. I refuse to cry in front of Grace.

Or about Grace.

Ever again.

"I have to go," I say, and hurry out of the yard.

GRACE

OCTOBER 12

MY STOMACH IS IN knots as I go back inside.

When Ally showed up here, I thought maybe . . . I thought maybe she was starting to forgive me. It's probably silly to think that's even possible, but I can't help but hope.

No matter what she believes, what I did two years ago wasn't personal. Not to her, not to Henry. I honestly, truly thought I was doing the right thing to get justice for Ms. Appelbaum.

And I knew if I told Henry and Ally first what I saw, I might never go to the cops.

"Did she leave?" Lara asks as I walk into the kitchen.

"Yeah," I say, pouring myself a glass of water. I can feel her eyes on me, watching, waiting for some sort of explanation.

"So, you're writing for the *Boar* again, Gracie?" she finally says. "And cowriting an article with Ally Copeland. What's it about? Why didn't you tell me?"

Knowing Lara, she's not going to let this go until I give her something.

"You've been so busy with wedding stuff, I figured I'd tell you after. And in terms of Ally—we aren't really cowriting. The second anniversary of Ms. Appelbaum's death is coming up and we're putting together a special section about her life for that week's paper. I offered to help since I knew her pretty well. Ally just wanted to talk about it. She's the editor in chief this year, you know."

My mom and Lara exchange a look and my jaw clenches. They could not be less subtle.

"*What?*" I say. "You're the ones always getting on my back about doing more extracurriculars for college applications. Plus, Ms. Appelbaum was important to me. I want to help." I take a breath and say what I know will get them off my back. "Even if it means hanging out with Ally. Temporarily. It's not a big deal."

"But with her connection to Henry . . . and the new trial . . ." My mom trails off. I know what she's leaving unsaid.

If I'm seen fraternizing with Ally Copeland, people might start to talk.

"It's not a big deal," I repeat. "The stuff for the paper doesn't have anything to do with Henry—*or* Jake. We're just writing about Ms. Appelbaum. Talking to a few people who knew her well. That's it. We're staying far, far away from the trial."

My mom frowns. "Just be careful, Grace. People might take it the wrong way if you start associating with her again."

And there it is. Is it any wonder that I've been so nervous about all of this?

"Yeah. Okay." I break eye contact. "I'll be careful."

GRACE

OCTOBER 13

MEGHAN HAS A SOCCER game this afternoon, after school. Some of our friends, including Matt, decide to go watch, which is why I find myself sitting in the mostly empty stands, cheering her on. It's been weird, hiding what I'm up to with Ally and Henry from her, but I don't think she'd understand. And I *know* some of our mutual friends would not.

It's getting old, though, worrying what other people think about me.

Speaking of. Macey Brown and Tim Martinez appear at the end of the stands. Macey waves.

"Grace, what's up? Where have you been? I haven't seen you around much, outside of Matt's party."

She hasn't seen me because I've been avoiding her as much as humanly possible over the course of the last week. It hasn't been that hard—we have different lunch periods, and the break has been necessary after all the nasty things she's said about Henry and Jake.

Honestly, if Meghan weren't a genuinely good friend and Matt weren't coming to the game, I wouldn't even be here right now.

"Hey," I say.

"Hey, Grace," Tim says as they settle next to me. Tim has never been my favorite person either, but he's always around, just like Macey.

I think back to what Ally said yesterday, about how we never used to like the people I hang out with now.

Maybe there was a reason for that. Maybe I lowered my standards because I was so lonely.

"Matt's coming soon," Macey says, nudging me. "He should be here—oh yeah, there he is." I glance over my shoulder and see Matt climbing up the bleachers toward us.

I haven't seen much of him recently either, but I'm not here because I missed him. I'm here because I need information. Information that I can bring back to Ally, to prove to her that I'm a useful part of the team. That they should keep me around. Because if I screwed up two years ago and the person I saw that night wasn't Jake, I need to fix it. No matter who it upsets.

"Hi, guys." Matt high-fives Tim, then scoots around Macey to take a seat next to me.

"Hey," I say, taking in the perfect side part in his blond hair, his broad shoulders, his icy blue eyes.

Two weeks ago, my heart would have skipped a beat, being this close to him. But now, after spending time with Henry again, it's not doing anything at all.

"How was your day?" I ask him. He needs no more

encouragement than this to launch into a five-minute recitation of his day. It's the polar opposite of what I do when asked, which is to assume the other person is just being polite and tell them "fine."

"Are your parents home yet?" I ask when he finally finishes talking.

"Ah, you got this!" he screams at the field and then turns to me. "What?"

"Just wondering if your parents are home."

He rolls his eyes. "Surprisingly, yes. My dad's on my back already, of course. Have you guys turned in your college apps yet? He seems to think I should have already submitted them, like, they aren't due for a month, bro. Chill— Nice shot!"

"I haven't yet," Macey says.

"Me either," I say, trying to figure out how to steer the conversation in the direction I need it to go. I'm going to have to throw Ally under the bus. "So . . . did you hear that the newspaper is doing a special edition about Ms. Appelbaum?"

Predictably, Macey's and Tim's heads swing in my direction. "Another one?" Tim asks. "Didn't they already do that last year? If you ask me, what they *should* be doing is a whole spread on why Jake Hanson is a fucking murderer."

Macey chimes in. "I can't believe they allowed that girl to be editor in chief of the paper. Who thought it was a good idea to let her have that position? She's best friends with the brother of a killer."

"Yeah," I say, like I'm agreeing with her. The word pains

me as it leaves my mouth. I attempt to change the subject back to Appelbaum. "Anyway. I can't believe the two-year anniversary is already coming up."

"Two years later and that psycho is already out of prison," Tim mutters. "She must be rolling in her grave."

Macey leans around Tim to look at me. "Are you going to have to testify again, Grace? At his new trial?"

"Oh man, *are* you?" Matt asks. His attention is finally off the game, and on me.

I shrug like the question doesn't bother me. "Not sure. We'll see what happens. I keep thinking about it, though . . . how weird is it that I was, like, right across the street from her house when it happened? It's creepy, you know?"

Everyone nods. I swallow.

"Do you guys remember where you were?" I ask, trying to keep my voice casual.

They look at each other.

"The night Ms. Appelbaum was murdered?" Tim asks. "I was at Baron's house with some of the basketball team. . . . Matt, were you there?"

Matt's attention is back on the game and it takes him a minute to respond. "What?" His eyes flick to my face and then away.

"I said, were you at Baron's house with us?"

"I . . ." Matt hesitates.

"Actually, now that I think about it, you weren't, were you? Where were you? I can't remember."

"I was out of town," Macey offers into the ensuing silence, like anyone cares. I ignore her, silently willing Matt to answer.

"Didn't you have some drama with Appelbaum be-fore she died?" Macey asks Matt, and I take back my rude thoughts about her. Sometimes her complete lack of tact comes in handy.

Matt's face flushes. "No."

"Yeah, you totally did," Tim says. "Your dad was super pissed because of that paper—"

"Nice goal, Meghan!" Matt yells, standing and clapping loudly. After a second, Macey and Tim and I follow. I blink. I'd forgotten where we are for a second. Meghan's out on the field with her arms in the air, her teammates cheering.

After the cheering dies down, Macey launches into an entirely different subject, Appelbaum forgotten. I try and fail several times to get us back on track, but Matt changes the subject every time.

Finally, I'm forced to pivot to plan B, aka the one I've been hoping to avoid.

I pull my phone out of my pocket, groaning loudly. "Shoot. I told Meghan I'd take some photos of the game, but my phone is dead!" I sound so fake; I can only hope Matt doesn't notice. I definitely do not have a career as an actress waiting for me after high school.

"What?" Matt asks without taking his eyes off the field.

"My phone." I clear my throat. "I told Meghan I'd take some photos, but it's dead. . . ."

"Want to borrow mine?" Matt asks, like I hoped he would.

"That would be awesome, thank you so much!"

"Yeah, no problem. Here you go." He unlocks it and hands it to me.

"I'm gonna go down to the field for a sec to get a better shot, if you're cool with it?"

He nods, distracted by the game again, and I head down the bleachers, heart thumping, holding his phone tight.

He acted so evasive back there, refusing to say where he'd been the night of the murder, pretending like his dad hadn't tried to get Appelbaum fired. Why is he being so weird about all of it?

Once I'm on the field, I turn to make sure they're all still up in the bleachers. Matt waves, and I wave back, guilt heating my cheeks. This is ridiculous. There's no way Matt murdered Ms. Appelbaum. He's probably going to Stanford or Columbia next year. Everyone loves him. He's so innocent he let me walk away with his unlocked phone.

Ally's voice rolls through my head: two kids in the Midwest murdered their teacher over a bad grade.

Maybe not so ridiculous?

I snap a couple of quick shots of Meghan in action and then flick over to his photos, scrolling until I get to December 2023.

Okay. Well. This is not what I expected to find.

Apparently, Matt takes a lot of selfies. Like, a *lot* a lot. The first few days of December that's all there are: pictures and pictures of . . . him. Lots of different outfits, different hairstyles . . . one where he's flexing in his bathroom mirror, shirtless and . . . pantsless?

Jesus Christ.

I almost drop the phone, feeling awkward all of a sudden, even though I didn't mean to see that. Matt works out, that much is clear. Could *he* be the person I saw that night, wearing Jake's jacket and a hat pulled down low? He's just about the right height.

I keep scrolling past the, um, naked picture, more selfies, party pictures of people who I'm friends with now but wasn't then.

Once I get to the fifteenth, I slow. Several pics of Matt in different outfits from that morning—who knew he was so vain? His friends in hallways at school, guys from the basketball and lacrosse teams making dumb faces. Bryce sitting behind the counter of some store, giving the camera the finger.

I reach a photo time-stamped 7:45 p.m. A selfie of Matt inside his car.

I zoom in. Over his left shoulder I can make out a few parked cars, the edge of an industrial building.

The next photo is from an hour and a half later, a sign that reads WELCOME TO DELAWARE.

I let out a breath. Matt wasn't lying. He *was* out of town the night Appelbaum died. He couldn't have done it. I quickly text myself the photo, then erase the evidence from his phone.

I sneak a look behind me. Matt is still talking to Tim, paying me no attention, so I swipe to the next photo.

My stomach sinks. It's a screenshot of a news article about Appelbaum's murder. She was killed on the fifteenth, but they didn't find her until the seventeenth, when her sister went into her house looking for her after she didn't show up for their planned lunch. Once she saw the scene, she called the cops and they found Appelbaum's body stuffed inside the freezer chest in her garage.

I swipe to the next photo: a random shot of the front of a converted warehouse with the street number 1642—the sort of building that's all over west Brawner.

I text it to myself, then delete the message.

Now that I have what I need, I should stop, but it's addictive, looking through someone else's private stuff.

I swipe to the next picture and my heart stops.

Is that . . . ?

I zoom in on the photo and—

"What are you doing?"

The phone slips from my hand and drops to the ground. I bend to get it at the same time Macey does, and manage to grab it first.

"Nothing. Taking some pictures of the game," I say, holding the phone close to my chest.

"That's not what it looked like to me." She's frowning. "That's Matt's phone, right? It looked like you were going through it. What the hell?"

"I wasn't." I'm struggling to keep my voice calm. I have no idea how much she saw or *what* she saw. I refuse to admit anything.

"I was taking some pictures of Meghan. Like she asked me to. Look." Before Macey can get a peek, I swipe back to the pictures I took a few minutes ago of the action on the field.

I hold the phone out to her. "See?"

Macey glances at the screen. "Yeah, well. I know what I saw. You were going through Matt's phone. You've been acting so weird recently. Ever since Jake's release was announced. I mean, I get that you'd be freaking out, but that doesn't explain why Emily Wensch saw you last week, out back of school sitting with Henry Hanson and Ally Copeland? What is *that* about? Are you talking to those freaks?"

"No!" I exclaim before I can stop myself. God, maybe Ally is right about me. Maybe I'm willing to throw the two of them under the bus to protect my own back. Maybe I've learned nothing. Maybe I'm kidding myself, thinking that I don't care what people think of me.

"Yeah, well, whatever it is, you better get it together and stop being so shady if you want Matt to stay interested in you. He has a lot of options. If I told him what I saw today . . ."

"I wasn't going through his phone!" I say again.

Macey snorts. "Right. Who do you think Matt would believe—me or you? We've been friends since kindergarten. If you don't want me to say anything to him, you better make it worth my while."

"*Excuse* me?"

"You're in Freeman's English class, right?"

"Yeah . . ."

"I'm in her other section. I hate writing papers. But I hear you're decent at it—you wrote for the newspaper for a while, huh?"

I stare at her.

"Our next paper is due in—"

"—two weeks," I finish for her, heart sinking.

"Yep. You can write two of them in that amount of time,

right?" She doesn't wait for me to respond. "Great. Thanks
so much. I'd like an A, please. Now you'd better get that
phone back to Matt, before he starts getting suspicious. We
wouldn't want that, would we?"

She gives me a smug grin and slinks away.

HENRY

"ALLY, I REALLY DON'T think it's a good idea for me to come," I tell her, again, as she drags me through the halls. The word *murderer* floats to us from somewhere nearby. I tense.

"Ignore it," Ally mutters. "They're not worth it."

I'm usually the one telling her that, but admittedly, today I'm feeling on edge. I'm sick of everything right now. My locker vandalized. Home egged. This morning I found a charming note someone had slipped through the vents of my locker that simply read FUCK YOU.

Whoever wrote it has a real future in greeting cards.

"Talking to the English teachers is important." Ally changes the subject back to what we've been arguing about for the last couple of minutes, since she met me outside of my AP US History class. "We need to see if they can tell us anything about the Matt stuff."

"I agree one of us needs to talk to them, but I have faith you can handle it solo. I'm Jake's brother, Ally. You go in there asking questions about Appelbaum with me in tow, and it's going to get awkward real fast."

We head into the stairwell that leads to the English department. We're walking against the flow of foot traffic, but thankfully it's less congested in here. Less chance of someone being an asshole.

"Henry, there are like *five* teachers we need to talk to. It'd take me forever to do it alone. I need you."

"What about Grace?"

Ally's mouth puckers. "I don't want to talk about Grace."

I sigh. Her response confirms my suspicions that something happened between the two of them. Hell if I'm going to get in the middle of it.

Everything with me and Grace started happening a few months before Ally's dad died. I didn't tell Ally, because at first I wasn't sure what to call it. I can't speak for Grace, but for me it was something like falling in love. Which sounds so lame and cheesy, but whatever. It's the truth.

I didn't start noticing Grace like that until seventh grade, and then it was like I couldn't stop. I never told Ally— I never told *anyone*—because what if Grace didn't feel the same way? I couldn't blow up our friendship like that.

But then one day, the summer before sophomore year, we were at my house hanging out and Ally left early. Grace and I ended up sitting under a blanket together watching some Netflix show. By the end of the episode we were holding hands.

It went from there. We started texting without Ally on the thread, hanging out just the two of us. Holding hands turned into kissing, which turned into even more. We were each other's firsts.

But we didn't tell Ally.

We had plans to—we really did—but then Mr. Copeland died unexpectedly, and everything started going to hell.

I almost crash into Ally's back when she stops on the second-floor landing with no warning. She's been in a weird mood all day, related I'm sure to the fact that yesterday was the anniversary of her dad's death. Around this time of year, it's always harder than usual to get through to her.

"Okay, yes. I agree you shouldn't be the one to talk to Glasgow or Freeman. They were both friends with Appelbaum. But isn't Berkeley sympathetic to Jake? Since he was his advisor and all? I feel like he might even be willing to tell you *more* because you're Jake's brother. I thought he came and talked to you after Jake was convicted and said if you ever needed anything, his door was open."

"Yeah . . . he did. But . . ."

But I haven't talked to him since. I've avoided him as much as possible, actually, in large part because I'm embarrassed. Berkeley tried so hard to help Jake—meeting him after school and tutoring him on weekends. I can't help but think he must resent wasting all that time, because Jake still blew up his life.

"So you should be the one to talk to him. And then there's Mr. Porter. . . . He's new, so he won't know anything—we can skip him. And I doubt Mrs. Sargent will tell us anything—she's the head of the department, so she probably had a lot to do with keeping the drama between Matt and Appelbaum quiet in the first place. We'll start with the other three. Okay?"

I frown. "Ally . . ."

"Henry," she snaps. "Just do it!"

I clench my jaw.

"Fine. So, what exactly am I supposed to ask him? Didn't you tell me that according to that police report you got, he told the cops he and Appelbaum barely knew each other outside of work?"

"Yeah, but he still might have heard some rumors floating around the department about it. Maybe he knows if Mr. Clark threatened Appelbaum."

"Her sister already told us Mr. Clark was pissed."

"Yeah, but she didn't give us any details. Sure, he was mad. But did he ever make any threats? That's what we need to find out."

There is absolutely no way Mr. Berkeley is going to tell me something like that, particularly since it involves a parent, but I'm tired of arguing.

"Fine," I say.

"Good. I'll meet you back here shortly."

I head to Berkeley's classroom. Jake spent a lot of time there during the end of his junior year and the beginning of his senior. Here and the stupid record shop where he worked. Where he met Nick.

Berkeley's at his desk, packing his bag. I knock on the open door. He looks up, eyebrows jumping when he sees me. He pushes his wire-rimmed glasses farther up the bridge of his nose.

Berkeley came to work at BHS the same year Appelbaum

did and was immediately popular. It helps that he's younger and attractive. Goes out of his way to help kids. He's always hosting study sessions on the weekends, tutoring kids after school.

"Hey, do you have a second?" I ask tentatively.

"Henry Hanson! It's good to see you. I was just about to head out, but for you, sure." He motions for me to enter. "Take a seat, if you want."

I slip into a chair in the front row.

"So what can I do you for? To be honest, I thought I might be seeing you now that Jake's out. How's he doing?"

"He's . . . okay. I guess." He's also the absolute last thing I want to talk about right now. "I'm actually here because . . . This is sort of random and probably a little strange, but I'm helping out my friend Ally with this newspaper article that she's writing . . . about Ms. Appelbaum?"

Berkeley stops what he's doing and stares at me. "Miriam Appelbaum? And *you're* helping with it? That seems . . ."

I bark a laugh. "Yeah. Like I said, strange. But Ally's going through some personal stuff right now, and I'm trying to be a good friend . . . you know."

Berkeley gives me an odd look, then his face relaxes into a smile. "Sure. Okay. How can I help?"

"Um." I pick at a stray thread hanging from the bottom of my shirt and stumble my way through my next question. "So, yeah. I hope this isn't inappropriate, but we heard that there was maybe some bad blood between Ms. Appelbaum and one of her students? Before she died? And, um . . ." I'm totally losing him. How does Ally manage to get people to open up?

Berkeley comes around his desk and perches on the front edge. He crosses his arms against his chest. "Okay, I'm going to stop you there."

"Yeah?" I say, hoping against hope he's about to tell me something useful.

"It sounds like what's really going on here is you're hunting for other people who had problems with Miriam Appelbaum before she died."

My face flushes.

"Right. I thought so." He sighs. "Henry, you're a good guy. I get that you want to help Jake. We *all* wanted to help Jake. You know I tried"—he rubs his palm against his forehead—"but you have to believe that if he's innocent—"

"He *is* innocent!"

Berkeley holds up a hand. "Again, *if* he's innocent, his team of lawyers will find a way to prove it. Okay? That's not your job. You're a kid."

I'm sure he means well, but even so, he's pissing me off. I'm a *kid*? Like any of the grown-ups in Jake's life are doing such a great job helping him.

I set my jaw. "Yeah, well, that may be, but like I said, I'm here because I'm helping out my friend with this article. Did you ever hear about any issue between Ms. Appelbaum and Matt Clark?"

Berkeley's kind expression slips off his face. I can tell I'm going at this too hard, but I don't know what else to do.

"Anything at all?" I push.

Berkeley stands. He grabs his bag from the desk and swings it over his shoulder.

"Henry, I barely knew Miriam Appelbaum beyond us

being colleagues. Also, I have to tell you that what you're asking isn't something appropriate for an article in the school paper, particularly given that one of the parties involved is deceased. I'd suggest you tell your friend that she should seriously reconsider what she plans to print . . . if this article actually exists."

He glances at his watch. When he looks at me again, his pleasant expression has returned. "And with that, I have to run. It was nice catching up, and please tell your brother Mr. Berkeley says *hello*."

Ally frowns at her phone like it's personally offending her as I steer my car onto her street. Post–English teacher convos, she's in an even worse mood than before.

Her conversation with Glasgow and Freeman went about as well as mine did with Berkeley. When she told them about the article she's writing, they told her a bunch of stories about how wonderful Appelbaum was in the classroom, but as soon as she tried to steer the conversation toward Matt and his dad, the two of them clammed up.

"You okay?" I ask as I pull into her driveway.

"I'm fine." She pauses. "Actually, you know what? Scratch that. I'm not fine. We're getting nowhere. How are we supposed to figure out if Matt and his dad are actual suspects if no one will tell us anything? Using the newspaper as an excuse only goes so far."

"Did you . . ." I hesitate. "Did you happen to ask Grace? About Matt? I think they're friends or whatever."

Or whatever. I feel sick.

"I think they might be dating, actually." She winces. "Sorry . . . I didn't . . ."

She might not have meant it, but her words still feel like a kick in the stomach.

"It's fine," I say, even though it's not fine. At all.

"I . . . yeah. I asked Grace about it. Matt's social media is pretty barren, and I don't know what else to do."

"Have you found anything on his dad yet?"

"I've been Googling him." She lets out a loud groan. "And I just found this. Here. Look."

She shoves her phone at me. I take it.

"He was at a conference. In Philadelphia."

On the screen is a photo of a stern-looking man standing behind a podium. The caption reads: *Keynote speaker Matthew Clark addresses crowd on final day of the summit.*

"Apparently he was giving that speech that night, during the time frame Appelbaum was killed. There's no way he could have been there and also murdered her. Dammit!" She smacks the dashboard with her palm.

"Well, at least we can cross him off our list." I pause. I hate to say this next part, but . . . "Also, do we really think Matt would have murdered Appelbaum solo?"

"I don't know. But our suspect list is tiny, Henry! It includes, thus far, the mystery person I overheard Appelbaum arguing with, freaking *Matt*, and the tiny possibility that it was a random act of violence. We *suck* at this. Matt's one of our only leads, so we need to keep exploring it. I asked around, and apparently his dad is a real dickhead. People snap under pressure. It happens."

"But if his dad was away—"

She ignores me, unstrapping herself from her seat and throwing the passenger door open with a thud. I trail after her into her house. She sits down at the kitchen table and drops her head into her hands.

"Ally . . ." What if she decides investigating is too much? Too hard? What if she decides to give up? She's stubborn, but still. She's so frustrated, and I can't do this without her.

"What?" she mumbles.

I'm scrambling for something to distract her from our failures. "Did you ever hear back from Appelbaum's high school friends? The ones that Mrs. Flowers mentioned? She said she'd bug them, right?"

She lifts her head. "Good question. I haven't checked my DMs since earlier today. Hold."

A few seconds later—"Rachael Wu! She wrote back!"

I crowd her shoulder. "What does it say?"

"It says, *Happy to chat with you. Miriam was a close friend. Not sure if you reached out to our mutual friend Lucy, but she should be around to chat as well if you're up for talking to two of us at once.*"

Ally lowers the phone, suddenly a lot more chipper. "This is great. Hopefully they'll be able to tell us *something* useful. I'm going to write back and see if they can talk tomorrow."

She's just finishing up when the doorbell rings.

"Hang on." Ally disappears out of the room, returning a moment later with Grace in tow. I straighten, pushing a hand through my hair to make sure it hasn't gone wild.

Then I notice that they're both frowning.

"It's Grace." Ally jerks her thumb in Grace's direction.

"I see that. Hey," I say to Grace, who's awkwardly lingering in the middle of the room, watching Ally.

"Hey," Grace says. "Sorry for just showing up like this, but I needed to talk to you guys. I talked to Matt earlier."

"You did?" Ally looks up with sudden interest.

"Yeah." Grace takes a few steps toward us. "I figured I might as well try to use the fact we're friendly"—my stomach drops—"to our advantage. Because I want to help," she adds.

Ally is quiet.

"What did you learn?" I ask, even though what I really want to ask is, *Are you dating him? Do you like him more than me? Have you guys hooked up?*

"Well . . ." She shifts from foot to foot.

"Do you want to sit?" I ask.

She glances at Ally, then shrugs. "Sure." She takes the chair next to me. "So I was with him and Macey Brown—"

Ally makes a noise of disgust. Macey Brown is one of Grace's newer friends and also happens to be one of the people who was most horrible to me right after Jake's arrest.

"And Tim Martinez."

Also a total dick.

"You have *awesome* friends, Grace," Ally says sarcastically.

"I know. I know . . . they're awful." Grace lowers her eyes to the table. "But not all of them are like Macey and Tim, I swear. Meghan and her girlfriend are cool—"

"Right," Ally interrupts. "I'm sure they're all lovely. Remember all those nasty notes they left in your locker, Henry?

Those were really cool. Almost as cool as Grace telling the cops that she saw Jake the night of the murder."

"Ally . . . ," I say, shaking my head. She glares at me.

"Jesus, Ally. First of all, there is no way those notes were from Meghan *or* Carmen. Second, I said I was sorry like one hundred times already. Okay? I'm trying my best to fix what I did. What else do you want from me?"

"Nothing. Just tell us if you found out anything." Ally dismisses her apology. "About Matt."

Grace chews on her bottom lip. She had to have known what would happen if she brought up Macey and Tim and Matt in front of Ally, but she chose to suffer Ally's wrath in order to give us information.

I can't help but feel for her. Ally would say I'm a sucker, but she doesn't understand.

"What happened?" I prod as gently as I can. Ally rolls her eyes.

"Yeah. We were watching Meghan's soccer game and I brought up the night of the murder."

She clears her throat. "I asked them if they remember where they were. Tim and Macey did right away, but Matt was, like, weirdly evasive? Apparently, Tim was at a party that night and Matt wasn't there, and Tim asked Matt where he'd been, and Matt said out of town, all vague. But the question clearly made him uncomfortable."

"Cool. Matt was out of town. Great. Thrilling. Did you come over here to tell us you learned nothing useful?" Ally asks. "You know, you could have just texted us that. Or, even better, said nothing at all."

Grace flushes. "Just listen, okay? I had a backup plan. Matt's, like, an obsessive chronicler of things—he's constantly taking pictures. I thought maybe if I could see them I might be able to figure out where he was that night. So, I stole his phone."

"You stole it?" Ally sounds impressed.

"Well, sort of. I borrowed it. But I managed to look through his pictures."

"And?" Ally prompts.

"He was definitely out of town. There's a photo of him posing with the Welcome to Delaware sign that night."

"Who takes a picture with the Welcome to Delaware sign?" I ask.

Grace shrugs. "I don't know. It's random, but it also means he couldn't have done it. But . . ."

"But?" Ally asks.

"I . . . I kept scrolling through his pics, and I swear to God the last photo I saw was of a bunch of baggies. Filled with white powder."

"White powder?" I ask. There's only one person that reminds me of.

Jake.

"Yeah. But it couldn't be—"

"If Matt's into that stuff, you should stay away from him," I say to Grace before I can stop myself.

Ally raises an eyebrow at me.

Grace just nods. "I mean, agreed . . . but I might have been misinterpreting it. I've literally never heard of Matt being into anything like that. Some of the other guys from the lacrosse team, sure, but not him. Either way, we can cross him off our suspect list. But I didn't find out anything on his dad, so he's still a possibility."

"Actually, we figured out he was at a conference in Philly that night. He couldn't have done it," Ally says.

"Oh," Grace says. "So where does that leave us?"

"With our suspicions of Nick Marion," Ally says. "And we still don't know who I heard Appelbaum arguing with that day at her house. Luckily, I just heard back from her high school friends and am setting up a time to meet with them. They might be able to give us the answer to that, which would be *huge*."

"When are you meeting them?" Grace asks.

"Don't know yet. I suggested tomorrow after school, but we'll see."

"If it's tomorrow, can I come with?" Grace asks, and I brace myself for Ally's inevitable *no*.

"I have something to do after school tomorrow, actually," I say quickly. It might be good for the two of them to spend some time together, alone. "So that works. Grace can give you a ride, Al."

"Great!" Grace says. "That works on my end."

"Oh . . . okay," Ally says slowly. "It might not even be tomorrow, but if it is . . . I guess you can come."

And then she kicks me under the table, hard.

ALLY

OCTOBER 14

GRACE AND I ARE on our way to meet Appelbaum's friends Rachael and Lucy at a café on the west side of Brawner.

Just the two of us. Alone.

All due to Henry Hanson's lying ass. He kept insisting that he wasn't—lying, that is—but I know he was. What does he have to do after school? Nothing, that's what.

He probably thinks spending some time alone together will make me and Grace best friends again, which . . . absolutely not. I'd rather stab one of my mom's knitting needles through my eye. I'd rather light myself on fire and then jump out of an airplane a thousand feet above sea level without a parachute. I'd rather—

"I think we're here." Grace interrupts my thoughts. "Are you okay?"

"I'm fine," I say defensively, and then realize I'm hanging on to the handle of the car door like it's a life raft.

Okay, so yeah. Maybe I'm a little stressed—so sue me. It's not every day that your best friend forces you to hang out solo with your *ex*–other best friend, who also happens to have turned your best friend's brother in for murdering your favorite teacher.

Why does my life sound like a soap opera?

The café is in a small strip of stores and restaurants that managed to survive the massive renovations happening all over Brawner in the last five years. My dad used to say it seemed like everything that gave the town character was disappearing. He was worried that Brawner was going to turn into a place with the same chain stores you see in every suburb across America.

We park in the lot beside the café.

"You stay here," I direct Grace.

"Um, *excuse* me? I'm not staying in the car. I'm not your chauffeur, Ally."

I give her a dirty look. "Fine. But let me do the talking. Got it?"

She rolls her eyes. "Whatever."

The café is dark, cool, and almost totally empty. I spot Rachael and Lucy immediately; they're the only people in here other than the waitstaff.

"Over there," Grace says quietly, nudging me with her elbow.

"Yeah, I know." Now that we're actually here, my mouth has gone dry. I've interviewed tons of people, but it's never mattered as much as this. If these two don't tell us anything worthwhile, I have no idea what to do next.

Their conversation grinds to a halt as Grace and I approach.

"Hi . . . are you Lucy Phillips and Rachael Wu?" I ask hesitantly.

"We are!" One of the women gets to her feet. She's white, about my height, with short blond hair and a small gold ring through her right nostril, and is wearing ripped blue jeans and a sweater. Honestly, she doesn't look that much older than me or Grace.

"I'm Lucy Phillips and this is Rachael Wu." She indicates the woman who's still seated, a pretty Asian lady with beautiful long black hair. "You must be Ally?"

I nod. "And this is my . . . cowriter. Grace. She's working on the article, too."

"Great." Lucy smiles at both of us. "Oh! Please, feel free to sit."

I take a seat next to Lucy and Grace slides in next to a silent Rachael. Unlike Lucy, she doesn't seem that thrilled to be here. She's studying Grace's face intently.

"You look familiar," Rachael says, just as I'm about to launch into my whole dissertation about the article for the *Boar*. "Have we met before?"

Grace shakes her head. "I don't think so? My sister went to Brawner, though; she was a few years younger than you guys, but you might know her? Lara Topham?"

Rachael's eyebrows jump. "Lara Topham's your sister? I remember her. Didn't she win some huge national prize for debating when she was a freshman?"

"Oh, I see the resemblance," Lucy says. "She got engaged not too long ago to someone from our class."

Grace nods. "Evan Miller."

Rachael and Lucy exchange a look I can't quite decipher. "What?" I ask.

"Nothing," says Rachael. "It's just . . . Lara's not the person I would have expected him to end up with. . . ."

Lucy jumps in. "I think she's trying to say that Lara's so smart. And Evan is . . ."

Grace lets out a little laugh. "Not the most intellectual person?"

"Something like that," Lucy says.

"Wait," Rachael says, snapping her fingers. "That's not why I recognize you. I recognize you from the *trial.* You're the one who helped put Miriam's killer behind bars, aren't you?"

Grace's cheeks flush red and she looks down at the table. "I . . . yeah."

Lucy's eyes have widened. "You are! Oh my god, your testimony . . . you're amazing. Thank you for doing that. I'm sure it couldn't have been easy, since you knew him and all, and—"

This conversation is taking a turn I really, really do not like. My stomach is starting to tie itself up in knots, and I hate it, I hate that if I defend Jake right now, the two of them will likely leave, but I can't sit here listening to this.

Luckily, Grace seems to be on the same page, because she interrupts Lucy. "I appreciate that, and actually that's sort of why we wanted to talk to you guys. Ally told you about the article we're working on for the *Boar*?"

The two of them nod, the subject of Jake thankfully falling to the wayside for the moment.

"Well," Grace continues, "we're trying to talk to people

who were important to Ms. Appelbaum, people who really *knew* her. We want to write about her life instead of how she died. She deserves more than that, you know? All people remember about her is she was murdered, and it's all gotten sensationalized. We want to remind them she was a real person, before all that."

They're both quiet after I stop talking.

Finally, Lucy speaks. "That's lovely, Grace. We'd be happy to talk to you about Miriam." She looks at Rachael. "Right?"

Rachael shrugs. "Sure, fine. That's a better angle than what I expected. Not just the same tabloid crap those websites keep putting out for clicks. What do you want to know?"

Grace and I exchange a glance. "Stuff like . . . stories from when you were in high school? How she changed over the years? You guys were friends for a long time," I say.

"We were," Lucy says. "We miss her. It was always the three of us, especially back then. She was a good friend."

"Mostly," Rachael adds.

"What do you mean?" I ask.

"She's just kidding," Lucy says.

"Am I?" Rachael mutters. Lucy laughs good-naturedly.

"What was she like in high school?" Grace asks.

"Smart. Kind. Always up for a good time." Lucy launches into a story about how Ms. Appelbaum volunteered at the local library in high school, and then another about how she started a home delivery service for seniors.

I jot down some fake notes, but I'm starting to get agitated. Hearing what an angel Appelbaum was is not going to help Jake. We need to know if she had bad blood with anyone.

I need them to tell us something useful.

I think back to our conversation with Mrs. Flowers. She told us about Appelbaum's drama with the Clarks when we asked her who we should avoid interviewing.

"Thanks so much for all that," I say once Lucy finally finishes talking. "It's super useful. I wonder if there's anyone else you suggest we speak to? Other grown-ups? We've already spoken with her sister and a few of the teachers in the English department—Ms. Freeman and Ms. Glasgow, who gave me some great stories—and Mr. Berkeley, although he said he didn't know her that well—"

Rachael lets out a loud snort. "He said *what?*"

"He—" I'm confused. "He said he didn't know Ms. Appelbaum well?"

"Um, ooookay," Rachael says. "I guess that's true if you don't count the two months they dated."

My heart stops in my chest. "Excuse me, *what?*"

"They *dated?* When?" Grace's expression mirrors what I imagine mine must look like: a mixture of horror, confusion, and—I have to admit it—delight. Because what is this, if not a lead? Catching Berkeley in a lie is potentially a major break in our case.

Particularly since, per the files I have, Berkeley also told the *police* he barely knew Appelbaum.

It's one thing to lie to Henry, but a whole other to lie to the cops.

"Back in 2022. Like, August, September, around then,"

Rachael says. "They kept it very much on the DL because they didn't want other faculty to get weird about it. Miriam especially wanted to keep it from AnnMarie and Nicole—er, I mean Ms. Glasgow and Ms. Freeman. They aren't his biggest fans, apparently. The relationship wasn't serious, but Miriam and Paul sure as shit knew each other."

Rachael picks up her straw and starts twisting it into little knots. "Men are such assholes. It's just like a man, isn't it—to totally disown a person once there's any drama."

"There was drama?" I ask, trying to keep my voice calm. This is even better than I'd hoped.

"Maybe I shouldn't have said that. It wasn't anything major, but when they broke up Miriam said he acted a little weird."

"How so?"

She shrugs. "She got a few texts from him saying stuff like 'she better not tell anyone' and 'she'd regret it if she didn't stay quiet,' which, like, chill out, my guy."

"Tell anyone what?" I ask.

"She assumed he meant he wanted her to stay quiet about the fact that they'd dated. Personally, I think he was embarrassed she'd been the one to break things off, even though it was clear he wasn't really that interested in her. Like, how serious could he have been? He never even invited her over to his house? God, the audacity. Men are like that. Their ego is the only thing they care about. Assholes."

Lucy sighs. "Rachael, don't scare them." She turns to us. "Ignore her. Her boyfriend broke up with her a couple of months ago and she's on an extreme anti-man kick right now."

"*So* sorry, Luce. Not all of us are lucky enough to be lesbians." Rachael picks up a straw wrapper from the table and shreds it into snow. "I wish daily that I didn't find men attractive."

"Did you guys tell the cops any of this? Them dating? The texts?" Grace asks.

They look at each other. Rachael shakes her head. "I mean, no. They talked to us once, but their questions were all about Jake Hanson. Plus, Paul might have been an ass, but Miriam was never scared of him. I'm sure the police knew; the cops had to have subpoenaed her phone records after she was killed."

Rachael's right. The cops must have looked over her phone records. I wonder what excuse Berkeley gave them to explain away those texts. I wonder if he even needed to give them an excuse, or if the cops were already so focused on Jake that they brushed it aside.

"Did Ms. Appelbaum date anyone else before she died?" I ask casually, hoping they accept this as a normal follow-up question, since we're already on the subject of Appelbaum's love life. Maybe the guy I heard her arguing with that afternoon was a new boyfriend.

Lucy's eyes flick to Rachael's face. "We . . . aren't sure."

"She didn't tell us anything specific," Rachael says. "But Lucy called her one weekend morning, early, and—"

Lucy jumps in. "And I heard a man's voice in the background. But when I asked her, she denied it. Said she was alone. But I know what I heard."

"Do you know who it was?" I ask.

Lucy hesitates. "I'm not sure," she says finally. "We told

the cops, but nothing ever came from it. I assumed it was probably a one-night stand." Her face turns bright red and she claps a hand over her mouth. "Oh God, sorry. I forgot for a minute that you guys are in high school."

I can't help but laugh at her embarrassment. "You're good. High school isn't what it used to be."

We leave the café a few minutes later and head to Grace's car.

"So that's interesting about Berkeley," I say as we walk through the mostly empty parking lot. The sun is starting to set, but the streetlights have yet to blink on. Grace's face is cast in shadows.

"Extremely." She beeps her car unlocked. "He lied about something major. Huge red flag. Were you the one who talked to Berkeley the other day at school?"

I shake my head. "Henry did. And he *definitely* said that Berkeley told him he didn't know Appelbaum outside of being work colleagues. . . . Hang on."

I take my phone out of my back pocket and dial Henry as we get into the car.

"Yeah?" he answers on the second ring.

Busy, my ass. I put him on speaker.

"I'm with Grace. We just finished talking to Appelbaum's high school friends, and get this—remember how Berkeley told you that he didn't know Appelbaum well?"

"Yeah?" Henry says.

"Well, her friends said not only did Berkeley *know* Appelbaum, they actually dated. Like, for two months."

"*What?*" Henry says. "Are you serious?"

"Yup," I confirm. "And he didn't just lie to you; he lied to the *cops.* Remember, he also told *them* he barely knew Appelbaum when they interviewed him. And his alibi was Nick Marion, who might have lied to us too. What if . . . what if the two of them agreed to tell the cops they were together because one or both of them was involved?"

"I keep thinking . . . ," Grace says. "Could it have been *one of them* who I saw that night? If we go off the theory that someone framed Jake, it actually makes a lot of sense. They both knew Jake really well. They knew about Appelbaum getting him expelled, about Jake freaking out on her that day at school. They knew where Jake lived and about how he always wore that jacket. . . . Nick definitely would have known that Jake always left it in his car."

"True, but back then Nick was almost a whole foot taller than Jake," Henry says. "I don't think you could have confused the two of them . . . but Berkeley . . ."

"Berkeley is short," I finish for him. "Short, and he lied about dating Appelbaum. And her friends said he got really weird after they broke up. Sent her a bunch of these texts telling her she'd better not tell anyone they'd dated. You know what this means, right?"

"Yup," Henry says. "It means we need to have another conversation with Mr. Berkeley."

HENRY

OCTOBER 14

AFTER HANGING UP WITH Grace and Ally, I continue to lay on my bed, staring up at the ceiling, mulling it all over.

Berkeley lied about his relationship with Appelbaum.

Berkeley told the cops that he was with Nick Marion the night Appelbaum died. But if he lied to them about his relationship with Appelbaum, he could be lying about that, too. Nick would have backed him up—Berkeley's a teacher, and he helped Nick get out of trouble a bunch of times, just like he did for Jake. Nick might have felt like he owed him.

Jake has made it perfectly clear that he doesn't want to talk about the case with me. He doesn't want me poking my nose into his business. But he's also the only person I have direct access to who knew Berkeley and Nick Marion well.

Plus, shouldn't *he* care more about all of it? Here I am, busting my ass to try and help him while he just sits up in his room, moping.

And sure, I owe him, but this is his future we're talking about—*his*, not mine.

I get off my bed for the first time in three hours and head out of my room, stopping in front of Jake's closed door.

He answers on the second knock. His eyes are heavy-lidded. I wonder if I woke him up. I wonder what he does in there all day, alone.

"What do you want?" he asks by way of greeting.

"I need to talk to you."

"Okay? We're talking right now."

"I mean, *really* talk. Can I come in?"

Jake glances over his shoulder into his dark room. "No."

"Then can you come out?"

He stares at me with an unreadable expression.

"Please?" It's taking all my willpower to keep my tone level. "It's important. It won't take long."

"Fine." He steps into the hallway and shuts the door behind him. "What?"

"Mr. Berkeley was your advisor," I say. "Before."

His jaw clenches. "Yeah, so?"

"Did you ever hear anything about him dating Ms. Appelbaum?"

"What? What are you talking about? This better not be related to your questions about Nick the other day."

"Look, long story short," I hurry, "I was talking to Berkeley recently, and he happened to mention that he didn't really know Ms. Appelbaum well, but then Ally talked to Appelbaum's friends, who said they actually *dated*, which—"

"What the hell?" Jake's face pales. "Now you're talking

to Paul Berkeley? And Appelbaum's friends? What do you and Ally think you're *doing*? I thought I told you to leave it to the professionals."

I've had about enough of him being a dick. "Are you serious?" I say, my voice rising. "We're trying to help! Help *you*. But it's like you don't even want to help yourself. I don't get it; I heard you last night with Kakova, barely saying a word. Why are you giving up so easily?"

He stares at me for a very long, very uncomfortable moment. "Be careful who you talk to," he finally says in a low, scary tone. One I've never heard from him.

"Be *careful*? That's all you have to say to me?"

"Just stop! Okay? Leave it alone." He moves closer to me, and my skin prickles with goose bumps. Suddenly our mom seems very far away downstairs. He's so close to me, I can feel his breath on my cheek.

He jabs his finger into my face. "Are you hearing me, Henry? Leave. It. Alone! You don't know what you're doing. And I have no way of protecting you this time."

"What's that supposed to mean?" I ask, but he's already stepped back into his room.

The door slams in my face.

GRACE

OCTOBER 15

"HE SLAMMED THE DOOR in my *face!*" Henry says for the fourth or fifth time as he rips a vicious bite from his sandwich. He's told this story on repeat since sitting down. Clearly what happened with Jake really shook him.

"He freaked out when I said I talked to Berkeley. I don't get it; it almost seemed like he was . . . scared?"

"Yeah," Ally says. "You said. Which, again, makes me wonder the following: Does Jake know something he's not saying? Berkeley was the alibi he originally gave the cops, right? We thought that he used Berkeley because he thought Berkeley would back him up and get him out of trouble—again—but what if we've been thinking of it backward? What if *Jake* was the one trying to protect Berkeley? Maybe he didn't realize that Nick had already agreed to be Berkeley's alibi, and was trying to give him one. Maybe Berkeley did something that night, and Jake knows it."

"Maybe," Henry says. "But if that's the case, why would

Jake take the fall? I can't ask him about it again. He made that really clear last night. He'll kill me if—" His face flushes. "Not literally, I mean . . ." He drops his head into his hands. "Forget it."

"We know what you meant," I tell him softly, my heart tugging for him. Since we started hanging out again, I've kept my distance, but he's so upset I can't help myself. Instinct takes over and I reach out under the table, tentatively placing my fingers on his upper thigh for comfort. His muscles tighten and then relax under my touch, and a moment later, his hand finds mine. Warmth fills my belly.

"Henry, Berkeley lied to you. If you can't talk to Jake, you need to talk to him directly," Ally pushes.

Henry scowls. "Do you actually think that'll work? What do you think will happen, I'll go in there and be all, *You lied,* and he'll be all, *Henry, you're right, I did, thank you for calling me out and also by the way I murdered Appelbaum, so sorry your brother was convicted for it*?"

"Probably not," Ally says, rolling her eyes. "But my dad always used to say that lies are almost as useful as the truth because they can tell you something about the person."

Ally is going to eviscerate me for saying what I'm about to say, but so be it. "I don't think Henry going to talk to him is a good idea. If Berkeley's involved . . . Henry shouldn't be alone with him. We should go to the cops."

"The *cops*?" Ally scoffs, exactly how I expected. "Yeah, because they did *such* a great job with all of this the first time? They barely *looked* at anyone other than Jake. Like, think about it: Appelbaum's friends are right. The cops must have seen her phone records, which would have included those texts Berkeley sent to Appelbaum, but they never did anything about it, outside of questioning him. *Once.* Most of them had zero experience with murder cases. They screwed it all up. Plus, what do you think we should tell them, exactly? That our teacher lied about dating Ms. Appelbaum? Last time I checked, that's not a crime. They'll laugh you out of the station."

"Yeah, but . . ." I want to argue, but as much as I hate to admit it, she's right. Going to the cops right now won't help.

"I'll talk to Berkeley at school," Henry says. "I'm sure it'll be fine. Public setting and all."

"I'll come with you," I offer. I'm not about to let him go alone.

"Are you sure?" he says, his fingers tightening around mine.

I shrug. "I actually have English last period, so I'll be over there anyway. And I had him freshman year, so he knows me."

"Okay, great," Henry says, and Ally snorts. I ignore her. This isn't just because I want some alone time with Henry. At least, that's what I'm telling myself. "Let's meet by the English classrooms after school. We'll catch him as he's packing up to leave. That's what I did last time."

"Okay. I'll meet you by his classroom."

I stop a few doors down from Berkeley's classroom three minutes after the final bell. Henry has yet to arrive. A group of giggling girls walks by me, and I flatten myself against the wall to wait. The minutes tick by and the stream of students slows to a trickle.

Henry is still nowhere to be seen. Where is he? I'm in the middle of texting, asking as much, when Ms. Glasgow appears from her classroom, bag slung over her shoulder.

"Hi, Grace," she says.

"Hi," I say.

"Are you waiting for someone?" She glances back into her classroom. "Most everyone's taken off, but . . ."

"Uh, sort of. I was waiting to talk to Mr. Berkeley?"

"Paul?" Her expression turns puzzled. "I didn't think he was teaching any senior English classes this year."

"Oh. Yeah. It's actually about . . . something else."

"Well, I haven't seen him, but you can check his classroom."

"Thanks." I don't move. She stares at me like she's waiting for me to go, and I can't take the awkwardness of the moment any longer.

"Um, thanks, I'll see you later?" I start walking quickly toward Berkeley's classroom as I text Henry yet again.

Where are you???

As I approach, I see that Berkeley's at his desk, typing on his laptop. I must make more noise than I mean to, because before I can slip out of his line of sight, he spots me.

"Grace?" he calls, snapping the lid of the computer shut. "What are you . . . ? Can I help you with something?"

"Hi, Mr. Berkeley." I step inside, palms slick with nervous sweat. I'm the one who wanted to go to the cops about this and now I'm stuck here, talking to this man alone. I make a mental note to yell at Henry next time I see him.

"So, what can I do you for?" he says.

I clear the lump from my throat. "Sorry to bother you. I actually . . . I don't know if you've heard about this thing the *Boar* is doing? On Ms. Appelbaum? Since the anniversary of her . . . of her death is coming up?"

His expression shifts. "This again? I'm not sure if you're aware, Grace, but I spoke with Henry Hanson already. I didn't know Miriam well. We worked together for a few years, but that was about the extent of it. Surely there are other people you can speak to, if you need sources. Ms. Glasgow and Ms. Freeman, for example."

I'm not good at this. *Ally's* good at this—challenging people, pushing for answers. The hardest thing I've ever done was tell the cops I saw Jake walking into Appelbaum's backyard, and look how that turned out.

"Grace?"

I twist my fingers together. Take a deep breath. I'm being ridiculous. We're on school property. There are people around. It's not like he's going to hurt me.

I can do this. I *need* to do this.

"Yeah. Henry mentioned that? But the thing is, um, well, we spoke with some of her friends from high school yesterday. And they told us that you . . . you two dated?"

He freezes, eyes locked on my face. "*Excuse* me?"

I'm going to throw up. I shouldn't be here alone, doing this. I am *bad* at this.

Berkeley is still staring at me.

I dig my fingernails into the palm of my right hand, so hard it hurts. There have been so many times over the last two years when I've stayed quiet. When I've walked away, instead of challenging people's awful behavior. When I've put myself and my fear of being a pariah before what I knew was right in my heart.

How much longer am I going to stay silent?

Something inside me snaps.

I start to babble. "Yeah. That's what they said. That you guys dated for two months. Which . . . I don't get it. If you dated Ms. Appelbaum, you must have known her, right? Why would you tell us you didn't? We're fact-checking things for the section and—"

"What exactly does my dating life have to do with your article, Grace?" His voice is soft, but there's something in his tone that knots my stomach. He rises out of his chair and walks around his desk, stopping a few feet from where I stand. Without thinking, I take a step backward and collide into the sharp corner of a desk.

"*Ow!* We're just trying to get the facts straight—"

"The facts of what exactly? I ask again: What does my dating life have to do with your article? If I chose not to disclose something to you all that took place outside of this building, that is *my* choice, do you understand? You do not go digging into my personal life. My personal life is personal."

Mr. Berkeley does not sound like a young, affable teacher anymore. He sounds very, very angry.

He sounds like someone who could kill.

"We were—"

"I repeat," he interrupts, "do not go digging into my personal life. It's a serious violation of my privacy and I'll have no choice but to report you to the administration if I catch wind that you're doing it again. Do you understand me?"

I press my lips together, blinking fast, trying to stop the tears threatening in the corners of my eyes.

"Do you?"

I nod.

"Good. Now, it's time for you to go."

I don't argue. I want to get out of here as much as he wants me gone.

Without so much as another word, I hightail it out the door as fast as humanly possible.

Henry's halfway down the hall, running toward me, his bookbag slapping against his back.

"Hi, sorry! Sorry! I got caught in hallway traffic and it took me forever to get over here from the science building. Are you ready to talk to—" he says, then notices the tears running down my cheeks. "Grace, are you okay?"

I fall into his arms and he wraps them around me, tight. For the first time all day—all week—maybe for the first time in two years, I am safe.

He strokes the back of my head. "Did something happen?"

I have to take several deep, shuddery breaths before I'm able to reply. "I talked to him."

Henry's arms tighten around me. "Berkeley?"

I nod into his chest.

"Okay, we should get out of here. Can you walk?"

"Yeah."

He lets me go, and I feel the loss immediately. I sniff,

wiping under my eyes to make sure I don't have pools of mascara there. I'm so embarrassed. Crying, because of what? Because Berkeley was sort of mean to me? Because I apparently can't handle any sort of conflict without falling apart? Henry's been dealing with stuff like this for two years. I need to get myself together. Do better.

"C'mon." He holds out his hand. I can feel a part of me hesitate, the horrible, small, fearful part that's still afraid to be seen with him, afraid of what might happen if people find out.

I don't want to listen to it anymore.

I take his hand and we walk toward the exit. Most everyone has left, but I catch a glimpse of Taylor from the newspaper as we approach the doors. She does a double take, but, to her credit, walks by without a word.

When we're outside, Henry stops. We haven't spoken since we started walking.

"Do you want to sit?"

He's still holding my hand.

"Yeah." I'm calmer now, away from Berkeley, still connected to Henry. We head to a bench away from the entrance, and I tell him what happened. As I talk, his eyes grow wide.

"Jesus. I'm so sorry that I was late. Does he really think threatening a student is a good look?"

"I mean, he didn't outright threaten me, but he was . . . I don't know the right word. Menacing? But that makes him sound like a cartoon villain." I sigh. "I might have overreacted."

"Hey. I absolutely do not think you did. Berkeley is

clearly hiding something. He lied about his relationship with Appelbaum—"

"He said that it's because he doesn't feel the need to share his personal life with students."

"Yeah, but—not to sound like Ally—he also lied to the *cops*. Lying to the police is not something an innocent person does."

We lapse into silence for a second, his hand still wrapped around mine. It reminds me of two years ago, all the hours we spent like this before the first time we kissed. Holding hands, talking, without acknowledging that something was going on between us.

"Grace . . . ," Henry starts. I look up, into his eyes. He chews on his bottom lip nervously. I wait, afraid to move for fear he might not finish his sentence.

A breeze kicks up, showering us in red and yellow leaves from the branches of nearby trees. Henry reaches out and snags one from midair with his free hand, examining it like it's the most interesting thing in the world.

Maybe I need to be the one to speak first. I am, after all, the one who created this mess.

"Henry, I'm so sorry—" I've already apologized, but this is different. Ally was there the last time, and even though she has every right to be angry, the person I hurt the most is the one sitting beside me. The person I should have talked to before going to the police. The person whose brother's life I destroyed.

"It's okay," he says over me. "You don't have to say anything—"

"I do. We only started hanging out again because I forced

my way into your investigation. We haven't really talked—
the two of us, alone . . . and then there's this." I pull our
clasped hands up so we can both see them. "I am so, so
sorry for what I did two years ago. I should have come to
you first. Before going to the cops. I don't know if it would
have changed anything, but I owed you that much, at least.
Because I . . ." I swallow. "I cared—I *care* about you? A lot?
And . . ."

Jesus Christ, this is hard. My parents aren't exactly shin-
ing examples of open communication, and I've spent more
of my life trying to bury my real feelings way down deep
inside myself.

Luckily, Henry jumps in to save me, like he always has.

"I understand. Why you did what you did." His jaw
sets. "We all screwed up back then. It wasn't just you. I was
angry at you, at *myself*"—he winces—"at all of it for a really
long time, but it didn't help anything, you know? And even
when I should have hated you, Grace . . ."

Our eyes meet and my heart jumps.

"I never did."

He reaches out and tenderly tucks loose strands of hair
behind my ear.

ALLY

OCTOBER 16

"WHERE THE HELL HAVE you been?"

I'm two steps into the newspaper office when Taylor greets me, irritated. Nothing new, except right now I sort of don't blame her.

"What do you mean?" I reply. I'm not about to admit that I know exactly what she means. I'm running severely behind on the article I'm supposed to write for next week's paper, and I sort of, maybe disappeared this week, leaving her to pick up my slack.

"What do I *mean*?" Taylor says loudly. "I haven't seen your face in this office all week! Ari, Mary, and I have been here, working our asses off to make sure everyone hits their deadlines and next week's paper gets out on time, and you've been totally MIA. Aren't you supposed to be writing an op-ed? Where is it? I'm not supposed to have to bug *you* to do your work."

"The editorial is almost done!" I snap. I'm lying, but I

can't deal with her right now. Yes, I'm behind, but I've been busy with more important things. Not that I'm going to share *that* with Taylor.

We're finally making actual progress on this case. We have a real suspect, and with him, a million new questions to answer.

Like: Berkeley started teaching here in 2021, but where was he before? And why did he lie about dating Appelbaum to both us and the cops?

"Well, hurry up and turn it in then," Taylor says. "You're supposed to set a good example, Ally. The EIC turning in articles late is unacceptable."

"It'll be done soon!"

"It better." She starts to walk away, but I stop her.

"Have you ever had Mr. Berkeley for English?"

She turns back, eyebrows raised. "What?"

"Have you ever. Had Mr. Berkeley. For English?" I say slowly. Taylor rolls her eyes.

"Yeah, thanks. I understood the words you were saying, but . . . random, much?"

"I'm just wondering if you've ever heard anything about him."

"Like in terms of what?"

"I don't know, like, whether you've heard anything about him not being as great as everyone says he is?"

Taylor blinks at me. "What does that even mean?"

"I don't know. I just thought maybe you'd heard something about him! Everyone loves him, but I wonder . . ."

"Wonder what? Are you saying he's *too* well-liked and

that makes you suspicious? You're so contrary, Ally. My mom would say you're probably like this because you're covering up some deep insecurity. You should probably talk to someone. Deal with your trauma."

"Jesus Christ, Taylor. Can you just answer the question instead of psychoanalyzing me? Your sister was at Brawner when Berkeley started teaching, right?"

Taylor's big sister, Dara, graduated a year before Jake was supposed to. And she was editor in chief of the *Boar*. If I were to psychoanalyze *Taylor*, I'd say it's a big part of why she's so pissy I won the spot.

"Fine. Yes, she was. He started working here her junior year, which I only remember because she was features editor, so she had to put together that stupid article about new staff that we print every year. I remember her complaining about him specifically because when she went to fact-check his bio with the people at his old school, they acted like they were in the CIA. They wouldn't just give her the information straight. It created all this extra work for her."

"What do you mean? Why?"

Taylor shrugs. "I don't know. I guess they were weirdly reluctant to talk about him? She thought it was probably because they were pissed at him for leaving. He's a good teacher, you know. Dara had him her senior year and loved him."

"What school was it?"

"I don't know, Ally. Why would I remember that? Why don't you use the research skills that got you your position and look up the piece in our online archives? It's literally so easy to do. Why are you asking about Berkeley anyway?"

She studies me. "Does this have something to do with Jake Hanson? Berkeley was his advisor before he got arrested, wasn't he? What are you up to?"

"Nothing, *God*," I scoff. "I was just wondering. I'm allowed to wonder about people."

"Yeah. Right. Well, if it does have something do with Jake, leave me out of it, okay?"

"Trust me, I would like nothing more," I mutter.

"Good." She puts her hands on her hips. "Now if you'll excuse me, I have to get some actual work done, since my editor in chief is clearly not going to."

She stomps off.

God, she is frustrating as hell.

We have about twenty minutes before the start of our editorial meeting. I probably should spend it actually writing my op-ed, but I can't help myself—I start searching the *Boar* archives for the profile Dara wrote on Berkeley.

I find it a few minutes later.

Also new this year is English teacher Paul Berkeley, who comes to Brawner from Southampton Academy, a small private school on Long Island. When we spoke to him, he expressed his enthusiasm for all things Shakespeare, and said that he has grand plans to create a senior-level elective focused on Shakespeare's plays. Mr. Berkeley says: "I'm thrilled to join the English department at Brawner High. I love teaching high school and can't wait to connect with the students here."

I immediately Google Southampton Academy. According to its website, it's a private school with a ridiculously large campus, a bunch of uniformed kids, loads of AP courses not offered at Brawner, and alumni who go to top-tier colleges. Must be nice.

Why would Berkeley voluntarily choose to leave a school like that and come *here*? Brawner's fine, but it doesn't compare.

There's no mention of Berkeley on the Southampton website, which I guess isn't a huge surprise considering he left the school five years ago. I'm about to do some more digging when I'm interrupted by Taylor's annoying voice.

"I think we should get the meeting started. Ally?" I twist around to find her staring at me pointedly from the front of the room. "Care to come up here and help me run this thing?"

Help her run things.

JFC. I'm absent for a few days and she's already trying to stage a coup.

After our meeting, I bolt, trying to avoid any more interactions with Taylor. As I head down the hallway, I text Grace and Henry.

> I found the name of B's old school. It's in the Hamptons. Some bougie private school. And get this—the Boar did a new teacher profile on him when he came to BHS, but when they called the school to ask about him, whoever answered the phone was super weird and would barely

tell them anything. Total red flag. We
should call them.

Henry responds immediately. *Weird. Why wouldn't
they talk?*

Idk but we need to find out. It's too late to
call tn but we can tmrrow

Grace enters the conversation. *What does this have to do
with Appelbaum? What we need to do is figure out if B's alibi the
night Appelbaum was killed is real*

And how do you propose we do that? I respond. *B won't talk.
Asking Jake about it was a dead end. Maybe something from his
past will give us a clue. Maybe he has a trail of dead girlfriends??*

Grace: *Idk seems like a long shot. Look I've been thinking.
Matt's having a party tomorrow nite and Nick Marion's always
there. We should go talk to him. Nick was B's alibi, right? If B was
lying about it, maybe Nick doesn't even know B told the cops they
were together. Maybe we can trick him into giving us info*

Is she actually suggesting we go to Matt Clark's house?
Clearly, she's lost her freaking mind.

I respond: *There is a zero percent chance Henry or I are going
to a party at that dickhead's house*

A second later, a message arrives from Henry: *I'll go.*

He must be kidding.

I say as much.

He replies: *Grace already talked to Berkeley alone. She
shouldn't have to do this by herself. I get you don't want to go, so
the two of us will handle it*

My stomach flips. *The two of us.*

I furiously type: *Are you serious?? Those people will murder you if they see you there*

I promise I won't let that happen, Grace responds, like she has any control over what those idiots do.

I can't believe I have to argue with them about this. But I guess they'll do anything to hang out alone. This reminds me so much of the old days, when they first started . . . whatever. Hanging out without me. Hooking up. Ditching me, right after my dad died. Right when I needed them most.

I hated it then, and if my shaking hands are any indication, I hate it now.

This is a bad idea

It'll be fine, Henry writes.

Great, from Grace, arriving at the same time I send, *Let me repeat: this is a BAD IDEA.* They ignore me and start talking about their plans.

Plans that suddenly do not include me.

I punch through the outer doors of the school, a blast of cool air assaulting me, my stomach in knots. Things are spinning out of my control and suddenly I feel very, very alone.

My mom's car sits in front of the school, waiting. I walk toward it, gnawing on my thumbnail, watching my phone as Henry and Grace message back and forth without me.

GRACE

OCTOBER 17

MEGHAN FINDS ME AT my locker on Friday afternoon.

"Oh, so you *are* alive?" she says, hurt written on her face. "I haven't seen you all week. Texted you like a million times and . . . what the hell, Grace?"

"I'm sorry," I say, trying to think of a reasonable excuse for being totally MIA.

I've been too wrapped up in Henry and Ally and our investigation to really even notice that I hadn't spoken to Meghan. I got all her texts, and I meant to respond, but then . . . I don't know. I just didn't. My brain is somewhere else right now.

She's not the only one I've been neglecting. Lara was on my back yesterday for slacking on my maid of honor duties. She asked whether I even cared about her wedding. Basically made me feel like a pile of garbage, but she has a point—her wedding is in just over a week.

I need to be better. Try harder.

"I've been—" Whatever Meghan's about to say is interrupted by Matt, who walks up to us, flanked by a couple of his friends.

He smiles. "See you two at my house tonight?"

"Definitely," Meghan says. She nudges me. Right. I'd almost forgotten that I'm supposed to be interested in him.

"Yep," I say, for lack of anything better. I'm a real verbal gymnast. I force the corners of my mouth up.

I'm nervous about tonight. Nervous to talk to Nick again. Particularly nervous to bring Henry, because I'm not dumb enough to think that Ally is totally wrong. There's no way it's going to go smoothly. People like Macey Brown and Tim Martinez are absolutely going to freak out when they see him there.

But after the week I've had, I think I'm finally over caring how they react. After the conversation Henry and I had outside of school yesterday. After I confronted Berkeley all alone and walked away (mostly) unscathed. After freaking Macey Brown *blackmailed me* on Monday afternoon. She's been texting me constantly since, asking if I've started working on her paper. *Let* her be pissed about Henry showing up. She can suck it.

"Cool, see you guys later then." Matt walks off, laughing at something one of his friends says.

Meghan studies my face. "What was that about?"

I swing my bag up and over my shoulder. "What was what about?"

She points in the direction that Matt disappeared. "*That.* You couldn't have seemed less interested. And honestly, it's been like that since Jake's release was announced. You're so distracted. I mean, I get that it's a lot and Matt might not exactly be your top priority, but what about me? We haven't really talked in *weeks*. You blow me off every time I reach out. What is going on?"

I chew the inside of my cheek as I consider how to respond. Can I trust Meghan? She's been a good friend to me over the past couple of years, but she's been friends with everyone else for so much longer. Most of them have been friends since kindergarten: her and Matt and Tim and Macey Brown. Even though I love Meghan, I can't help but wonder: Where do her loyalties really lie?

I can't chance it.

"I'm sorry. I've just had a lot on my mind and . . . yeah. You're right. I guess the thing with Matt has fallen by the wayside. But I'm really sorry I abandoned you."

"I get it," she says. "I can't imagine what it's been like, having Jake back, basically living in your backyard. It's just . . . I miss you."

"I miss you, too. And I'm sorry. But tonight will be fun!" Although, with Henry there, I'm not sure *fun* is the right word for it.

She looks skeptical but doesn't push. "Just answer my texts next time, okay?"

"Of course," I say, forcing a lighthearted laugh.

The party is already well underway when Henry and I make our way up the edge of the drive, skirting under small tree branches and around bushes. A car honks as it catches us in its beams and Henry ducks, almost crashing into me. I reach out to steady him and we lock eyes.

It took me the whole car ride here to convince him that he should enter Matt's house through the front door, rather than sneak in through the side yard. I get it; he doesn't want to make waves, but as I told him—he deserves to be here as much as anyone. We can't keep letting assholes dictate what we do and say.

"Hey," he says. We're inches apart. He smells like he used to, of fresh soap and a hint of citrus. I lean into him without really thinking about what I'm doing—old habits, the moonlight soft on his face, his brown hair falling over one eye.

"Do you—" he whispers, but another honk interrupts him. I jerk back, and the moment's gone.

"We should . . ." He motions in the direction of Matt's. I nod.

We're almost to the house when my phone buzzes in my hand.

It's from Henry. *We're here,* he's written in our group chat with Ally.

It's nice of him to keep Ally up-to-date, even though it's pretty clear she's mad at us. She hasn't replied to the thread since yesterday afternoon, when she made it clear she thinks this is a terrible idea.

It's starting again, the awkwardness between the three of us, particularly between her and me. I failed her in so many ways after her dad died. Back then I was so self-centered, wrapped up in Henry and my feelings for him. I think one of the reasons that she turned on me so viciously after Jake's arrest was because I'd already hurt her so much.

The group thread stays dark.

I shake it off. I can't think about Ally right now. There's too much that could go wrong tonight. Nick might not show up. He might have already been here and left. Matt's friends might decide they want a fight.

The house is a hundred feet in front of us and my bravado is starting to fade. Maybe I'm being ridiculous. Naive. Putting my own desire to prove that I care about Henry before his safety.

But it's too late now.

We're at the front door.

"Do we just . . . walk inside?" Henry asks.

I nod.

Everything is okay at first. Loud, crowded, but okay. Henry keeps his head down, hat pulled low to hide his face. No one notices him.

"Follow me." I grab him by the arm and pull him through the foyer, dodging small clumps of people.

The first time I ever really hung out with any of these people—Meghan, Matt, Tim—was at a party just like this one, toward the end of my sophomore year.

Meghan and I had Spanish together, and we'd started talking a bunch after class. I was hesitant to make a new friend at first. Things had ended so terribly between Henry and Ally and me, and after, the only people who seemed to want to be my friend were the ones who vocally—violently, even—hated Jake. The ones who tortured Henry in the halls, who kicked his ass one day after school during Jake's trial, who slashed the tires of his car.

They thought I was some kind of hero for turning Jake in. It made me sick to be around them. It wasn't what I wanted. I didn't want any of it; I just wanted things to go back to how they'd been a few months prior.

Meghan was persistent, though, and after a while I realized she wasn't like the others. She was cool and thoughtful, and her girlfriend, Carmen, was really nice, and even though the questions and comments about Jake and the trial started coming once I started hanging out with her extended group of friends, I dealt with it.

I hadn't realized how lonely I'd been until I wasn't alone anymore.

I had an entire new set of friends, and my old ones wouldn't even wave when they saw me outside my house.

"Through there," I whisper in Henry's ear, pointing to the door to the back porch. Nick is always out back, even in the dead of winter. "He hangs on the far side of the pool in the shadows."

We step outside.

The porch lights are off. Through the dark, I can only make out vague outlines of people gathered around the pool.

This is good. Maybe no one will even notice that we're here. We can get in and out and—

"*Grace!* Where have you been?" Meghan destroys that dream. She walks up to us clutching a red plastic cup with Carmen in tow.

She's leaning in for a hug when she catches sight of Henry.

Her eyes widen, her mouth pulling down into a deep frown. She backs up, away from me.

I'm about to say something—what I don't know, maybe try to explain—when, over her shoulder, I catch sight of Tim Martinez and two other guys from the lacrosse team heading in our direction.

HENRY

OCTOBER 17

"HENRY . . ." GRACE GRABS MY arm, hard.

I think she's about to say something about Meghan. Instead, she points at something behind me.

I turn. Three guys, coming toward us. Through the dark, I make out Tim Martinez's angry face.

My mouth goes dry. I'm not a fighter. Never have been. Jake and I always preferred yelling to punching.

"Hey!" one of them—Jeff something?—yells. "Hey! What the hell you think you're doing here, Hanson?"

I consider my options. I could run back into the house? Across the yard? Either way, they would probably catch me in about two seconds. I haven't exactly been working out much lately. I've had other stuff on my mind.

"Oh God," Grace breathes. "Tim looks pissed."

"Hey," I say. I have no idea what comes after that word, but it doesn't matter. It's too late.

Tim is on me.

"What the fuck is this?" He grabs my arm, fingers digging into my flesh. I try to yank away, but he holds tight, jerking my elbow. A bolt of pain shoots down my arm.

"Get off me!" I sound like such a wimp.

"I knew I saw you over here. Is he harassing you?" he asks Grace. Her cheeks have drained of color.

She shakes her head, silent.

For a long, awful moment, I think she might not say anything at all. Or worse, say that I just showed up. That she doesn't know what I'm doing here. That she doesn't know me.

Tim's fingers tighten around my arm and I try to pull away again, harder this time. Hard enough that he lets go. He tilts off balance and stumbles back a few steps.

Fury flashes across his face. He comes at me, fast, slamming into my midsection with his shoulder and taking my breath with him.

I topple backward to the ground. Crash against it, bones shaking, soul crushing. Above me, Tim looms.

"Stop it! He came with me!" Grace yells, stepping between us.

Tim freezes, tilting his head, confused.

"What?" he asks.

She crouches down next to me, smoothing my hair away from my forehead, and looks up at Tim. "He came with me. He's my . . . my friend."

Tim blinks. "Your *friend*? Grace, what are you talking about?"

"Just leave him alone. Okay?" Her voice is soft, pleading. "We just need to talk to one person here and then we'll leave. Don't start something over nothing."

Tim's upper lip curls. *"Nothing?* His brother murdered one of our teachers in cold blood. You call that nothing? This piece of trash has the same blood running through his veins." He spits at my feet. "For all we know, he helped his brother that night."

"I was *with* him that night, you idiot," Grace says with disgust. She turns to make sure I'm okay. My ribs are smarting, but my ego is more bruised than anything. I shrug her off me and climb to my feet.

Grace's friend Meghan shoves through the growing crowd, offering a hand to help Grace up.

"Jesus, people. What's going on out here? You idiots are going to get the cops called on us again—" Matt Clark comes through the back door, freezing in his tracks when he sees me. "What is he doing here?" He looks around for an answer.

"Bro, that's what I'm trying to find out," Tim says. "He clearly wasn't invited, but Grace claims they came together. Which . . . I know they used to have a thing or whatever, but I thought *you* two were—"

"*You* invited him?" Matt is staring at Grace, his expression unreadable.

She steps closer to me.

"I see."

"We just need to talk to someone really fast—" she says.

"Who cares why he's here?" Tim elbows Matt in the side. "We should kick his ass for trespassing."

"Tim, let it go," Meghan says.

"Well, well, well. What do we have here?" A nasal voice cuts through the noise.

Macey Brown. This is like a literal hit list of my least favorite people at school.

Matt is still staring at Grace.

"Hello?" Macey says to no one in particular. "Isn't someone going to do something about the fact that Henry Hanson is in the backyard?"

"You're just here to talk to someone?" Matt asks Grace quietly.

She nods. "We're . . . I'm helping Henry with something. We need to talk to Nick Marion."

"*Marion?*" Matt says sharply. "Grace—"

"It's for—it's for a school thing. It's a long story. We'll be gone soon. I promise."

"I . . . fuck, man. All right. But you know, Nick is . . ." Matt trails off, worry furrowing his brow. I might hate the guy, but he clearly cares about Grace.

"I know," Grace says.

"You know." Matt runs a hand through his hair. "Okay. . . ."

Meghan looks between me and Grace. "What do you have to say to Nick Marion?"

Grace hesitates, and I jump in to try and help. Which, clearly, is a mistake.

"It's nothing—" I start, but Matt cuts me off.

"Don't push it, Hanson," he says grimly. "Nick's on the far end of the pool. Go. Before I change my mind."

Next to him, Tim groans. "You're just going to let him walk away?" He grabs at Matt's arm, but Matt shakes him off.

"Let it go," Matt snaps.

"Grace. Wait—" says Meghan.

"I'll call you later," Grace says.

"But—"

Grace turns away from Meghan, tugging on my arm. "C'mon. This way."

She still has her hand resting on my bicep as we walk across the porch, down to the pool deck, into the shadows. My ribs ache. I'm vibrating with adrenaline, anticipation, fear. The warmth of Grace's hand on my skin.

On the far side of the diving board is a group of chairs pushed together. A guy sits on one.

Nick.

I haven't seen him in two years. He looks awful. Cheeks sunken and pockmarked with acne, hair stringy and long. I can't help but wonder if this is what Jake would look like now, if it weren't for prison.

He rises off his chair when he spots us. "What the— Henry Hanson? You should not be here."

"And, you"—to Grace—"I thought I told you to leave things to the grown-ups, but instead you show back up with his little *brother*?"

Back to me: "Didn't she turn your bro over to the cops, man? Does Jake know you're hanging out with her again?"

"We need to talk to you," I say, pretending like his words don't hit like sharp arrows.

He snorts. "Oh yeah?" He shoves his hands into the pockets of his baggy jeans.

I glance at Grace. "You told her you didn't see Jake. After the murder."

"Yeah. That's 'cause I didn't."

"No. You did. You came over after they took Jake in for questioning the first time. That night. I swear to God you did, even though he says—" I stop.

"What does he say, exactly?" Nick asks. "I bet he agreed with me. Didn't he?"

I'm silent.

Nick lets out a humorless laugh. "Right. That's what I thought. Ever think maybe *you're* the one remembering wrong? Now that we've cleared that up—"

"We're here because we're trying to help Jake!" I say. "Don't you want to help him? You guys used to be best friends."

"Right. Sure. You two are regular old detectives. Like I already told your friend here, I don't know shit. Leave it to the professionals. Et cetera, et cetera. Now can we all get back to our nights?"

God, I hate this guy. As far as I'm concerned, if Jake had never met him while working at that record store, he'd be in college right now. Anger surges inside me. I'm so sick of this—of everyone hating me and my family, of not being able to go anywhere without someone wanting to fight me. Of Jake and his stupid trial.

Of hating myself for my part in it all.

"No, we can't. Where were you the night Appelbaum was killed?" I ask. "Huh? We know you hated her. She failed you. Almost got you held back. Maybe *you* stole Jake's jacket. Maybe you were the one Grace saw in her backyard."

I fall silent, heart pounding. I shouldn't have said that. Next to me, Grace has stopped breathing.

My anger drains away. All that's left now is fear. It's so

rare these days that I let my mouth get ahead of me. Nick is going to kill me.

He takes two steps forward, leans in close to my face. His breath smells stale. I might throw up.

His voice is low. "Are you really accusing me of murdering that teacher?"

"No! I didn't mean . . . obviously you didn't do it. That came out wrong."

He rubs the scruff on his chin. "Did it?"

"I wasn't trying to say *you* murdered—"

"It sounded like that's exactly what you were trying to say."

"No. We're here because we need to ask you a few questions. Mr. Berkeley lied to us. He told us—and the cops—he told *everyone* he didn't know Appelbaum well, but we found out they dated. That seems really suspicious, don't you think? You were his alibi—"

"Why are you asking around about Berkeley?"

"Because—"

"He has nothing to do with this."

"But why would he lie unless he had something to hide?"

"I don't know. I'm not a psychologist."

"But—"

Nick's teeth are gritted. I'm almost his height, but right now it doesn't feel like that. Right now, I feel about three inches tall.

"Do not go asking around about Berkeley. Do you understand me? Does Jake know what you've been up to? 'Cause if he did, he'd say the same thing. I feel for your brother, I really do. But there's nothing I can help you with here.

And there's nothing you can do either. You need to leave this alone. For your own good."

Grace speaks for the first time. "Do you really think Jake did it?"

Nick's upper lip curls. "Aren't you the one who saw him? Don't *you* think he did it?"

"Not anymore," Grace says. "I think I made a mistake. And I'm trying to fix it."

Nick turns on her now. "What did I tell you the last time we talked?" he growls. "Leave it alone. Let Jake's people handle it. Drop it."

Nick's all up in her face and Grace has gone rigid.

"Back off!" I say, trying to figure out how I can wedge my body between them. "We get it. Okay? We get it."

He glares at Grace for another few beats before nodding. "Good. Now if you'll excuse me, I have business to conduct."

And with that, he stalks away.

ALLY

OCTOBER 17

MY MOM AND I are sitting on opposite ends of the couch, watching TV. I'm half paying attention as I scroll on my phone. Henry texted earlier saying he and Grace had gotten to the party, but there's been nothing since. I'm still so pissed at them for not listening to me, for going even though it is so clearly not a good idea. But it would be nice to get an update.

"Are you okay?" My mom interrupts my thoughts and I realize I'm frowning. "You seem . . ."

I tilt the corners of my mouth up.

"Yeah. Sorry. I was reading a story about Jake and made the mistake of looking at the comments. People suck."

She frowns. "How is he? Have you seen him?"

I shake my head. "Henry says he's mostly been holed up in his room. I haven't been over to their house since he got back. It sounds like it's pretty tense."

"I bet. It's a shame they decided to retry him so quickly.

Sucked the joy right out of his arrival home. I should check in with his mom. See how she's holding up."

My mom flips through a few channels, then throws the remote onto the coffee table. "I'm about done for the night. Feel free to change to whatever you want to watch."

"I'm good."

"All right. Night, honey, don't stay up too late." She kisses me on the cheek and heads upstairs.

I wait until I hear her bedroom door shut before getting up. An ache throbs in my chest. Moments like this make me miss my dad so much. He was a night owl like I am, and after my mom went to bed, I'd find him in his office still working. We'd have long conversations about whatever piece I was writing for the *Boar*. About his adventures freelancing, before he settled down as a staff writer. We'd even talk about Appelbaum sometimes; he knew her from a program he'd run for aspiring high school journalists back in the day, and always said she was one of the most talented students he'd ever had. He loved that I was able to work with her, although he was surprised that she ended up back in Brawner.

Unbeknownst to my mom, I still go into his office at night sometimes, particularly when everything feels like too much.

Entering his office is like falling through a portal into another time. Hanging on the walls are framed articles, awards he won throughout his career, photos of the three of us. His ghost is everywhere in this room.

"Hi, Dad," I whisper. I sit down at his desk, folders and old copies of the *Brawner Times* still piled high on top of it.

Tears well in my eyes.

"I miss you."

The room is silent in response.

A few tears leak down my cheeks. I wipe my wet face furiously with the sleeve of my hoodie. That's about enough of that. I stand.

Recently, I've been going through my dad's things. I want to understand everything about him. How his brain operated, how he put together the stories he wrote. And— I'd never tell my mom this—part of me hopes that maybe I can find answers to the questions that have bothered me since he died.

Why did he leave his office in such a hurry that night? What story was he working on? And why couldn't any of his colleagues tell us where he was going or who he was going to see?

I've never told anyone about my questions. Back then, Grace and Henry were in their own world. My mom was shut up in her room, crying.

Then, two months later, Appelbaum was murdered, and everything went even more to shit than it already had.

Reading through my dad's papers has been interesting, but I haven't found anything about that night. He wasn't very organized—I keep finding pieces from eight years ago filled with stories he wrote the month he died, and it's taking me forever to get through all of them.

I head to the closet, one of the few remaining spaces in this room I haven't searched, and yank open the door.

I'm greeted by dust. Two years of neglect will do that.

Hanging from the wooden rack are a bunch of coats.

One for every season. I reach out and run my hand down the arm of one. I remember the last time he wore it.

It's too much. I shove the coats away from me, into a corner of the closet, and sink to the floor, more tears escaping down my cheeks. *Dammit.* I didn't come in here to cry. I came in here to . . . to . . .

I don't know.

I'm probably an idiot, thinking I'll ever find anything useful in here.

Grace and Henry are together right now, probably happy that they're alone and making progress on the investigation, while I sit here feeling sorry for myself. I have to get it together. I sniff in a huge breath through my nose, exhale through my mouth.

Better.

I pull up into a crouch. With the coats pushed into a corner, I'm able to see what they'd been hiding. A few boxes. A couple of pairs of shoes. My dad's old briefcase.

He always took it to the office filled with notebooks and his laptop and whatever else he needed for the day. I didn't realize it was in here.

The sight of it is like a kick in the stomach, but I can't help but grab it and fling it open. He had it with him the day he died. What if there's something inside that will give me a clue about why he was where he was that night?

The first pocket yields a half-dozen yellow legal pads and some pens. The pads are filled with his writing and what looks like some of the research he did in 2021, when he was working on a series of articles on the renovation of downtown Brawner.

The renovation was super controversial. On one side were all the small-business owners, who were afraid of losing their livelihoods and who wanted to make Brawner a Main Street community again—one where the downtown was revitalized, sure, but in a way that preserved its history. And on the other side, the Miller family. The same family that Grace's sister, Lara, is marrying into in a couple of weeks.

Eventually, the Millers won.

There was a huge uproar after City Council decided to allow the Millers to go ahead with their vision for the renovation—lots of protests, angry op-eds written in support of one side or the other, that sort of thing. My dad covered it all.

I thumb through a couple of thick legal documents, minutes from some town hall meetings, and then find a small blue planner with 2022 embossed on its cover. My dad once lost an article he'd been working on for weeks when his computer ate it. After that, he went old-school, printing out his work, filing hard copies of everything, keeping his calendar offline.

I open the planner at random to late August, two months before he died, and flip through the days. Almost every block is filled with appointments: car maintenance, a doctor's visit, lunches, work meetings.

My eyes catch on an entry. August 29. *Miriam @ Bar Louie—2 p.m.*

My heart stops.

Miriam?

There's only one Miriam I ever heard my dad talk about. Miriam Appelbaum.

I stare at the entry. Could it be? She and my parents were

always friendly and my dad knew her from the mentorship program at BHS, but what was he doing meeting her at a bar in the middle of the day? I guess maybe they were talking about journalism?

I grab my phone off the desk and Google Bar Louie. It's located on the west side of Brawner, in a hotel.

I head into September. On the ninth, there's another note, my dad's handwriting: *Miriam @ Bar Louie, 5 p.m.* Another on the fifteenth, the twentieth. If they were catching up, talking about journalism—hell, if Appelbaum was planning to leave BHS and was picking his brain about how to get a job as a staff writer—why meet so often? In person? Across town? At a hotel?

As time passed, he started using her initials: *MA.* Some of the entries include *w jg.* With *jg*? More initials? I have no idea.

There are more Bar Louie meetings into October, right up to the fourteenth. The day he died.

Two notes there.

MA @ Bar Louie—3 p.m. w jg

Three hours before he died. Was that the reason he wasn't in the office that evening, like he said he would be?

Did they spend his last few hours together? If so, why didn't Appelbaum ever mention it to me?

What is *jg*?

The second note is an address. *2295 Hydraulic Road.*

I flip through the rest of the book, into days my dad didn't get to see. He was supposed to meet with Appelbaum again, the Monday after he died.

A sick feeling, creeping in my stomach. Before he died, my dad had been acting weird. Coming home late without calling. Missing dinners. He said he was working on a big story, but he wouldn't tell us what it was, which wasn't like him.

What if—

Am I really wondering whether my dad and Ms. Appelbaum—my favorite teacher, our neighbor—were having an affair?

They knew each other when Appelbaum was in *high school*. That is disgusting.

I'm going to throw up.

My phone buzzes—a welcome distraction from these dark thoughts. I shove the planner out of sight, into the pocket of my hoodie, and pick up my phone.

It's Henry. *You awake?*

I want to tell him what I found. Except, what if he's still with Grace? The thought of him sharing this with her is too awful to imagine.

Plus, if I tell someone else, it might make it true. And it can't be true. It can't.

I shove everything I pulled out of the closet back into it and shut the doors with a bang. If I can't see it, it doesn't exist.

I turn my attention to my phone: *Yes. What happened? Did you see Nick?*

Yeah. He got VERY upset when we
mentioned Berkeley. Told us that we

**needed to walk away. Said Jake would
say the same thing. We didn't even get
a chance to ask about B's alibi bc he
freaked out so hard. He wouldn't care so
much unless he knew something, right??**

I sit back on my haunches, glad to have something else to think about.

> hang on

I was so annoyed about Henry and Grace going to Matt's party that I didn't look further into Berkeley's background. It's not like I actually think I'm going to find an article about him being a serial girlfriend murderer, but maybe there's something that will tell us more about him.

I Google *Paul Berkeley, Southampton NY.* A bunch of those creepy people-finder websites pop up, listing various addresses for different Paul Berkeleys. Halfway down the page I find one that could be him.

Paul Berkeley (32)

I click. Listed under the name are a bunch of addresses in Southampton: apartments on different streets, a house.

I take a screenshot of the page.

Next, I try *Paul Berkeley, Southampton Academy.* The first thing that pops up is an article from the *Southampton Tribune,* titled "2017 top teachers around East Long Island." Berkeley's photo is halfway down the page.

My search is interrupted by another message from Henry.

Hello??

Give me a minute. trying to see what I can
find about Berkeley.

I navigate back to the story. Under the photo is a brief
write-up.

*Shakespeare lover . . . teaches junior and senior English as
well as electives . . . came to Southampton after graduate school
at Fordham . . .*

Nothing helpful there. I backtrack, keep scrolling down
the Google results until I see a link to a Facebook group:
Southampton Academy Parents.

I click, but it's listed as private.

Dammit. I log in to Facebook, which I haven't used in ap-
proximately one thousand years—it's lucky I have my password autosaved—and request to be a member.

Back to Henry: *I found a FB group for parents at Berkeley's
old school but it's private. Just requested to be a member. I'll let
you know if I'm accepted.*

Ok

There's a pause and then: *Al, pls don't say I told you so, but
you were right. Going to the party was not the best idea.*

Are you okay??

**Yeah but it was on the verge of getting
bad. Matt Clark had to step in and help. I**

**can't live like this. We need to find out who
killed Appelbaum. Soon.**

I grip the phone tight as I type my response, trying to tell myself I'm only motivated by an altruistic desire to help Henry and his family, not by what I found in my dad's closet.

I think we need to do the one thing we haven't. Get into Appelbaum's house. See if we find anything the cops missed. They weren't looking for clues about Berkeley— they were focused on Jake. And her house has barely been touched since.

**How do we get inside? We can't exactly
walk in the front door.**

We'll figure it out, I promise. We're going to go in there. No matter what we need to do.

GRACE

OCTOBER 18

"ABSOLUTELY NOT," I SAY, apparently the only rational person in Ally's basement right now. "We are not breaking into that house. First of all, that's a felony. And second, she was murdered in there! And it's been sitting empty for two years. It's creepy."

"Scared?" Ally smirks from her chair. She's been particularly unpleasant to deal with this afternoon, which I assume is because she's still pissed about Henry and me going to the party. She's such a child.

"No!" I spit at her. "It's just a ridiculous suggestion. And one we could get into a lot of trouble for. Remember those kids who broke in right after the murder to do a séance? They got caught and ended up spending the night in jail. I heard—"

"I'm sorry, a *ridiculous* idea is what you pulled Henry into last night," Ally interrupts. "I tried to warn you—"

"Ally, stop," Henry says.

"I'm just saying—"

"Let it go. *Please.*" He sits forward on the couch, pushing his fingers into the bridge of his nose. "I'm fine. Grace didn't make me do anything; I went because I'm trying to help Jake. And speaking of—"

He turns to me. "We need to do this. I'm sorry. I know you're worried, but Ally's right." Ally sticks her tongue out at me. Mature. "There might be something in there. An important clue. Something about Berkeley."

The thought of going into Appelbaum's house makes me want to hide under my bed. It's bad enough living across the street from it, but to actually go *inside*?

No thank you. But I can't disappoint Henry.

He continues. "I think we should wait a few hours, until the sun goes down."

"Yeah, that makes sense." Ally turns to me. "You know, Grace, you can always go home. *We* can handle this alone."

I bristle. Her message is clear: I'm expendable.

I guess after last night our brief truce is over.

"No," I say. "I'm coming with you."

We spend the next few hours waiting. Ally and I mostly ignoring one another while staring at our phones, a Netflix show on in the background. It's weird, being in this basement. I used to spend so much time down here, whole weekends, and I treated it like it was my own.

Now I'm curled into a little ball in the corner of the couch, wishing I was anywhere else.

Finally, night falls.

Ally leads us out the back door. Her mom's still at work—she has this cool-ass job as the event manager at a local winery, so a lot of what she does happens in the evening. Until tonight, I hadn't given much thought to the fact that since her dad died, that's meant Ally has eaten dinner by herself almost every night.

Earlier, we decided our best bet was to enter Appelbaum's property the back way, so we head through Henry's yard, into the thicket of trees behind Appelbaum's. Their long, high branches block the moonlight, and I tap on my phone's flashlight.

"Grace!" Ally hisses. "What are you doing? Turn that off!"

"It's dark!"

"Yeah, but now people can see us. Turn. It. Off."

I swear to God, sometimes I want to throw a brick at that girl. I let out an angry hiss, but snap off the light. One second later, a fallen tree branch trips me and I almost crash to the ground.

Brambles scratch at my jeans, my arms, my face. We dodge around piles of rotting leaves and walk through tall patches of overgrown grass, before entering Appelbaum's property.

Ally's breath catches. "I can see this from my house, but it looks so much worse close-up. Didn't her garden use to be right here?" She nudges at the remains of a plant with the toe of her shoe.

"I'm surprised your mom hasn't complained to the township about it," I say. "Mine certainly has."

Ally winces. "I think it's because she knows what it feels

like. To not want to get rid of someone's stuff, just because they're gone."

"Oh," I say. I'm an idiot. "Right." We fall silent as we head toward the house over cracking patio stones.

"How are we going to get inside?" I ask as we come to a stop at the bottom of the stairs leading to the back porch. It's covered in dead leaves and downed branches.

"Well, there are two options to get inside. The porch, or that one." Ally points to a flight of concrete stairs that disappear into the earth. "Those lead to the basement. The porch has a sliding door—"

"We should try that one first," Henry says. "Sliding doors are easy to pop off their tracks. Plus, it's less visible."

Ally and I exchange a glance, momentarily connected by surprise.

"How do you know that—about the doors?" she asks him with a raised eyebrow.

He shrugs. "I watched a lot of TV when Jake was on trial."

We head up the stairs. I'm trying not to think too deeply about any of this, about what happened here two years ago, about the fact that one day Ms. Appelbaum walked up the stairs and didn't even know it was for the very last time.

The porch is coated in two years' worth of pollen and peeling white paint. Henry lets out a loud sneeze.

"*Shh!*" Ally scolds.

Henry rolls his eyes. "It's not like that was on purpose. You need to chill, Al."

"Well, even so." She stops in front of the sliding door with her hands on her hips. "Okay, how do we do this?"

Henry flattens his palms against the glass. "So . . . if you apply a little pressure and lift it up a bunch of times, the lock should unhook. . . ."

He tugs on the door handle and it slides open.

"There we go."

He looks at me and smiles.

"Impressive," mutters Ally.

A stale, musty odor wafts out of the house and I gag. It smells nasty—like decay and wet socks. After Appelbaum died, after Jake was arrested and the cops closed the case, I remember seeing a cleaning crew inside, but I'm pretty sure they were the last people in here.

"Should we . . . ?" Ally sounds much less brave than she did in her basement.

"Yeah . . . ," Henry says, motionless beside me.

"Or we could just go back home?" I say. Sweat rolls down my sides, even though it's a cool fall night. "There has to be something else we can do. . . ."

Henry clenches his jaw. "No. We're already here."

He disappears through the door.

"I'm going in," Ally mutters under her breath, then follows him.

Do I want to go in there? No. Zero parts of me want to do that. But I want to help Henry. I want to make up for what I did.

Dammit.

I pull my shirt up over my mouth and step into the house.

In the kitchen, Henry lets out another loud sneeze and rubs his eyes. "Jesus, this dust is killing me."

"Okay. I know the layout in here from cat-sitting," Ally

says. "Two bedrooms, two bathrooms, a study, living room, kitchen. Plus, the garage . . ."

The garage. Where Gabrielle found her, stuffed inside that freezer, with that rose under her hands. I shudder.

Ally's face is pale. She was the closest of us to Ms. Appelbaum because of the school paper.

"The living room is through that archway," Ally continues, pointing. "And her study's at the end of the hall. That's where we should start."

The living room is where she was killed, by the fireplace. The cops found the most blood spatter on the hearth. Their theory was that Jake smashed her head against the bricks, and she bled out there.

How hard is it to get blood stains out of brick? I assume hard enough that the cleaners Mrs. Flowers hired probably weren't able to get it all. If we looked hard enough, would we see some?

Ally disappears from the kitchen with Henry on her tail, leaving me alone. I grip the edge of a counter, trying to get myself together. Past and present are tangling in my head. I half expect Appelbaum's cat, Penny, to wander into the room.

Shut up, Grace. I need to stop thinking like this or I'm going to give myself a heart attack.

"Grace?" Henry calls.

"Coming!" I take a deep breath and move.

The living room is darker than the kitchen, curtains drawn against the outside world, hiding the front windows of the house. There's a couch, a coffee table, a bookshelf that still has framed photos on it. The rug is missing large chunks, and a handful of bricks are missing from the hearth of the fireplace. I can't stop staring at it.

"The cops must have done that," Ally says. "Forensics and stuff, you know?"

"Yeah. Right."

To the left of the curtained window is the front door of the house.

"The study is that way." Ally points to the hallway, her voice wobbling.

"Are you okay?" I ask, moving toward her, reaching out a hand to her without thinking.

She flinches. "Yeah. Why wouldn't I be?"

"Ally . . . if you need—"

"Let's just get this over with. I'm fine. Okay?"

She is very clearly the opposite of fine—eyes darting every which way, chewing her bottom lip raw—but I nod.

We head down the short hallway to the study, passing two closed doors on our way there.

"Appelbaum's bedroom and bathroom," Ally says by way of explanation as we walk by them.

Inside the study, I see a small desk at the back of the room, two bookshelves against the closest wall, a couch. Everything seems to be in a reasonable state of order—the cleaners must have put the room back together after the cops went through it.

"Okay, we're here." I stop next to Ally. "What are we looking for?"

She frowns. "I don't know, Grace. Why do *I* always have to be the one making these decisions?"

God, I am so sick of her and her moods. If she's still this pissed off that Henry and I went to Matt's party, she needs to get a life.

"I don't know, *Ally*, maybe because you're a total control freak and every time someone else makes a suggestion, you totally shoot it down or tell us why it's stupid? Like Matt's party. We went. Get over it. Henry's still here, in one piece. Plus, we did what we set out to do—we talked to Nick. What did *you* do last night that helped us?"

Her jaw juts forward, eyes narrowing.

"Guys—" Henry says.

"Screw you, Grace," she says in a low voice. One that's more hurt than angry.

My anger evaporates. I hadn't even considered that last night probably reminded her of before, when Henry and I disappeared on her. A lot of her anger right now is probably my fault.

I sigh. "This is all so weird and sad, and . . . I'm sorry. Not just because of this, but . . . after your dad died, I wasn't the friend I should have been. It wasn't fair to you. I never told you that. I should have."

She blinks at me in surprise.

"I should have been there. I'm sorry," I say again.

A few tears have sprung into the corner of her eyes. She wipes at them furiously. After a moment, she speaks.

"Thank you." She clears her throat. "I . . . I'm sorry, too. I have to tell you guys something. I . . ."

Her voice cracks.

"What?" Henry asks.

"Ally, are you okay?" I ask gently.

"I don't know." She pushes a palm against one temple and drops her head. "Last night I went into my dad's office because . . . I sometimes do that? When I'm upset or sad or whatever . . ."

"Right . . . ?" I say, glancing at Henry to see if he knows what's going on with her. He shrugs.

"I've been going through his stuff. Trying to figure out why he was where he was the night he died. Because no one at his office had any idea. So, last night, I found his planner. From the year he died . . ."

She pulls her phone out of her back pocket. "I took some pictures of what I found. Here." She holds out the phone. Henry takes it.

He studies the screen, frowning.

"Does this say Miriam?"

I walk over to see. Henry flips through the photos again so I can see them. *Miriam @ Bar Louie,* then, later, *MA @ Bar Louie.*

"Wait. Are these— Was your dad meeting up with Appelbaum before he died?" I look at Ally.

"It certainly looks that way, doesn't it? Who else could Miriam or MA be? It had to have been her."

"But why?" I ask.

Her mouth pulls into a frown. "I have no idea. And at a bar? Which, by the way, I Googled. It's at a *hotel.* My dad was acting weird for weeks before he died, but I always assumed it was because of whatever he was working on— everyone at his office said they thought it was a big story, even though no one seemed to know what it was about. But, what if he . . . what if they . . ."

She sinks to the sofa and buries her face into her hands. When she speaks again, her voice is muffled.

"What if they were having an affair?"

"No way. Your parents always seemed so happy," I say.

"I know!" She raises her head and wipes under her eyes. "But those last couple of months before he died, it was different. He was coming home late, missing dinner. . . . I'd hear them arguing sometimes, when I was trying to fall asleep. Something was up. And my dad knew Appelbaum, remember? He ran that journalism mentorship program when she was still at Brawner. She was one of his mentees. He always talked about how great she was, how surprised he was when she moved back here after college instead of getting a job at a paper in a bigger market. . . . Oh God, and remember how Appelbaum's friends told us she was seeing someone new before she died? What if it was *him*?"

"Ally . . . ," Henry says, walking over to sit next to her. He pats her on the arm. "I'm sure it wasn't that."

She groans. "You don't know that! They were meeting at a hotel. If they were just having friendly chats, why drive all the way across town? I need to figure out if something was going on between them."

"Are you sure that's what you want?" I say gently. Ally and her dad were always close, and she admired Appelbaum so much. It will kill her if she finds out they were having an affair.

Her leg bounces; her hands are balled into tight fists. "*Yes.*

I know it might seem like it doesn't matter because they're both gone, but I can't wonder about it for the rest of my life. I have to know. If there's something in here that can give me a clue, I need to find it."

Henry sighs. "I get it. Grace and I will take Berkeley, all right? See if we can find anything related to him in here. You see if you can find anything about your dad. I really don't think you will—"

"You don't know that," Ally interjects.

"Where are you going to look first?" Henry asks, ignoring her.

"The desk," she says.

"Okay. Grace?"

My gaze lands on the closed door of the closet.

"There," I say, pointing. Henry nods.

I head to the closet and pull the door open, revealing a row of coats. On the floor are some rolls of Christmas wrapping paper, a few empty cardboard boxes, and a small metal file cabinet.

"Do you need help?" Henry says behind me.

"Sure." I move to the side so he can get a better view.

"Do you think she's okay?" he murmurs softly, close to my ear.

We lock eyes, then his drop to my lips for the briefest of moments. My stomach tumbles.

"I don't know. I hope so." I turn back to the closet, gnawing on the inside of my cheek, trying to calm down. "You take the file cabinet, I'll take her jackets?"

"Sure."

I inhale deeply to ready myself, then shove my hand into

the pocket of the first coat. I pull out some old gum wrappers and a pen. The next one also has nothing of note. I keep going with similar results. Crumpled tissues. An unpaid parking ticket. A pair of old wired headphones.

Henry laughs. A rectangular keepsake box rests in his lap, and there's a note card between his fingers.

"What?" Ally walks over, hugging a stack of file folders against her chest.

"Read this." He holds up the card and Ally takes it.

"Parting is such sweet sorrow, that I shall say good night till it be morrow," she reads. "Ew. So cheesy. What is this?"

"A florist note. See the logo? Anny's Florist."

I peer over Ally's arm to look at it. "That quote's from Shakespeare. I remember it from freshman year, when we read *Romeo and Juliet*. Berkeley was obsessed with that play. He must have sent that to Appelbaum."

"Probably. It's dated August 2022," Henry says. "That's when they dated."

Ally makes a face. "I don't blame Ms. Appelbaum for dumping his ass if this is the type of thing he sent her. Where'd you find it?"

"Here." He holds up the box. "Found this in one of the cabinet drawers. The lock was broken—I assume by the cops?—and there's a bunch of personal stuff in it—"

He's interrupted by a loud *thunk* from the hallway.

We all freeze.

"What was that?" Henry whispers.

"I don't know," Ally says. "It sounded like something falling?"

We're all quiet, listening.

"Maybe it was noth—" Ally starts. An even louder thump cuts her off, followed by what sound like footsteps.

"What *is* that?" I whisper, the hairs on my neck standing at attention.

Henry rises, clutching the box. "We need to get out of here."

"It s-sounds like there's someone out there." Panic shakes my voice. "How can we leave if there's someone out there?"

"It might not be," Ally says. "It's probably not, right . . . ?" She looks to us for reassurance, but none comes.

A scraping sound, like something heavy is being dragged.

"It's getting closer!" My heart is in my throat.

Because all I can think is: What if it's Appelbaum?

What if she's back?

It's not rational; it makes no sense—I *know* that it makes no sense—but she was murdered here. What if she haunts this place?

What were we thinking, coming inside?

Someone touches my arm and I jump before realizing it's Henry.

"You're shaking," he says. His hand is warm against my skin.

I lick my lips. "I'm fine," I lie.

Another loud noise, even closer.

"We need to go." Ally's voice quavers. "Before whatever that is comes in here."

"We need to run," Henry says.

"On the count of three, okay?" Ally starts to count. "One . . ."

I dig my nails into the soft flesh of my thumb.

"Two . . ."

Is it almost here?

"Three."

We take off toward the entrance to the room. I reach it first. Fear almost stops me, but Ally shoves me through the door into the hallway.

It's not until I'm rounding the corner into the living room that I see it.

The front door to the house, hanging open.

We didn't come in that way.

Fear seizes me. I stop without thinking and Ally crashes into me.

"What the—" she says, and I point.

"The door," I say. "It's open. There's something on it."

A piece of paper, fluttering in the breeze.

We huddle, staring at it from the edge of the living room.

"Where did that come from?" Ally asks us, voice tight.

"I don't *know!*" I'm near tears, barely keeping myself together. "How did the door get opened? It wasn't open before."

"Do you think . . ." Ally trails off.

"Should we take the paper?" Henry whispers.

"We need to go!" I tug on Ally's sleeve.

Henry nods, but Ally ignores me. She steps toward the door.

"Someone must have put it there. . . ."

"Ally!" Henry hisses. "What the *fuck* are you doing? Grace is right. We need to go."

Ally isn't listening.

"Ally!"

She's at the door now and pulling down the piece of paper, then darting back.

"I got it. Let's go." She takes off running toward the back porch without another word.

GRACE

OCTOBER 18

"JESUS," ALLY SAYS. SHE'S bent over, breathing hard.

I'm slumped against the railing of her back deck, unable
to move. Blinking back tears.

Shaking.

Worry creases Henry's face. "Are you okay?" He puts a
hand on my arm and manages to lead me to a chair.

"Sit." He takes off his hoodie. "Put this on. You need to
warm up."

I sink down onto the chair, wrapping myself in his sweatshirt, then drop my head to my hands. A hand settles on my
back, helps ground me.

We're back at Ally's. Safe.

At least for the moment.

My nerves finally calm enough for me to raise my head.
I'm surprised when I realize it's Ally crouched beside me,
not Henry.

"Are you okay?" she asks, her voice gruff.

I nod, and she pulls a piece of paper from her pocket. "This is what was on Appelbaum's front door."

Henry comes over. "What does it say?"

Ally flattens the paper and holds it so we can all see. Written in thick black marker, in all caps: *STOP DIGGING.*

I jerk back, away from the words, my mouth dry. "Someone was *there*. In that house, with us. What if they killed Ms. Appelbaum? We need to go to the cops!"

Ally folds the paper in half. Shakes her head, a smile playing at her lips. "No way. This is good. Means we're on the right track. We're clearly looking in the right places if we're getting warned off. This is our first concrete sign that whoever killed Appelbaum is still out there."

My mouth drops open. "Are you serious right now? This isn't *good*. Whoever left that . . . they know what we're doing. They could have killed us back there, Ally! We have to go to the cops."

I shove up and out of my chair. Ally reaches out, trying to stop me, but I shake her off.

"Would you please relax?" she says. "All the note says is *Stop digging.* That could mean a million different things. The cops aren't going to care. Plus, what are we going to do? Tell them we're conducting our own investigation into who killed Ms. Appelbaum? That we broke into her house? I'm sure they'd be *thrilled*."

"But if it's from the killer"—I shiver and wrap my arms tight against my chest, try to keep myself together—"it means they're watching us. They're close. What's stopping them from hurting us next time?"

Ally's mouth sets, firm. "Nothing. Don't you get it? We're not going to be safe until we expose them."

"Ally's right," Henry says softly, walking over to me. "I'm sorry, Grace, but we have to keep going. They framed Jake for murder. We can't let them scare us off with a stupid note."

My teeth grind. Henry's right. They framed Jake, but I'm the one who claimed I saw him that night. This is my fault, the fact that we're even in this situation—the fact that Jake was in *prison*.

"Okay," I say in a small voice.

Henry brushes the hair from my face, nods. "Thank you."

Ally looks away.

"Not to change the subject"—he bends down and picks up the keepsake box from Appelbaum's and sets it down on the table—"but I grabbed this. Maybe there's something in it that can help. I only got through the top layer before . . ."

He opens it and starts pulling things out. "Lemme see. Newspaper clippings—"

Ally sucks in her breath. "By my dad?"

Henry shakes his head. "No. Looks like articles Appelbaum wrote for the newspaper up in Philly. There are a couple hotel key cards, a yearbook . . . her birth certificate—this seems like a bad spot for it; shouldn't she have put that in a safe? A bunch of postcards . . . a stack of old photos of . . . I think her grandparents? A few ticket stubs . . . That looks like most of it."

"Nothing else?" I ask hopefully. "A diary maybe?"

"Nope. Nothing like that." He sighs, running a hand through his hair. "Well, that was a waste of energy. This is all pretty useless."

"Let's go inside," Ally says. "I still haven't looked through these folders; maybe there's something in one of them."

I'm about to agree when my phone vibrates in my pocket. I pull it out and see a text from Lara.

> **Where are you? I thought you were helping me with the wedding seating chart!? And Evan and his parents will be here in an hour for dinner. Or did you forget that too?**

My stomach drops. She sounds *pissed*. And, to be fair, I did absolutely forget about both of those things.

"Guys, I'm so sorry but I gotta go."

As the words leave my mouth, I realize I'm relieved to have an excuse to leave. I need time to calm down, to get rid of this awful feeling that's settled in my stomach.

"You're *leaving*? Why?" Ally asks.

"Lara. I told her I'd help out with wedding stuff and—"

Ally doesn't let me finish. "Oh."

"I'm the maid of honor," I say, defensive. Annoyed. Why am I explaining myself to her?

"Fine, then. Go." She picks up the folders and walks inside.

"You okay?" Henry asks.

I nod, but I'm not. Not even close. "I really do have to go. I'm already late. . . ." My voice wobbles.

"Hey," Henry says. "It's okay. Ally is . . . you know how Ally is. She gets tunnel vision about stuff. It's not personal."

He's totally lying, and we both know it. It's very personal. It's always been personal between Ally and me.

"Yeah," I say, allowing him the lie. "I know."

"Anyway." He holds out his hand. I take it, and he strokes my palm. "She'll get over it. We'll see you later, okay?"

"Okay." But I stay, my gaze locked with his, until Ally yells, "Henry, are you coming or what?" from the kitchen.

"I gotta—" He nods in the direction of the door.

"Yeah. Me too." I drop his hand. "I'll see you later."

I head home to face Lara.

HENRY

OCTOBER 18

"THIS FOLDER IS FULL of articles my dad wrote." Ally shoves it across the coffee table. It stops just before it slides off. "This is gross. She was clearly obsessed with him."

I frown at her from the other end of the basement couch. The stuff from Appelbaum's is scattered around us. I have the box beside me, and Ally has the stack of folders on her lap.

"How many have you looked through?" I ask.

"Just two so far, but still. It's disgusting. My dad—"

"Your dad wouldn't have done that," I say. Even though I'm trying my best to control it, I can feel myself growing more annoyed at every mention of her dad.

"Please," she scoffs. "You don't know that. I told you, he was acting so weird before he died."

I make a frustrated noise. "Ally, stop. You're being ridiculous. Your dad was not having an affair with Appelbaum, okay? But even if he *was*—which he wasn't—could you please . . . I need you to stop. Jake's retrial is coming up soon. We have limited time to figure out how Berkeley is involved in everything. Because otherwise Jake is screwed. Remember? My brother? Who might go back to *prison*?"

Two spots of red bloom on her cheeks. "Yes, of course I remember." She picks up another folder from the table.

"Well, have you checked whether you got into that Facebook group for Berkeley's old school yet?"

"I . . . no. I've been distracted. But I will. I'll finish looking through these and then I'll check. I promise. You know, if Grace was here, this would go a lot faster, but I guess she has better things to do."

As if Grace is the issue. She's the one who talked to Nick Marion and to Berkeley. The one who intentionally put herself in harm's way.

Whereas Ally is just bossing us around.

"At least Grace is helping," I mutter.

"Oh my God." Ally throws the folder in her hands down on the table and turns to me with anger flashing in her eyes. "Can you please get your head out of your ass? *Grace* turned your brother in to the police for murder. *Grace* got him locked up for two years. But somehow you still think she shits gold. It's ridiculous. You forgave her for all of that in a heartbeat, but *I* take two seconds to figure out whether my father was having an affair with my favorite teacher and you treat me like I'm committing a crime! For real, Henry; I want to know. What is your problem? Do you really just have no pride? How could you let everything go so easily with Grace?"

And there it is.

The question she's been dying to ask me for days, out in the open.

"I'm not . . . I don't . . ." I don't know what to say. Do I tell her the truth? The thing that's been crawling around inside me for the better part of two years? The horrible truth I've tried to bury somewhere deep inside myself?

The fact that, sure, yes, Grace screwed up when she told the cops she'd seen Jake, but it's my fault Jake went to prison, too.

"What?" There's still anger in Ally's eyes, but there's something else too. Something that makes my heart hurt.

Betrayal.

"Make it make sense."

I have to tell her.

She's going to hate me.

"Hello? Henry?" She snaps her fingers in the air.

I chew on my bottom lip. "I can't tell you."

Ally makes a face. "Great."

"No, I mean because, if I do, you'll hate me."

She makes a noise halfway between a groan and a sigh. "Henry, are you stupid? I stuck with you through all of this, but you still don't trust me?"

"No. It's not that. I do trust you." My heart's pounding hard in my chest. "Look. The stuff with Grace. It's because . . . because I understand. I get what it's like to mess up royally and then try your best to fix it."

"What do you mean?"

I pick at a loose cuticle on my thumb until it starts to bleed.

"I mean . . . *God.*" I wrap my fingers around the pain.

"You remember those messed up DMs they found in Appelbaum's Instagram? The middle-finger emoji one and the other two that were sent from that spam account? The cops traced the IP address back to my place and everyone assumed Jake had been the one who sent them? The defense used them as evidence that he hated her even before she caught him dealing?"

"Yeah . . ." I watch as realization dawns on Ally's face. Her mouth goes slack.

"Henry. Was that *you*?"

"It was stupid! I was pissed off! I had perfect grades that whole semester and then she apparently hated my paper on *Romeo and Juliet* so much she gave me a C-minus. It messed up my whole average. So, yeah. I made a dumb spam account and sent her a couple of rude messages. I didn't know she was going to get killed a month later!"

"Why didn't you tell anyone?"

"I—" This is the worst part of all. "I was scared. They already had so much other evidence against Jake . . . and I thought . . . I thought it didn't matter."

"You thought it didn't matter," Ally says flatly.

I cringe.

"Oh God, Henry." She sits back, shaking her head.

"I'm trying to fix it!"

"You need to tell someone."

"It wouldn't make any difference. Also, remember what that reporter told Grace about lying under oath? What if this is similar? I would be in so much trouble. Plus, my mom and Jake would never forgive me. We're on our way to proving that he didn't do it. Right? That's way better than me fessing up to some stupid DMs."

"Well, at least this explains why you're being so nice to Grace." Ally laughs, but there's no humor in it.

I sigh. "Yeah. I screwed up. But I'm trying to fix it—just like Grace. It's why I need to help Jake—I need to make things right. I'm not trying to be a dick about the stuff with your dad, but . . . this has to be my priority right now."

She stares at me silently for so long I start to worry she's going to argue. Tell me that she's not going to help anymore unless I tell someone what I did.

Finally, she speaks. "I get it. I don't like it, but I get it." She picks up her phone. "Let me check Facebook and see if that group accepted my request."

"Okay. Thanks," I say meekly.

"Hang on. Lemme get into my account. . . ." She sucks in a breath. "Yes, they did! Come look."

"They did?" I slide to her end of the couch and lean over so I can see the screen. "Is there anything about Berkeley?"

"I don't know. . . . I'll search for his name. . . ."

A post pops up, dated May 8, 2021, written by an Anna Sandin.

> Does anyone else find it totally unacceptable that parents have been left in the dark about why, with only three months left in the year, Paul Berkeley left Southampton? The administration needs to tell us what happened. He was my daughter's favorite teacher and he just disappeared one day.

It's unprofessional. Stuff like that is traumatizing
when you're a kid. The administration owes us an
explanation.

"Twenty twenty-one was the year he started teaching at
BHS, wasn't it?" I ask Ally. "In September?"

"Yep." She scrolls down the page. "Most of these comments are people arguing about whether Berkeley has a
right to privacy. . . . wait, wait! Look at this one. *My kid
writes for the SHA newspaper. She said there've been some rumors floating around about him. I agree with OP. We deserve to
know what happened.* From Madeline Toussaint."

"Rumors? Like what?"

"It doesn't say. A bunch of people gave her shit about
spreading fake news, and she never posted again. I'm
going to message her. She left the comment four years
ago; maybe she'll be willing to talk since so much time has
passed?"

Ally types out a quick note, saying she's a student of
Berkeley's and has been assigned to write a profile of him
for the school paper.

"*I wonder if you might be able to tell me what sort of teacher he
was up at Southampton? He's very popular at Brawner.* There."
She sends the message and sits back.

Silence falls. I'm praying she doesn't bring up what I just
confessed.

"What else is in the folders?" I ask to steer the conversation away from the subject.

Ally pokes the stack beside her. "Not sure. It might just

be . . ." She hesitates. "Might just be stuff that has to do with my dad. Which I know isn't helpful to Jake."

It's possible I might have been a bit harsh about her dad.

"That's okay. It's important to you. I shouldn't have given you such a hard time."

She cringes. "Yeah. Well. I know you're worried. I'm still going to help Jake, obviously. But what if my dad was really having an affair with her? It could lead us to other suspects. Like what if . . ."

"What if?" I ask.

She plays with the drawstring of her hoodie. "What if my mom found out?"

I stare at her. "What are you saying?"

"I mean . . . what would she have done? Would she have lost it? My mom's pretty chill generally, but . . ."

I clearly underestimated how much this is messing with her mind. She cannot really be wondering if her mom murdered Appelbaum.

"Weren't you at home *with* your mom that night?"

She shakes her head. "I looked back in my calendar. She was at work. Allegedly."

"Ally. There is no way."

She doesn't respond.

"I'll prove it." I pick up my phone and dial the winery where Mrs. Copeland works. After two rings, someone answers.

I drop my voice. "Um, yes. Hi there. This is . . . Reed McCracken from the IRS. I'm calling to verify a few things about someone in your employ: an, um, a Jennifer Copeland? For tax purposes."

"Okay?" the bored-sounding person on the other end replies.

"Can you confirm she worked the following dates: December fifteenth, sixteenth, and seventeenth of 2023?"

"Twenty twenty-*three*?" the person says. "Uh, that was like a million years ago. Lemme talk to my manager. Hang on."

I pull the phone away from my ear. "They're asking their manager."

The seconds tick by. Finally, someone on the other end of the line says, "This is Meredith Autrey. You're asking about Jennifer Copeland?"

"Yes ma'am," I reply. "For tax purposes."

"Gotcha," she says. "Well, I can confirm she was at work the fifteenth and seventeenth of December. I was here with her. Not the sixteenth, though. Hope that doesn't get her into any trouble? She's one of our best employees. What did you say your name was?"

I hang up. "She was at work. She didn't kill Appelbaum. Okay?"

Ally sighs. "Okay. Thank you. I could have done that myself, but I was . . ."

"Nervous?"

"Yeah. I guess."

"Okay, now that we've established your mother is not a murderer, can we get back to it? You take the folders, I'll go through the box again. Sound good?"

She nods.

I grab the box and pull off its lid. On the porch, I'd

stuffed everything back inside and now the yearbook is on top of the pile. I hold it up. "Is this from Appelbaum's senior year?"

"Twenty fifteen? Must be. Lemme see." Ally takes it from me and flips it open. "Oh my God, look at these clothes. Hideous. Let me see if I can find Appelbaum in here. No . . . no . . . no . . . oh wait, yep. There she is." She taps the page. "In the photo of the *Boar*'s staff."

I lean over to look. "Weird. She's so young."

"Yeah." Ally turns the page. "More clubs . . . Spanish, LGBTQIA+, theater, debate . . . *Oh*—there she is again! Front row. Check out her hair."

Ms. Appelbaum is wearing a huge grin and leaning into the guy sitting next to her. "Look who it is," I say, pointing.

"Oh yeah! Grace's sister's fiancé. Evan. They were the same year in high school." She turns back to the page with the *Boar* photo. "It's so weird to me, how she wrote for the *Boar* in high school and then was its advisor after college. Why did she move back? I'd never. Once I go to college, I'm gone. Speaking of, have you finished your applications?"

"Not yet. Working on them," I lie.

"Yeah, I get that. It's been hard to concentrate on anything but this stuff recently. Did I tell you that Taylor got all pissy with me the other day? Claimed I'm slacking on newspaper duties."

She rolls her eyes, but guilt snakes into my chest. The newspaper is the most important thing to Ally. I don't want her wrecking her life to help my family.

"Wait, what? You didn't tell me that. If this is too much . . ."

She waves my words away. "It's fine. I'm mostly kidding. Taylor's harmless. And Jake is important to me."

"I just—"

"I'm not arguing about this." She shuts the yearbook and picks up her phone.

"Ally, c'mon."

She ignores me, scrolling.

"Ally—"

"Wait, *ohmygod.*" She sits forward.

"What?"

"The woman already wrote back! Old people really do hang out on Facebook constantly, don't they?"

"The one from Southampton?"

Ally nods. *"Hi, Ally. Nice to meet you. It's interesting to hear where Paul Berkeley ended up . . . I haven't thought of him in many years. In terms of what sort of teacher he was . . . I think it would be best if you talked to my daughter Sophia about that. She goes to GW down in DC, which I know is not far from you. I told her you might reach out, so feel free to text or call her at your earliest convenience. Her number is 631-555-2421. Thanks, Madeline."*

Ally looks at me. "I'm going to call the daughter." She dials the number and puts her phone on speaker.

It rings once and we're kicked to voicemail.

Ally hangs up. "She probably didn't recognize the number. I'll text her."

She dashes off a text explaining who she is, and then we wait. A minute ticks by, then another.

I'm trying my best not to get ahead of myself, but I can't help but hope that this will give us some answers. Berkeley lied about his relationship with Ms. Appelbaum. Told the cops he barely knew her. Ally told me that her friends said he texted her after they broke up, warned her about talking. They assumed he didn't want her blabbing about them dating, but what if that wasn't it? What if he thought she'd found out something about him? Something that has to do with why he left his old school suddenly, in the middle of the school year? Something that could potentially ruin his life?

What if it sent him over the edge?

Ally's phone vibrates with an incoming call.

"It's her," she breathes.

ALLY

OCTOBER 18

"ANSWER!"

I nod and put the phone on speaker.

"Hello?"

"Hi . . . Ally?"

"Yes. Hi." My throat is dry. This could be it. Our big break.

"My mom said you were asking about Mr. Berkeley? He's teaching at your school now?"

I nod, then realize she can't see me. "Yeah, he is. I'm doing a little research on him and found a post in the South-ampton Academy Parents' Facebook group from a few years ago, saying he left in the middle of the year, but no one knew why. Your mom left a comment, said you'd told her about some rumors going around about it?"

"Mom," Sophia mutters. "I told her to delete that comment, but I guess she never did. My senior year there were a

232

ton of rumors about why Mr. Berkeley left. The administration was so tight-lipped about it all—they claimed he *left to pursue other opportunities*—which was so vague and shady it made everyone way more curious, you know?"

"Makes sense. What were the rumors? Can you say?"

Sophia is silent for a moment. "What did you say this is for?"

I look at Henry to see if he's on board with me telling her at least a portion of the truth. We have nothing to lose by being honest with this girl, and she might be more forthcoming if we are. He nods.

"It actually has to do with a teacher from our school who died a couple of years ago." I lick my lips. "She was murdered. Berkeley claimed he barely knew her to both me and the cops, but I found out they'd *dated.* It got me curious. Because why lie about that unless you have something to hide?"

"Wow," Sophia says. "That's wild. Your teacher was murdered? And it was never solved?"

"Um . . . ," I say.

"Lie," Henry mouths.

"Yeah, it's a cold case," I tell Sophia. "Since I caught Berkeley in that lie, I've been looking into his background. Ran across the post that said he left your school in the middle of the year, which sounds weird. It didn't have anything to do with someone dying, did it?"

"Unfortunately—or fortunately depending on your point of view, I guess—it did not. I definitely would have heard about it if that had been the case. Whatever it was, it was something the administration was able to keep really quiet."

"Oh." My shoulders slump. "What do you think it was, then?"

"Not sure. The two major rumors I heard were that he'd been sleeping with a student—he was popular and young and fairly attractive, if you swing that way. Creepy and majorly illegal, but not out of the realm of possibility. The other was that whatever happened involved a few kids in my grade, including this obscenely wealthy kid, Dave Adani. No one seemed to know exactly why or how. I don't know if it's true, but it *would* explain how it was kept so quiet. The Adanis were huge donors to the school. Like, in the millions. Honestly, though, whatever it was, his leaving didn't surprise me too much."

"What do you mean?"

"I don't know. Everyone thought he was awesome, but . . ."

"But?" I prod.

"But . . . I don't know. I always got a weird vibe. Like, he was almost *too* involved with the students. He co-owned this record store in town with his cousin, and they hired all these kids from school to work there. Which I guess makes sense in one way—cheap labor—but in another . . . boundaries much?"

"No—" I start. Henry grabs my arm, hard.

"Ow!" I mute the call. "What the hell?"

"Berkeley owned a record store?" he hisses. "And he hired kids from the school?"

I arch an eyebrow, rubbing my arm. "Yeah? And?"

There's fire in his eyes. "What do you mean *and*? *Jake* worked at a record store."

"Yeah, but does Berkeley have anything to do with the store?"

"I mean . . . not that I know of, but—"

"Hello?" from the phone. "I'm sorry I can't be more helpful, but I have to run to class. . . ."

"Shh," I say to Henry, and take the call off mute. "It's okay. I appreciate you talking to me." A thought occurs to me. "Hey, before you go. Whatever happened to the Dave kid? Maybe we could track him down and see if he'll talk?"

Beside me, Henry is practically bouncing out of his seat.

"Last I heard, he was playing lacrosse at Bates. He graduated with the rest of us. It could be because the rumor was fake, but it could also be because his parents paid off the administration to let it go. It wouldn't be the first time something like that happened. If you want to try to get in touch with him, go for it, but I doubt he'd talk. He was always a total douchebag. One of the biggest dealers in our grade *and* he worked at Berkeley's store, even though he clearly did not need the money. Guess he thought slumming it with the plebes made him edgy—"

Henry snatches the phone out of my hand, interrupting Sophia's rant. "What was the name of the record store?"

"What—who is this?" Sophia says.

"Ally's cowriter for the article. Sorry, I should have introduced myself earlier and I know you have to run, but do you remember the name of it?"

"Sure," Sophia says. "The Phoenix."

"What—"

I grab the phone back. I know he's excited, but we need to let her go. "Sorry," I say into it, elbowing Henry in the ribs.

"It's okay," Sophia says. "Feel free to text with any other questions."

As soon as I hang up, Henry explodes. "Why didn't you let me talk? Did you hear what she said? Berkeley owned a record store there. He hired kids from school to work there. Maybe it's related to the place Jake worked. . . ."

I hate to poke holes, but his theory is weak. "Yeah, I don't know. What are you thinking? That Berkeley has a connection to the place Jake worked? Don't you think we would have heard about it, if that was the case?"

"Jake and I weren't talking much by then. . . ."

"Right, but . . . I know we're not the most popular kids at school, but I think we would have heard if one of the teachers at our school owned a record store. I'm a *journalist*."

He winces. "True. *Dammit.* I thought maybe we actually had a lead." He throws his head back, staring up at the ceiling. "This sucks. One dead end after another."

I consider him for a moment, then shrug. No lead left unexamined, right? That's what my dad would have said. "Well, who does own it?"

He lifts his head. "The record store?"

"Yeah."

"I have no idea. It had just opened when Jake started working there, though."

"What's the name of it? Record something, right?"

"The store? Favorite Record."

I Google it and it comes up right away. "Okay, the

website says *Favorite Record, named after owner Joe Fontaine's favorite Fall Out Boy song, opened in December 2021 and sells B-sides and otherwise hard-to-find vinyl.* That's it."

"No mention of Berkeley," Henry says, his voice flat.

"No. None . . ." I'm staring at the photo on the website. Joe Fontaine. A burly, bald man around Berkeley's age, smiling stiffly in front of a sign that reads FAVORITE RECORD. I've definitely seen that face before. Where? "Wait, Henry, look at this." I turn the phone so he can see the screen. "Does this guy look familiar or am I losing my mind?"

He examines the photo. "Wait. He does."

"Where have we seen him?"

He's staring at Joe's face. "I think . . . I think that's the guy who was in Berkeley's car, that morning we were meeting Grace in Grant Park before we went to talk to Appelbaum's sister!"

"Yes! I remember now. You almost slammed right into them."

"I did not." He rolls his eyes. "Anyway, he and Berkeley clearly know each other! What if that's how Jake found out about the job at the store? Through Berkeley's connection to it? Sophia did say that he used to hire a bunch of students at the store up there. . . ."

"True," I say.

"Jake started getting into trouble right around the time he started working there. I always thought it was because he became friends with Nick, but what if . . ." He stands and starts pacing. "What if was bigger than that? What if it was what was going on at the *store* that got him into all that crap? Sophia also said that kid, the rich one, was the biggest dealer in her grade. And he worked at Berkeley's old store. What if it's all connected—Berkeley leaving Southampton, Joe Fontaine, the store, the drugs, Jake and Nick . . . Ms. Appelbaum? What if that's what Berkeley thought Appelbaum had figured out? What got him fired from Southampton Academy! What if he's a drug dealer and he uses the businesses as a front?"

"Okay, right," I say, turning his words over in my head slowly. "But then why isn't Berkeley listed on the store's website? Why haven't we heard anything about him being connected to it?"

As I talk, I'm typing *joe fontaine* into Google's search bar.

"Sophia mentioned that Berkeley co-owned that store in Southampton, right?" Henry says. "Maybe—"

I interrupt him. "Hang on."

"What are you doing?"

"Gimme a minute." We lapse into silence as I start to deep dive. "I'm seeing if I can figure out how they know each other, Berkeley and Fontaine. I'm back on Facebook, looking for Fontaines on Long Island, where Southampton is, and . . . *shit.* There are a bunch of them."

"Any Joes? Joeys? Josephs?"

"One Joe, but his profile is private, and his profile pic is of a car, but . . . I can see his friends list. He's connected to seven different Fontaines. I bet at least one of them has a public profile." I start clicking through the Fontaines, one by one, to see what I can find. Rhonda Fontaine has a public profile with tons of photos anyone can see. "You know, people are really ridiculous with the amount of info they share online. I mean, haven't they heard of identity theft? Deepfakes? It's—"

The next picture I click on makes me lose my train of thought. It's of a group of people wearing formal attire, standing on the steps of a church. The caption reads *Celebrating my niece Margaret's wedding with family*.

My eyes land first on Joe. Second row, third from the right.

And then they land on another, even more familiar face. Berkeley.

"Jackpot."

"What?" Henry grabs my phone and reads the screen. "With *family*? Sophia said it was Berkeley's cousin who he owned the store with, right? What if, I don't know, what if they both moved to Brawner? Reopened the store here, but for whatever reason, this time Berkeley didn't want his name involved? If he took such huge pains to hide it, he would have been *pissed* if he thought Appelbaum had figured it out, don't you think?"

"Extremely," I say, and check the time. "It's after seven. The website says they close at six and open at ten. We should go there first thing tomorrow to check it out. Sound good?"

"Perfect." His eyes shine. "We might have actually done it, Al. We might have figured out who murdered Ms. Appelbaum."

GRACE

OCTOBER 18

I'VE BEEN CAMPED OUT in my kitchen with my mom and my sister, talking about the seating chart for the wedding for what seems like hours. I know less than half of these people. A lot of them are business associates of Evan's parents, so I haven't been much help figuring out where to put them. To her credit, Lara doesn't seem to mind. I think she wanted me here for moral support; even though I'd never say this to her, she looks totally exhausted.

After much debate—mostly with herself—Lara finally settles on another table grouping. "I think we're about half-way done," she says with a tired smile.

My mom checks her watch. "I hate to break this up, but I have to get dinner going soon."

Lara chews on her bottom lip. "Oh man. I didn't realize what time it is. We can pause for tonight. We'll do more over breakfast. I'll bring bagels." She turns to me. "I hate to ask, but we really need to finish this tomorrow since we got such a late start on it today. Can you help in the morning?"

A twinge of guilt. "Yeah, no problem. This was fun," I say, trying to sound like I mean it.

"Great, thank you." She stands. "I've got to run and get changed before Evan and his parents get here."

I head into the family room to get my phone. When I got home from Ally's, I was distracted, looking at my phone every five seconds to see if she or Henry had texted with any updates. Lara started getting annoyed and my mom forced me to leave it in here.

There are a bunch of messages from Henry.

I sink down on the couch to catch up on what I missed.

A lot, apparently. I read the texts, my stomach sinking as I see how much they learned while I've been helping my sister. I missed so much. They might have solved the case without me. They didn't need me there at all.

"You okay?" Lara asks, startling me. I was so engrossed in my phone I didn't hear her come in.

"Fine," I say, but I've never been a good liar and she raises an eyebrow.

"I can tell when you're upset, Gracie," she says. She takes a seat next to me.

I glance down at my phone resting on my thigh and then back up to her eyes.

"I just . . ."

I've been keeping so much from her. Suddenly, I want to unload this whole ridiculous mess, like I used to when I was little. Tell her that Ally and Henry and I are trying figure out who really killed Appelbaum. Tell her that I made a mistake when I told people I saw Jake the night of the murder and it's been eating me alive.

But how would she react if I admit I ruined Jake's life? Lara has never done something so awful. She's perfect. She'd never understand.

So instead I lie again. "Meghan's just stressing. She and her girlfriend had a big fight and I've been trying to calm her down all day. . . ."

"Ah. Sorry to hear that." Lara's clearly lost interest. She pats my leg. "I'm going to see if Mom needs help."

My phone, sitting between us on the couch, vibrates as another message arrives.

We both look down at it. My heart drops.

On the screen is the name Ally Copeland.

I shove the phone under my thigh, but I know it's too late. Lara had to have seen it.

And sure enough, when I cut my eyes to her face, a deep V has formed between her brows.

"It's for the paper," I say, stumbling over the words in my rush to get them out. Lara and my mom made their feelings about Ally and Henry quite clear the other day; I really don't want to deal with another lecture about who I should and should not be seen with. "The article I'm writing? Anyway, when are Evan and his parents getting here?"

Lara clears her throat. "About fifteen minutes," she says, standing. "Are you going to change?"

I glance down at my outfit, which I thought was perfectly acceptable up until this moment. To be fair, I've been wearing the same thing all day, and since we were inside Appelbaum's dusty house it's possible it smells.

"Yeah. I'll go change now," I say, moving to get up. Lara's the furthest thing from stupid, and I want to get out of here before she starts grilling me about why Ally's texting me about the school paper on a Saturday.

"Great." She pauses. The only sound is my heartbeat in my ears. And then: "After you're done, come help in the kitchen?"

I breathe a sigh. "Sure. Of course. Happy to."

As soon as Lara is gone, I check my phone.

Ally's text reads *Meet at my house tomorrow morning at 10. we're going to the record store to check it out.*

My stomach sinks. I just told Lara I'd help her in the morning, and she's already so edgy with me. But this is important—more important than a wedding. Jake's future is at stake. I already missed so much of the investigation by leaving earlier.

I'll figure out how to handle Lara.

I'll be there, I type, then press Send.

Evan and his parents arrive promptly fifteen minutes later. My mom answers the door in a cloud of perfume, not something she normally wears, except for special occasions. Which, I guess, she thinks this is.

My parents have done well for themselves—my dad is a dermatologist and my mom works part-time fundraising for a nonprofit—but whenever they get around Evan's parents they act like they're about to have a meal with British royalty. It's ridiculous.

"Anthony, Caroline, it's *so* lovely to see you," my mom says.

"Hello, Jill. Hi, dear." Mrs. Miller kisses Lara on both cheeks and smiles at my mom. I'm standing at the bottom of the stairs just behind them, but Mrs. Miller says nothing to me. It's always like this with Evan's parents—I'm invisible to them. I'm not sure they even know my name.

Not that I care. His mom is pretentious, always name-dropping, and his dad is puffed full with self-importance, unwilling to accept that he might not be the center of the known universe. Like this: The last time we went out to dinner with them, he spent the first twenty minutes of the meal complaining that our seats were too close to the kitchen. I wanted to slide under the table and die, but no one else seemed fazed.

The one thing that makes me not completely hate them is the fact that they absolutely love Lara. The times I've seen them around her, they ask her questions, respect her opinions—almost more than Evan's.

"Can I get anyone a drink?" My dad appears from the kitchen. "Wine? Bourbon?"

"A chardonnay with two ice cubes, please." Mrs. Miller takes off her coat and holds it out like my mom is the butler. My mom takes it with a smile.

"Good to see you." Mr. Miller slaps my dad on the back. My dad winces. "Bourbon sounds great."

"Great."

We all head to the kitchen, where my dad pours drinks.

"Lara told us she made the dean's list again *and* was invited to be a member of the law review." Mr. Miller takes his drink from my dad. "Impressive, that daughter of yours. Evan's a lucky guy to have landed such a fine woman. She really helps keep him in line. We're lucky he grew up after college and didn't end up staying out in California"—he says the word like it tastes bad—"like he wanted to—"

"*Dad*," Evan interrupts, irritation flashing across his face.

"So! Dinner should be ready soon!" My mother, incapable of dealing with conflict no matter how mild, claps her hands and changes the subject. "Grace, do you mind finishing up the salad? The rest of us can take our drinks to the living room."

"Sure," I say, thrilled to have an excuse to avoid listening to their small talk.

Everyone heads into the living room but Lara hangs back. She watches as I start chopping the green pepper.

"Want me to do that?"

"I'm good," I say. "Thanks."

"Okay." She's quiet. I'm so tense I could crack.

I'm allowed to talk to whoever I want, I think defiantly, stabbing the vegetable even harder.

"What's going on with you, Grace?" Lara says. "Recently it's like you're only half here."

I put the knife down. That is not what I expected her to say. "What do you mean?"

"I mean . . . you're not acting like yourself. You're distracted; you're making up excuses not to help with wedding stuff. That afternoon when I was here, and you said you had too much homework? I saw you sneak out of the house. Then when I got here today, you were nowhere to be found. I had to text you to come home. All of it makes me feel like you don't care about one of the biggest days of my life. And it hurts. You're my maid of honor."

My cheeks heat up as I hear the truth in her words. Lara's right. My heart—and my brain—have been miles away from her and her wedding, which isn't fair to her.

She must see my face fall, because she sighs. "Grace, it's okay. I'm not angry. I'm just . . . disappointed, I guess. You're my *sister.* I had all these ideas about how it would be, and . . ."

A pit opens in my stomach. I hate disappointing people. I hate disappointing *her.*

"I'm sorry. Your wedding is important to me, I swear. I've just been dealing with a lot."

"I get it. I'm sure it's messing with your head, Jake coming home and everything. I'm trying to be understanding here . . . but my wedding is in a week. I need you by my side, Gracie."

Tears well in my eyes. For most of our lives, I've been the one who needed Lara. I never stopped to consider that maybe she needs me, too.

"I'm sorry," I say again, around the lump in my throat. "I'm here for you. I really am. I promise."

She pulls me into a hug. "I appreciate that. We're so much better when we stick together." She steps back. "Okay, I have to get into the other room, but I'm glad we talked. Tomorrow morning, though, right? We'll finish the seating for the reception together?"

I think about Ally's text, my response, my plans to ditch Lara again. I can't do it, not now. I need to be a good sister.

I plaster on a smile. "Absolutely," I tell her. "Can't wait."

ALLY

OCTOBER 18

WE'RE SO WRAPPED UP in Berkeley that it isn't until Henry leaves for the night that I remember the other folders I took from Appelbaum's.

They're still sitting on the coffee table where I left them earlier, waiting.

I sit down in front of them. Maybe Henry's right. Maybe I'm being ridiculous. My parents were happy. . . . Except what about all the arguing toward the end? What about the fact that my dad told us he was working late the night he died, but wasn't at his office? What about all those meetings with Appelbaum at a hotel?

What if Ms. Appelbaum was so kind to me after he died because she'd lost someone important to her, too?

The thought makes me sick.

I wish I was the type of person who could walk away from things when I know they might hurt me.

But I'm not. I open the top folder.

Inside, under the two articles I already saw, are several more, all written by my dad. They cover a variety of topics: town hall staffing changes, recent elections, and downtown renovations. I flip through them, but there's nothing that tells me why Appelbaum would have kept them.

I set the folder aside and open another. More articles, although this time a few are by other people.

The next folder seems more promising. Inside are pieces of notebook paper with Appelbaum's handwriting.

A few notes are scribbled:

8/3–703-555-3845—call to make sure JG legit?

8/18—meet JG @ 2:45—Leesburg Coffee

get in touch with MC—might help?? No date on that one.

What do they mean? MC has to be my dad—Michael Copeland—but who is JG? And why did Appelbaum drive to Leesburg to meet them? That's a solid forty-five minutes away.

I flip to the next paper and read.

Talked to JG @ office (9/29/22). hasnt heard/seen anything.

meet MC @ Bar Louie, 6:15

The next piece of paper isn't dated. There's only one thing written on it, circled in the center of the page:

connection to MCE????

I pull my phone out of my pocket and type in the number written on the first piece of paper: *703-555-3845*. It rings twice.

"Town Hall, how may I direct your call?"

I hang up quickly.

What the hell? Why does Appelbaum have the number for town hall in her notes? How does it connect to her, my dad, and the fact they were spending time together? Who is JG? MCE?

This is doing nothing to alleviate my confusion.

I reread the notes, then stand. My dad's planner is tucked away in my desk upstairs. If I compare them side by side it might give me some clues about what it all means.

Back in my room, I grab the planner and settle onto my bed. Spread everything out in front of me.

It jumps out at me immediately.

The initials *JG* in Appelbaum's notes, next to the phone number for town hall.

They're also in my dad's planner, written on the day he died.

MA @ Bar Louie—3 p.m. w jg

I sit back against my pillows to think. My dad used Appelbaum's full name at first, but quickly switched to her initials. He wrote Bar Louie out in full every time.

It seems likely that JG are the initials of a person. I rack my brain, trying to remember the names of my dad's colleagues, his friends, but I can only remember a few.

I pull up the *Brawner Times* website and check the masthead. There aren't any names on it that match those initials, but it's been two years and I'm sure there's been turnover.

My phone dings. A message from my mom.

**Will be home shortly. Hope you're
asleep!!!**

I realize with a start that it's almost midnight. I've gotten sidetracked again with this, just like Henry asked me not to earlier tonight. I need to get it together, stop obsessing about something that might not have even happened between two people who are dead.

I set the planner and the folders on my bedside table. There's a lump in my throat I ignore. I'll come back to this later.

The important thing right now is Jake.

BRAWNERNOW.COM

Murderer's new trial set for January
Am I the only person who cannot believe that
the criminal justice system in this town is so
broken that Jake Hanson, a convicted killer,
will be living in his comfortable home for the
foreseeable future while awaiting retrial? He'll
celebrate the holidays with his family, while
the family of the teacher he murdered in cold
blood grieves.

Incidentally, we've gotten word that the
police have been called out to the Hanson
house several times since Jake's release. One
can only surmise that it has something to do
with the return of the prodigal son. Perhaps
the Hanson family has found living with a

violent psychopath more difficult than they anticipated?

District Attorney Cassie Flynn is clearly incompetent. Jake Hanson should be back behind bars *tomorrow*. In fact, he should never have been released. If Flynn can't do her job properly, I think we should start a recall campaign. Let the voting public decide whether we think she's serving our needs.

Who's with me? Let me know at the address below, or better yet, email Cassie Flynn's office direct at info@da.brawner.gov and let them know your thoughts.

Thoughts? Questions? Want to tell us we suck? Write to editor@brawnernow.com.

HENRY

OCTOBER 19

SUNDAY MORNING BEGINS WITH a double whammy—another scathing editorial (if you can even call that trash an editorial) on that piece of shit tabloid website *BrawnerNow* *.com* and the news that someone smashed our mailbox to bits during the night. I see the opinion piece almost immediately upon waking thanks to my dad. He texted it to the family thread we hardly ever use anymore, along with the message: *JUST THOUGHT YOU SHOULD SEE THIS.*

Gotta love that guy. No communication ninety-nine percent of the time, but he somehow finds the time to send that. Priorities.

On top of all my worries is the memory of my confession to Ally about those stupid DMs I sent and let Jake take the blame for.

It's a beautiful start to the day.

I hide for a couple of hours after waking, distracting myself from my anxiety by playing Candy Crush on my phone.

At precisely 9:52 a.m., I hop off my bed.

I drive around the block to Ally's house and find her waiting out front, shivering in a thin blue hoodie. The clouds overhead are low and gray and it can't be more than forty degrees.

"Where's Grace?" I ask after she hops in the car.

She rolls her eyes. "Hi, Henry. Can we turn the heat up?"

"Sorry. Hi. Yeah, go for it."

"Thanks." She twists the dial a full turn to the right. "To answer your question, I don't know where she is. Haven't seen her. Are you sure she's coming?"

"She told you she was." I check my phone, but there's nothing. I send a message.

Where are you? Are you coming?

We wait for her reply, Ally sighing and shifting in her seat as the minutes tick by.

Finally, she leans forward and slaps her palms against her thighs. "Can we please go? She's obviously not showing."

I hesitate.

"It's been fifteen minutes, Henry."

"Fine." I sigh, turning my attention to the road.

Even though Jake practically used to live there, I've never been to Favorite Record. I was always sort of intimidated by it. Jake. Nick. All their friends who worked there.

The clouds open up as we drive. Rain spatters against the

windshield and I slow to a crawl. It was raining the night Ally's dad died and driving in the rain makes her nervous.

I glance over. Sure enough, her hands are balled into tight fists in her lap. When she catches my eye, she pulls a smile.

"I'm fine."

"You sure?"

"Yeah. We're almost there, right?"

I nod. According to my phone, we're less than two minutes away. We've been driving toward the west side of town—the one area of Brawner that the Millers haven't gotten their hands on yet. It's full of older homes, crumbling apartment buildings, small family businesses that have been around for decades.

At the next stop sign, I turn onto Long Branch Avenue, which is lined with warehouses converted into businesses—a trampoline park, a dance studio, the record store.

"There it is." Ally leans forward again. "Sixteen forty-two."

Last night, we decided I should go into the store alone so Ally can keep watch out front. Just in case something happens.

I park at the far end of the parking lot, then freeze, my hands curled around the steering wheel.

"You okay?" Ally asks.

Am I okay? Not really—I'm freaking out.

"Yeah. I'm fine," I say, trying to convince myself of it. It's the middle of the day. A public place of business. Nothing bad is going to happen. I'll just walk inside and check things out.

I can do this.

"I'm going."

Before Ally can respond, I'm out of the car and walking toward the entrance, gripping my phone tight like a lifeline.

Inside, the lights are low, and loud pop-punk plays on the surround sound overhead. A bored kid who I recognize from school—his name is Bryce, I think—sits behind the register, playing a game on his phone. He doesn't even look up when I walk in.

I text Ally: *BHS student working the register??*

She responds immediately: *Another connection to Berkeley!! Fits with what Sophia told us. Keep me updated*

I thumbs-up her message and head deeper inside, past racks of vinyl, posters of bands, stuff you'd expect to find here. Nothing that indicates an illegal operation is being run out of this place. But then again, it's not like they'd advertise it.

A loud crackle of static overhead makes me jump.

"Shit," Bryce says loudly. I turn back. He's up out of his seat and fiddling with something in a cabinet.

The door to the shop opens and Matt Clark walks in.

I duck behind a large cardboard cutout of Han Solo and peek around Harrison Ford's hair.

"Is he here yet?" Matt asks Bryce, who slams the cabinet door shut with a grunt.

"I don't know, man. I've been kind of busy—"

"Oh yeah?" Matt asks. "With all these customers?"

"I . . ." Bryce trails off. "Whatever, bro. You have legs. You can check the offices."

"Great, I will." Matt heads down an aisle, passing by

my hiding spot, and disappears through a door at the back. It's clear he knows where he's going, that he's been here before.

Does he *work* here?

I remember Sophia's story about Dave both dealing and working at Berkeley's store. Is Matt Clark dealing drugs?

Bryce settles behind the counter again, face buried in his phone. I don't think he's noticed me. He seems entirely unconcerned with his surroundings.

A text from Ally arrives. *Any luck?*

Maybe. text you shortly

I wish Grace was here. Not just because her presence calms me, but because she knows Matt.

Even though she ghosted us earlier, I message her.

Are you around? At Favorite Record
& have some questions

No response.

I need to follow Matt.

I glance at Bryce, still enraptured with his phone, then walk quickly toward the door Matt disappeared through and pull it open.

On the other side is a narrow, empty hallway.

No sign of Matt.

I start slowly inching my way down it.

Voices leak out from an open door farther down the hall, but they're too quiet for me to make out individual words.

I lick my lips, take another step forward. Stop in front of the closest door, which is cracked open. I push through it into a dark room and pull the door shut behind me. Flicking on my phone's flashlight, I see I'm in a supply closet, surrounded by stacks of large wooden crates.

I push at the lid on the closest one, but it's nailed shut, impossible to move. The next one is too. And the one after that. I keep at it, finally reaching one tucked in a corner with its lid cracked open.

I yank the lid off and set it gently on the floor, then shine my flashlight inside. All I see is plastic packaging. I grab a handful. Pull it out, holding my breath.

Under it are a bunch of nice-looking stereo speakers. My shoulders slump.

Exactly what you'd expect to find in the storage closet of a record store. What did I think I was going to find back here? Kilos of cocaine?

Annoyed, I reach in and pick up one of the speakers. It's heavier than I expect, and try as I might, I can't get a grip on it. It slips out of my fingers, crashing down loud into the crate. I can hear it splintering.

My heart thunks in time with the string of curses running through my head. I duck behind the biggest crate and crouch down, snapping my flashlight off. I can only hope the closed door was enough to muffle the noise. If anyone opens it I'm screwed.

I wait a minute, then two, and my pulse slows.

Finally, I stand. Tap my flashlight on and climb out from my hiding spot. I need to assess the damage I caused, put the lid back on that crate, and get out of here.

I look over the edge of the crate and my entire world tilts sideways.

The speaker is cracked in half at the bottom of the crate, and peeking out from its innards are two small baggies about the size of my fist, taped up tight.

I've seen bags like that before.

Jake's room, the summer before his arrest. By that time, we were no longer on speaking terms, but I kept hearing more and more stuff about him at school. That he wasn't just selling low-level stuff—Ritalin, Xanax, and weed—anymore. He'd gotten into more serious drugs. Stuff like cocaine. I snuck into his room one day because I had to know for myself. I found what I was looking for on his closet shelf, stuffed into a shoebox.

Coke. In little baggies. Exactly like these.

Holy crap. Ally and I were actually right.

I reach into the crate, grab one of the baggies, shove it into the waistband of my pants, and turn for the door.

All I need to do is get back into the front of the store. No one will touch me there. There would be too much risk of exposure.

I pull open the door, peek around the corner. The coast is clear. I'm about to head out when a familiar figure emerges through a doorway at the far end of the hall.

Tim Martinez with a large blue duffel bag clutched under one arm.

I tuck myself back in the closet.

Did he see me?

Footsteps coming closer . . . closer . . . and they pass. I exhale.

I wait a few long seconds, then move.

I'm almost to the door leading back into the front of the store. I'm reaching for its metal handle, when there's a loud shout behind me.

Without thinking, I turn. A big, bald man is coming toward me—not just big, *huge*—and he's red-faced and angry. I recognize him from his photo.

Joe Fontaine.

"Hey, kid!" he yells. "What the hell are you doing back here? This area is strictly off-limits."

Fear chokes me and I stumble sideways, slamming my hip against the side of the wall.

"I'm not . . . I didn't . . ."

"Joe? What's going on?" someone calls out from one of the rooms.

"There's some kid out here!" Joe shouts without taking his eyes off me.

"A kid?"

Berkeley appears in the hall, Matt Clark and Nick Marion behind him. His mouth drops open when he sees me.

"Henry?" he says, confused.

Nick's face goes white. We lock eyes.

There's a beat where no one moves. Then Nick mouths at me, clear as day: *Run.*

And my legs wake up.

I spin around, stumble, and I'm knocked off my feet, flying headfirst into the wall. White-hot pain explodes behind my eyes.

I crumple into a ball, coughing, acid rising in my throat.

"Henry, what are you doing here?"

Berkeley.

I have to get up. Go. Ally will be wondering.

I struggle to my knees, but Berkeley's already there, in front of the door, blocking my exit.

I can't catch my breath. "Nothing. I just"—I gasp—"I just got lost."

"What's this?" Joe bends down next to me. He yanks the baggie out of my waistband. Hands it to Berkeley.

"This doesn't look like nothing, Henry," Berkeley says, turning it over in his palm. "I think the two of us should have a conversation in my office. Joe, can you help make sure this young man gets there safely?"

Joe nods and yanks me to my feet, hard. Behind Joe, Nick is watching.

Matt Clark has disappeared.

"I can walk there myself!" I say, trying to yank away from Joe, but the room spins.

He ignores me, his fingers tight around my arm as he drags me down the hall and into Berkeley's office.

GRACE

OCTOBER 19

ALL MORNING LONG, MY stomach's been aching. Henry texted earlier, asking where I was, and I couldn't bring myself to respond.

Even though I promised myself I'd be on my best behavior once Lara arrived, as the hours have ticked by the ache has deepened, destroying my ability to concentrate.

Case in point: "Grace?" Lara says loudly, startling me. She's staring at me from across the table, brow furrowed. I have a feeling it's not the first time she's tried to get my attention. I blink at her. "What?"

She looks annoyed. "I asked whether you thought Aunt Judy would be okay at table three? Like five times?"

"Oh, right, yeah. I think that's fine," I say, attempting to inject a little bit of energy into my voice.

"Great," Lara says, her voice tight, and marks down the name on the chart in front of her. She and our mom talk about the next table and the next, and all the while, my brain drifts, imagining what Ally and Henry are doing right now, if they've found anything at the record store. Anything about Berkeley.

Finally, I can't take it anymore. "I have to go to the bathroom," I say, getting up without waiting for a response and rushing into the family room, where I left my phone earlier.

No new texts from Henry or Ally. I deflate.

Ghosting them was not my most mature move.

I drop to the couch, wrapping the hoodie I'm wearing around me, tight. Henry's hoodie, the one he let me borrow on our way to Appelbaum's yesterday. I'd planned to give it back to him when I saw him today, but now . . .

I don't want to have to face him when I return it; I don't want to have to explain why I disappeared. And he's not home right now.

I stand. I can just leave it on his front porch, and I'll be back to help Lara in no time at all.

I can't bring myself to use the shortcut through Ally's yard, so instead I walk around the block to get to Henry's street. I wonder if either of them will talk to me anymore after today. I wonder if I made a huge mistake, not going with them.

I think I might have.

Henry lives at the end of Hawthorne in a two-story brick house I used to know as well as my own. Years of my life were spent on this street and inside his house.

I walk up his driveway, nervously clutching the hoodie to my chest. I'm going to leave it on the front porch so he'll see it when he gets home.

A part of me hoped he might be back already, so I'd be able to explain myself to him, but his car is gone.

I'm trying to decide where to put the hoodie when the front door swings open.

I whirl around and come face to face with Jake Hanson for the first time in two years.

He's wearing a ratty T-shirt and stained sweatpants, his hair greasy like he hasn't showered in days.

He stares at me. I think back to all the people who kept asking whether I was afraid when he was first released. How my parents thought about getting security for our house.

"What the hell are you doing here?" he growls.

"I—I—" I stutter. I hold Henry's hoodie out between us like a shield. "I was returning this."

His eyes land on it, then swing back to my face. "Why do you have my brother's sweatshirt?"

"I—" I'm scrambling for an excuse. I have no idea what Henry has told him. "He lent it to me," I say finally.

"When? Recently?"

I nod, then shake my head. "No. Yes. I'm sorry . . . he lent it to me last night. . . . I was just returning it. I know he's out. I wasn't trying to trespass or be weird or anything, I promise."

"How do you know he's not home?" Jake's expression darkens. "He told me that he talked to you, but he claimed it was just a one-time thing."

"It's not like that," I mumble.

"Then what's it like?" he says, holding out a hand. "Gimme that."

I move forward hesitantly, tossing the hoodie to him with several feet of space between us. "It's . . . Look, I don't know what he's told you, but I've been thinking about what—*who*—I saw the night Appelbaum was murdered," I say. "I've been second-guessing what I saw. Henry and Ally and I decided that we needed to figure out whether it was you."

His lip curls. "*Whether* it was me?"

I swallow. "Wait, no. That's not what I meant—"

"Are you seriously standing here, telling me you suddenly *changed your mind*? That now you think it wasn't me? Because you certainly sounded sure when you sat up front in that courtroom and told everyone you saw me that night." His mouth sets in a hard line.

"I thought I was," I say quietly, "but now I'm pretty sure I was wrong."

"You're *pretty sure you were wrong*?" He barks a humorless laugh. "How cute. You do get that I spent the last two years in *prison*?"

"That's why we're trying to help—"

"Do you really think you're helping by tromping around town with my dumbass brother, playing detective? That is literally the last thing I need. Don't you think you've done enough damage? Stop dragging Henry into your shit."

I flush. "Look, I get that you hate me, all right? But I'm trying to help!"

"Grace." Jake's voice is sharp. "Are you listening? You need to stop. Do you understand?"

I swallow. Normally, I'd walk away right about now, but this might be my only chance to be useful today.

I plunge forward. "You used to work at that record store—Favorite Record—with Nick, right? Was Berkeley connected to it somehow?"

"What?"

"Um." I chew on my bottom lip, trying to remember exactly what Ally and Henry texted me last night. "Well, we figured out that Berkeley used to own a record store on Long Island. And the one you worked at is owned by this guy Joe Fontaine, who lived on Long Island, too, and there's a Facebook picture with the two of them in it. Which is way too weird to be a coincidence, so Henry and Ally went to the store to check it out—"

"They did *what*?" Jake yells. He steps out onto the porch, his face suddenly white.

"They went to Favorite Record?" I whisper, wishing I'd walked away when I could. "Anyway, I'll go—"

"When did they leave?"

"Around ten? Maybe a little after?" I add, remembering the time they must have wasted waiting for me.

"What time is it now?"

I fish my phone out of my pocket. "Ten-forty-five?"

"It takes fifteen minutes to get there . . . ," Jake says. "Jesus Christ, you are all idiots."

"What do you mean? We're trying to help—"

"*Help?*" He mutters a few choice expletives and starts pacing up and down the length of the porch, running his hands through his hair. "There's that stupid word again. I told Henry how he could help: Stay out of it. Let the grown-ups handle it. But does he listen? Of course not. Who do

266

you think you are, Scooby-fucking-Doo? Berkeley is a *drug* dealer. I used to deal drugs for him. You know how originally I told the cops I was with him that night? That's because I *was*. But Berkeley didn't want anyone looking at him too closely, so he sent Nick to my house to tell me that I had to tell the cops I was lying about my alibi."

I stare at him. "But why would you do that?"

"You still don't get it. Berkeley isn't who he pretends to be. He and his cousin, you don't mess with them. I argued with Nick—I told him there was no way I would do that because if I did, I was screwed—and then I got a message from Fontaine later that night on the stupid app he made us all use so our stuff couldn't be traced. All the messages disappear right after you read them. You know what it said? If I didn't cooperate, he'd come to my house and slit my mom's throat. And then Henry's."

I freeze. "What?"

"Yeah. *That's* the reason I changed my story. That's the reason I went to prison for something I didn't do. I told my mom that I was guilty, to leave it, but she didn't believe me. Said I was saying that to make her feel better about all of it. The woman won't quit. Then this new lawyer had to go and get me out of prison, and now those morons are there, probably getting themselves killed . . . *goddammit*." He slams his fist against the front door.

I'm panicking. "We need to do something! We need to call the police and tell them—"

"Tell them what?" Jake interrupts. "As soon as they hear who's involved, I can guarantee they're not going to lift a finger to help. By the time they send someone—*if* they send someone—it's going to be too late. You have a car, right?"

I nod.

"Good. Let's go."

"It's up ahead—there." Jake points through the windshield. "On the left. Second warehouse. Sixteen forty-two."

"Sixteen forty-two?" I repeat. Something about the building looks familiar, but I'm having trouble figuring out why—I can't remember ever being here before.

I turn into the parking lot and spot Henry's car immediately.

"There's his car . . . ," I say, driving toward it. "Someone's inside."

"Maybe they didn't go in yet," Jake says, his voice hopeful.

I pull closer and see Ally, staring down at her lap. She looks up and her mouth falls open when she sees us. I park and she climbs out of Henry's car.

"*Jake?*" she says. "I thought you were on house arrest."

"I am," he answers. "Where's my brother?"

"He went inside a while ago. . . . I'm starting to get nervous. He stopped responding to my texts."

"You two stay here," Jake says, and takes off running toward the store.

"When's the last time you heard from him?" I ask Ally.

"Eight . . . no, twelve minutes ago." She's looking at her messages. "The last thing he said was he hadn't seen Berkeley and he'd update me soon. What is going on? Why is Jake here? He's going to be in massive trouble when the cops find out he left the house."

"He freaked out when I told him where you guys were. Ally, he said Berkeley deals drugs. He said he *was* with Berkeley the night of the murder—his first alibi was true. But when Berkeley heard Jake had told the cops that, Fontaine threatened to murder Ms. Hanson if Jake didn't change his story."

Her face pales. *"What?* Oh my God. We have to get Berkeley to confess." She's gone before I can stop her.

"Ally, wait!" I scream, but she ignores me. She reaches the front door and disappears inside.

"Crap." I look around the parking lot. It's quiet. I'm all alone. The me of three weeks ago would probably get back in the car and hide, too afraid to put myself out there for someone I love.

But that's not true anymore.

I wipe my sweaty hands on my shirt and jog toward the store.

Bells chime overhead as I walk inside and loud music envelops me. The checkout counter is empty.

A hand lands on my arm and I let out a frightened yelp. It's Matt Clark. My mouth drops open.

"Grace, what are you doing here?" he hisses.

"What are *you doing*—" I say, but suddenly it clicks. Why this building looks so familiar. I saw a picture of it on Matt's phone. Right before the picture of the drugs.

Matt's eyes dart to the door, then back to me. "You should go," he says, and I yank my arm away.

"I'm staying," I tell him.

"You don't understand—"

"Do you work here?" I interrupt.

"I . . ." He trails off like he's not sure how to answer. "No. Well, sometimes, sort of . . . Can we talk about this somewhere else? I gotta go." He reaches for me, but I dodge him.

"Go then," I tell him.

He hesitates.

"Bye," I say, and wave for him to leave.

"Come with me," he says in a low voice.

"No."

"You—" he starts, but he's interrupted by a shout from the back of the store. His face pales. "Okay, fine. Have it your way. But you're going to regret it."

He takes off out the front door.

"Grace." Someone taps me on my shoulder and I yelp again. I spin around. It's Ally this time.

"*Shh!*" she hisses.

I lower my voice. "You scared me."

"Are you and your boyfriend done chatting?"

"Who?"

"Matt Clark."

"We're just—" I'm about to say *friends,* but I'm pretty sure that's not going to be true after today. "Yes. Done," I say instead.

"Good. Come with me." She drags me farther into the store, then stops behind a big cardboard cutout of a man. She points to the door at the back marked by a bright-red Exit sign. "I got here right as Jake disappeared through that. And then people started shouting. . . . I haven't seen Berkeley yet."

"We need to call the cops."

Ally nods. I take my phone out of my pocket, hands shaking, and press the numbers into its keypad.

A woman answers. "Nine-one-one, what's your emergency?"

"My friends are in trouble," I whisper.

"What? Miss, can you speak up? I can't really hear you over the music. Can you turn it down?"

"Please—"

Something knocks into my arm and my phone clatters to the ground.

"I thought I warned you." Nick Marion's angry face, inches from my own. He grabs my phone from the floor and presses End Call. "Why couldn't you just listen?"

There's shouting from the back of the store. Nick's jaw clenches.

"You two need to get out of here," he says.

I press my lips together and shake my head.

"No way." Ally echoes my thoughts. She glares at Nick. "Did you know Berkeley was with Jake that night? Of course you did. You told the cops that you were with Berkeley. That Jake wasn't. You let your friend go down for *murder* and—"

Another, even louder yell and Nick's head swivels toward it.

"Do you have your phone?" I whisper to Ally. She nods, slipping it out of her pocket and dialing. But before she can press Send, Nick's back, pulling it from her hand.

"Get off me!" She shoves him, but he holds the phone out of her reach.

"C'mon," he says tiredly. "Please. Just cooperate. Don't make things worse than they already are."

The back door slams open, making me jump and revealing Jake, wrapped in the arms of a muscular man with a goatee.

"Get your hands off me, Joe!" Jake's face is beet red, veins popping out of his forehead. He thrashes wildly, but Joe doesn't lose his grip. "Where is my brother?"

"I thought we were very clear about what would happen if you ever talked," Joe says. "But it's clear you didn't take that seriously enough, what with your brother showing up here. . . ."

"I *didn't* talk. I swear to God. He's an idiot; he doesn't know anything, okay? Do whatever you want to me, just let him go."

"Shut. The fuck. Up." Joe tightens his grip, and Jake lets out a shriek of pain.

Ally takes a step toward them, but Nick grabs her by the shoulder.

"Don't you dare."

"Get your hands off me!" she hisses, twisting away.

There's a loud shout as the front door opens.

"Police! Nobody move. We're looking for Jake Hanson."

Two uniformed officers appear, hands on their holsters, taking in the scene.

Joe has released his grip on Jake and backed up against the wall, hands above his head. Jake's staring at the cops, his jaw set.

"Jake Hanson?" the female officer says to Jake as she walks toward him.

"That's him, Officers," Joe says.

The second cop speaks. "Jake Hanson, you've violated the conditions of your house arrest—"

Before he can finish, Jake spins around and bolts.

"Stop!" the male officer yells, lunging for him and missing. Jake disappears through the back door, the cops on his heels.

"Wait! Jake isn't the one you want!" Ally cries. "He has an alibi!"

"*Don't—*" Nick says, but she's already gone, running after the cops.

I take off after her, following her through the back door and into a short hallway. The male officer has Jake's arms pinned to his sides. Jake's face is red with fury. Berkeley's at the end of the hall, talking to the female officer. Jake lunges at him, but the cop pulls him back.

"My brother is back there! You have to help him! He might be hurt!" Jake screams at the cops.

"Son, if you don't stop struggling you're going to make this much, much worse for yourself," the male cop tells him.

"You see?" Berkeley says loudly to the officers. "Just as I was saying. He's violent. He and his brother attacked us out of nowhere. Thank God you showed up when you—"

"Check the crates," Nick interrupts. I turn. His mouth is set in an angry line. "In the storage room. First door on the right. Then I'll tell you everything."

ALLY

OCTOBER 19

THIS STUPID METAL FOLDING chair is digging into my back.

I lean forward, trying to get comfortable, but it's impossible. I've been in this tiny room for about a billion years, staring at myself in the two-way mirror on the wall. Literally my only entertainment since they took my phone.

Two officers asked me a few questions, then left me here to rot.

"Hello?" I say into the empty room, hoping someone's watching me from behind the mirror. "Can someone please send Officer Kapoor back in? Or at least tell me what's going on? Are my friends okay? Is Jake?"

When Nick told the cops to check the storage room, Berkeley tried to outrun the cops, but Grace tripped him as he tried to pass her. He sprawled on his face, and I'm pretty sure he broke his nose. Another cop responding to the call caught Bryce and Matt outside trying to sneak away.

The cops found Henry in Berkeley's office, tied to a chair,

face bruised, but in the ensuing chaos we didn't get to talk to him. I haven't seen him since.

The door swings open and Officer Kapoor appears. About time.

"Hi, Ally. Your mother is here. I hope you understand how lucky you are to be going home right now. You're eighteen. We could hold you overnight. Charge you."

I fold my arms across my chest. This lady doesn't scare me. "What laws did I break, exactly?"

She frowns. "That's not the point. You and your friends could have been seriously hurt back there. You're all very lucky that Jake Hanson's ankle bracelet alerted us to his location before it was too late."

"Are you letting him go home?"

She narrows her eyes. "That's really none of your concern, Ms. Copeland. You do understand he broke the terms of his house arrest?"

"He only left his house because he knew his brother was in trouble! Like you just said, if he hadn't gone, you wouldn't have shown up and who knows what could have happened. He saved Henry's life. Also," I say, barely stopping to breathe, "did you talk to Berkeley yet? He needs to tell you—Jake has an *alibi* for the night Appelbaum was killed. They were together, but Berkeley threatened him and forced him to lie about it. Jake is innocent!"

She stares at me. "I don't know what you think you're playing at, young lady, but it needs to stop. Immediately. You are not a police officer. You are not a lawyer. You are also *not* in charge of what happens to Jake Hanson. What you are is a high school student who apparently thinks she's above the law, which is not going to serve you well in the long run, believe me. I would recommend you go home and take a long, hard think about your future. You got it? As I said, your mother is waiting. It's time for you to go."

My mom, Grace's mom, and Henry's mom are in the lobby sitting on ugly plastic folding chairs as they wait for us. My mom is deep in conversation with Mrs. Topham; Mrs. Hanson sits a few seats away from them. She's crying.

I can't imagine what it's like for her, being here, at the police station. All the horrible memories it must trigger.

And this time, *both* of her sons are here.

"Shit," a voice says behind me.

I turn and find Henry, a large, bright blackish-blue bruise blooming on his forehead.

"Are you okay?" I ask. I'm not sure if I'm talking about his head or everything.

"She's going to kill me," he says right as his mom spots him.

"Mom, I'm—" He hurries to her and sits, wrapping his arms around her small frame.

My mom sees me then.

She stands, brushing invisible lint off the front of her black yoga pants. "It's time to go home, Ally," she says in a clipped tone. My heart sinks. I'm in deep trouble.

"Is Grace coming?" Mrs. Topham asks, rising halfway from her chair.

The last time I saw Grace was when the cops separated us at the station. "I don't know," I say. "I can ask Henry?"

276

My mom shakes her head. "Absolutely not. We're going home."

"It'll only take a second—"

"Ally Copeland," my mom says. "Now."

We don't speak the whole way home.

My mom's fuming behind the wheel. I stare out the window, thinking. Wondering if what we did today is going to help.

What if Jake's put back behind bars because he left his house?

I let out a sigh. This is not going how I thought it would.

"What the *hell* were you thinking?" my mom says as she pulls into our driveway. She stops the car and turns to me, her expression a mix of fear and anger.

"Honestly, Ally. You put yourselves in an extremely dangerous situation, and for what? Police business should be left to the police. Do you understand?"

I let out a loud snort. "Because they did *such* a good job handling Ms. Appelbaum's case?" I ask.

"Ally, that is enough," my mom snaps. "I have been so patient with you. I know you want to help Jake; I know you think he's innocent—"

"He *is* innocent, Mom!"

Her lips tighten. "That might be, but no matter whether he's guilty or innocent, he's in deep trouble right now."

"He was trying to help us!" I yell, beyond frustrated.

"He broke the conditions of his release."

"That's ridiculous."

"Ridiculous or not, that's the law," she says. "And speaking of the law, Jake has a team of lawyers—*grown-ups*—working on his case. He does not need the three of you interfering. Do you understand?"

"He has an alibi! He was with Berkeley that night! He couldn't have done it!"

My mom sighs. "Ally, I'm not sure what you're trying to prove. Even if it's true"—she holds up a hand against my yelp of protest—"even *if* it's true, Mr. Berkeley will likely deny it. And even if he doesn't, even if he decides to come forward with that information after all this time because, I don't know, because he has nothing left to lose or has some moral awakening, it *still* doesn't mean anyone would believe him. He's been arrested for possession of drugs. He's not exactly the most reliable source of information."

I'm so, so close to losing it. So tempted to lash out at her, to hurt her like she's hurting me.

All I want is to get this awful feeling out of me, even if it means spraying it all over somebody else.

But I don't.

I turn my back on her and get out of the car.

As I storm into the house, I can't help thinking that if she's right . . . if she's right, then we might have done all of this for nothing.

We might be no closer to helping Jake than we were when we first started.

THEBRAWNERTIMES.COM

Teacher arrested on drug conspiracy charges

BY KATE CHAKRAVORTY

Yesterday, while responding to a house arrest violation, Brawner police discovered large quantities of cocaine, marijuana, and other illegal drugs in the back room of local record shop Favorite Record. Owner Joseph Fontaine, along with several other individuals, some of whom were minors, was arrested on charges of possession with intent to distribute. Also arrested was Mr. Fontaine's silent business partner and first cousin, Paul Berkeley.

The town of Brawner is reeling from the

allegations. Mr. Berkeley is an English teacher at Brawner High School. He's described by many as a popular member of the faculty. It now appears he acted as a supplier to several students who were dealing inside the school.

Police are still investigating, but at the moment it appears that Mr. Berkeley and Mr. Fontaine were the primary source of the majority of the drugs flowing through the school's halls.

This is a developing story.

Kate Chakravorty is a senior news reporter for the Brawner Times. *She can be reached via email at katec@brawnertimes.com.*

GRACE

OCTOBER 20

I'M HALFWAY THROUGH MY bowl of cereal when Lara storms into the kitchen.

"I cannot believe you would *do* this to me," she says, seething. My spoon clatters down into my bowl.

"Lara, let me explain," I say, but she's not listening.

"You think I want to be here right now, Grace? I need to go to *work*. I need to study for my law school exams. I have a lot going on—too much. But I refuse to do this over the phone. Why do I have to be the voice of reason for everyone? What happened to you being a good maid of honor? I've spent years of my life supporting you, talking to you about your issues and helping you through them. And you can't give me a few *weeks* of your time? Instead, you're off hanging out with Ally Copeland and Henry Hanson and getting into all sorts of trouble, trying to—Jesus Christ, I can't believe I'm about to even say this—prove Jake Hanson is innocent. He was *convicted* of *murder*, Grace. Or do you not remember testifying against him? You almost got yourself killed yesterday. I mean, how absurd can this get? It's absolutely ridiculous! Evan is freaking out—his parents were the ones who called us about it. You know they have family on the police force. How am I supposed to explain this to them?"

"Lara—"

"No." She holds up a hand. "I don't want to hear it right now. My wedding is this weekend. I am getting *married*. Do you understand how important that is? Do you understand it is one of the biggest days of my life? Because it doesn't seem like you do. And it definitely doesn't seem like you care."

"I care! But listen—"

"Honestly, Grace," she interrupts me. "No. I'm done listening. And with the way you've been acting, I'm starting to wonder whether I want you to stand with me at my wedding."

Tears spring into my eyes. I push my cereal away, appetite gone. "You don't mean that."

She drops her eyes. "I can't talk about this anymore. I have to go. You're supposed to come to dinner tonight with Evan and some of his extended family. I hope you can make it there without getting arrested."

"I'm sorry," I say, but she's already out of the room, headed for the front door.

Another person mad at me. This morning, I woke up to a text from Meghan. I guess she heard what happened at the record store. She wasn't as angry as Lara, but she said she feels left in the dark and she doesn't understand me anymore.

Why don't you trust me, Grace?

I drop my head into my hands. I thought I was helping, thought I was standing up for what's right for once in my life, but instead everything is falling apart.

Jake's back behind bars. My parents are upset and worried. Meghan's angry.

And my sister hates me.

I'm in my car in the school parking lot, unable to make myself go inside. I'm going to be late, but I don't care. I'm too tired to face everyone.

After Lara left, my phone started buzzing. I guess word about Matt and Bryce is out, because I've been getting nasty messages all morning, saying I should watch my back, wishing me dead. Macey Brown accused me of being a narc, like she thinks I pulled a long con on them all, inserted myself into their group two years ago just to bring her friends down.

If only I were that cunning. If only I'd known about Berkeley's drug ring back then, maybe none of this would have happened. Jake would have had an alibi right from the start.

A knock on my window interrupts my spiraling thoughts. Henry.

Can I come in? he mouths, pointing to the passenger seat.

I nod. Heat rushes through me, like it always does when he's around.

I unlock the doors and a moment later he's inside.

"Hey, are you okay?" he asks. "Everything that happened yesterday . . ."

I squint through the windshield, out into the gorgeous fall day. "Where's Ally?"

I'm trying to change the subject. I don't want to tell him what I'm thinking, that I need to stop all of this, that I can't do it anymore.

That I can't help Jake.

"Her mom dropped her off this morning," he says, suddenly very interested in the zipper on his bag. "I . . . I needed a little space, to be honest. My mom was very unhappy earlier. She basically told me I messed everything up for Jake. I mean, he's back in jail, Grace. Because of *me*."

His mouth scrunches the way it does when he's trying not to cry. My heart aches for him. I've been so busy moaning about my own life, I forgot to consider how much worse this is for him.

I reach out tentatively and touch his hand with my fingertips. He immediately turns his palm up and clasps my hand in his. We lock eyes.

My breath catches as I see what I'm feeling mirrored back at me.

"Grace, I . . . ," he starts, then pauses like he's trying to decide whether to finish his sentence. He runs his free hand through his hair, and it falls back down around his face, framing his square jaw, his chin.

He continues after a long moment. "I don't know what to do. I wanted to help Jake, but according to pretty much everyone, we've managed to do exactly the opposite. Kakova says it doesn't even matter if Berkeley tells the cops that he *was* with Jake that night, because he's lost all credibility. Since he's a drug dealer and all."

Before I can respond, my phone buzzes with another message. Henry glances down to where it sits on the armrest between us.

He reads the screen and anger flashes across his face. *"Traitor?* Are they serious right now? Who sent that? Are people harassing you? I'm going to—"

"It's okay," I interrupt. The last thing I need is for Henry to get into it with those assholes. "I can handle it. They're just pissed off because of Matt and Bryce."

"They do realize you didn't force those idiots to work for Berkeley, right?"

"Apparently not."

Henry sighs, leaning his head back against the headrest. He closes his eyes for a long moment.

I watch him, quiet. Everything is welling up inside me—the fact that Jake's in deep shit because of last night, Meghan's message, Lara's threat to banish me from her wedding, my parents' disappointment.

"I think we need to stop," Henry says finally, like he can read my thoughts. He takes a deep breath and hunches forward. Our fingers unclasp.

"Stop?" I don't want to assume I know what he means.

He nods. "The stuff we're doing . . . this investigation . . . we need to stop. We're not helping. But Ally's going to be so pissed."

"Don't worry about Ally," I say, even though that's easier said than done.

"Yeah. It's just . . . you know she's not great at giving up on things. Which is good in some ways—she stood beside me through all of this."

He doesn't say it, but I hear it anyway: *Unlike you.*

I wince. "I'm sorry."

"No, that's not what I meant. . . ." He sighs. "I need to tell you something. I already told Ally this, but I screwed up majorly back then too. Remember the DMs everyone thought Jake sent to Appelbaum from that burner account?"

"Yeah?"

"Well . . . they weren't. From him, that is. They were from me. I was pissed off about a bad grade she'd given me, so I made that account and . . . it was so stupid and petty. And then I let everyone think Jake had sent them. What sort of person am I if I can do something like that? I should have told someone, but I was scared and everything was happening so fast. You're not the only one who screwed up. And he's my *brother.*"

His mouth trembles. I reach out, my hand on his arm. Up to his bruised cheek.

He closes his eyes, leaning into me. Rests his head on my shoulder, my hand curling through his hair.

"I love you," I whisper, so quietly I'm not sure he hears.

We sit like that until the bell has rung its final warning.

ALLY

IT'S FINALLY LUNCHTIME. I shove my books into my bag, hurrying so I can go meet Henry and Grace.

School has been a madhouse today. The news of Berkeley's arrest broke early this morning and the reporters are back—even more than before, including ones from CNN and MSNBC. There are mobs of them in front of the school. It's a mess.

The administration called for an all-school assembly first thing, during which we were subjected to a very boring speech about the dangers of drugs. It, of course, skirted ever so carefully around the fact that one of our teachers is now in jail for running a drug ring on school grounds.

Everything was fairly calm until the end, when the cops showed up and hauled three more members of the lacrosse team out for questioning. People are saying that the police offered Matt and Bryce a deal to testify against Berkeley and

Joe Fontaine, and I guess part of the deal is ratting out the rest of their friends who were involved.

I push through the crowded hallway, keeping my head down to try to avoid attention. People have been coming up to me all day asking how we figured out Berkeley is a drug dealer. These are, of course, the same people who ignored me and harassed Henry for the past two years.

It's interesting how all of a sudden they seem to think we're friends.

Behind the school, Henry and Grace are already at our table, their heads bowed close together. It reminds me of the beginning of sophomore year, finding them at the lunch table sitting close like this, when I knew something was up but before they bothered to tell me they were dating.

"Hello," I say. At the sound of my voice, they jump apart, red-faced. I frown and take a seat next to Henry.

"Hey," Grace says. She's definitely nervous.

"What is going on?" I look between the two of them. "What were you just talking about?"

They have a silent conversation with their eyes. It's clear that whatever they were discussing has something to do with me.

I decide to ignore it. If they want to tell me what's going on, great. If not, even better.

"My mom was so pissy last night," I say. I take my lunch bag and the stuff from Appelbaum's house out of my backpack, placing it on the table in front of me. "She claims that even if Berkeley tells the cops he was with Jake the night of the murder, it's not going to help. Which is ridiculous, right? Clearly it *would* help, because then Jake would have an *alibi,* and that would mean he couldn't have murdered Appelbaum. Look, I brought all the stuff we took from her house so we can go through it again. See if we missed anything . . ."

Henry and Grace exchange another uneasy look.

"What?" I snap. So much for my plan to play it cool, but seriously? They're being flat-out rude at this point.

"Ally . . . ," Henry starts, fidgeting with the corner of a sandwich bag in a way that only makes me more pissed off. "We . . . I . . . Look. First of all, my mom heard from Jake's lawyer this morning. Last night, Nick told the cops that he and Berkeley were both with Jake during the time frame Appelbaum was killed—"

"That's great!" I interrupt.

Henry holds up a hand.

"Hang on. The thing is, is that there's no physical evidence to back up his claim. I have no idea if Berkeley told the cops the same thing, but even if he did, it sounds like it won't make a difference unless there's concrete proof. I guess the word of drug dealers doesn't go far with the police."

My heart sinks. "But . . ."

"Yeah. It sucks. My mom's pissed. I mean, Jake's back in jail. . . . We made a real mess out of everything."

"But we aren't done!" I protest. "If the cops aren't going to listen to Nick or Berkeley, we need to do *more.* What about the guy I overheard Appelbaum arguing with at her house that day?"

Henry and Grace exchange another look. This is just like the old days—they were always on the same side, the same page, the same team. And I was left out in the cold. Three is not always a good number in a friend group.

I keep talking. "Also, I didn't tell you what I found in these."

I tap the small stack of folders in front of me.

"After you left the other night, Henry, I looked through them and found a few pages of notes in Appelbaum's hand-writing. I don't think she and my dad were having an affair, not anymore. There was a phone number, which I figured out is for town hall, and some initials I haven't figured out yet. What's interesting is that Appelbaum and my dad *both* referenced someone with the initials JG—look at this."

I shove the piece of paper with JG in front of them. "Appelbaum made a note about calling town hall to '*make sure JG is legit.*' It sounds like whoever JG is might work there. And JG is probably important. I mean, from my dad's notes it sounds like the three of them—Appelbaum, my dad, and JG—met up the afternoon my dad died. What if . . . I don't know. What if JG knows why my dad wasn't at his desk that night?"

Henry is staring at me.

"Or," I continue hurriedly—there's only one thing that will get him to actually care about this, and it's not my dad—"what if JG has something to do with Appelbaum's death? We should go check it out—"

"*Ally.*" Henry cuts me off, his voice sharp. "You're not listening."

"Lara's so mad." Grace finally speaks. On the table, her

hands tremble and she balls them into fists. "She said she might not want me to be her maid of honor. She hates me."

"Yeah," Henry says. "Your mom can't be happy either, Al. We've made everything worse, which is the opposite of what we wanted. I don't think we should do this anymore. I think we should stop investigating."

I cannot believe what I'm hearing. "You just want to give up because of one minor setback?" My voice rises.

"It's not giving up," Grace says.

"Or minor," Henry mutters.

It's happening again. Them against me. Just like after my dad died. An awful fizzy feeling starts inside my nose. I stood by Henry for the past two years, and this is how he repays me?

"Oh, wow, so you talked about this *together*? Without me? How cute. Are you two dating again? Thanks for the heads-up."

"We're not—" Henry starts, but he cut his eyes to Grace.

"Whatever," I interrupt. "So, what? You want to leave it up to the court to decide Jake's fate? I remember how they treated him the first time around. Don't you care that there's a murderer walking around Brawner? Don't you want justice for Ms. Appelbaum? For your brother?"

Grace lets out a sigh, like she thinks I'm talking to her. I'm not. This is between me and Henry. "Of course we do. But yesterday was awful. Look at Henry, Ally. His cheek. His ribs are bruised. If Jake and I hadn't shown up, who knows what Berkeley might have done."

Now *she's* trying to take credit for rescuing Henry? How cute.

"I would have figured something out," I snap.

"Ally, I'm not saying you wouldn't have," she says. She needs to stop saying my name. "I'm just saying . . . it was bad. Henry could have gotten hurt—*really* hurt. And now Jake is in more trouble than ever. We need to cut our loses and admit we're not getting anywhere with all this. We have college to think about. Our futures."

She sounds just like that stupid cop back at the police station.

Henry nods in agreement. "Grace is right. We need to back off. And we're out of leads anyway."

My frustration bubbles over. I stand up, slamming my knee into the table hard.

"Dammit!" I yell. The pain makes me even angrier.

"Are you okay?" Grace says kindly, and my anger triples.

"I'm fine." I twist away from them, blinking hard. I will not cry. "I'm *fine*. I have to go."

Ignoring the pain shooting up my knee, I scoop my stuff back into my bag and stalk across the lawn to the building.

If Grace and Henry aren't going to help me figure this out, there's no reason to wait around. I'm going to town hall. I'm going to figure out who JG is and why Appelbaum and my dad were meeting with them. I've never cut school before, but there's a first time for everything.

I head to the front of the building, waiting for someone to stop me, but it's surprisingly easy to leave.

It's not until I'm outside that I remember I don't have a car.

Well, technically I *do*, but I've only driven it a handful of times. It mostly sits in the garage, a birthday present from my parents when I turned sixteen, two months before my dad died.

After his accident, I couldn't get behind the wheel without having a panic attack. Eventually, I stopped trying.

It hasn't mattered much. Usually I can hitch a ride with Henry or my mom, or someone from the newspaper if we work late. Today, though, there's no one to help me. I'm going to have to Uber and cross my fingers that my mom doesn't get pinged by the charge.

The reporters are still in front of the school, so I circle around the building to the side and cut across the soccer field, through a small thicket of trees, and emerge onto a two-lane road near the bus stop.

Now to get an Uber. I open the app, which I use maybe once every six months, only to find the nearest car is twenty minutes away. Thanks, suburban Virginia.

I sink down onto the bus stop bench to wait.

I cannot believe Henry and Grace are giving up so easily. Who cares if their parents are mad? My mom's pissed off too, and you don't see me quitting. And we're *not* making anything worse—yes, sure, it wasn't exactly our plan to have Jake end up back in jail, but it's temporary.

I don't care what they say. I can't stop. I refuse. There are too many dangling threads—Appelbaum and my dad's meetings, town hall, and *JG*.

I don't know if any of the threads are related to Jake, but I need to find out, especially since it involves my dad. I've spent so much time trying to help Henry's family, and he can't even spare a few hours for something that matters so much to me? Maybe he's not the person I always thought he was.

I squeeze my eyes shut, trying to concentrate, to block the awful thoughts out.

My dad used to work in DC before I was born, writing for a much bigger publication, but he and my mom moved here when they had me. He was always supportive of my dreams, my writing. It's why I was so disturbed when I thought he might have had an affair.

Could he and Appelbaum have been meeting about me? My work on the *Boar*?

My eyes snap open.

Wait. My dad was running that high school program, mentoring students when Appelbaum was a student at BHS. He always said she was talented, that he didn't understand why she stopped pursuing journalism full-time.

What if they were working on a story together?

My Uber finally arrives fifteen minutes later and the ride downtown goes by in silence. I'm in no mood for small talk.

The driver drops me off on the curb outside town hall, a three-story redbrick building.

I've never been inside, and now, standing on the street looking up at it, I imagine walking away, going back to school, forgetting about all of this. Refocusing on the newspaper, my classes . . .

But I know I can't do that. I'd never forgive myself. I need answers.

I head up the stairs and enter.

Inside, it's quiet and dimly lit. Across the lobby, an older woman sits behind a desk, chatting on a landline. I stand in front of her, and she smiles, holding up a finger to signal that she needs a minute.

"Rita? Let me call you right back," she says into the phone, then sets it back in its base.

"How can I help you?" she asks.

"Um, well, I'm looking for someone?" I say hesitantly.

"Who might that be, dear?"

I hesitate. If I tell her that I'm not sure, I'm afraid she'll kick me out.

"Actually, is there, like, a staff directory I can look at?"

She points to a nearby table with two clunky desktop computers sitting on it. They look like they've been there since before the turn of the century.

"You can take a look on one of those if you'd like. Under the Government tab. Staff Directory."

"Thanks." I head over and take a seat at one of the computers. On its screen is the City of Brawner website.

Of course. I should have thought to do this. I could have searched for JG without even coming here.

When I navigate the cursor to the Government tab at the top of the screen, a drop-down menu appears.

There it is. Staff Directory. Alphabetized by last name.

I click G, and a list of about twenty names pops up. My eyes land on it immediately.

Jamel Gallant.

He's the only JG in the directory. Next to his name, under department and title, it doesn't say anything. Which is strange. All the other names have something under those columns.

I head over to the woman behind the desk, who's back on the phone.

"Sorry . . . ," I say when I reach her.

"Hang on," she says to the person on the other end of the line. "Yes, dear?"

"So, I'm looking for Jamel Gallant? Can you tell me where I might find him?"

"Jamel Gallant?" A frown flashes across her face. "I think . . ." She types a few things into her laptop, her expression shifting as she reads the screen. "Yes, I was right. His office is in the basement. Room B33."

"The basement?"

She presses her lips together. "That's right."

"Okay . . . thank you." I turn to leave.

"Be careful, honey."

"What?" I spin back around.

The woman blinks at me. "What?"

"Did you—" She tilts her head, curious. Am I losing it? "Never mind."

The basement is . . . very basement-y. Low ceilings, limited light, a general sense of dread. Empty.

Not a place I'd want to work, personally.

Midway down the narrow hallway, I find room B33.

My hands are balled into sweaty fists by my sides.

I'm all alone down here. This might be my absolute worst idea ever.

What am I doing? Walking into a totally unknown situation, solo? This is exactly the scenario that any sane girl knows to avoid. Yet another stupid, impulsive decision by Ally Copeland in a long line of stupid, impulsive decisions.

I need to get out of here.

Except, before I can, the door in front of me swings open.

I tense, ready to run if need be.

In front of me is a guy in his midtwenties wearing a confused expression.

We stare at each other, frozen, for a long moment.

Then he says: "Ally?"

I'm so startled to hear my name, I scream.

ALLY

OCTOBER 20

"OH MY GOD. I'M sorry! I'm sorry!" the guy says, panicked. "Please stop. People are going to hear—I didn't mean to startle you. I'm Jamel. Jamel Gallant. I knew your dad?"

My heart stops. It's what I was expecting, but it still jars me, hearing it out loud.

"My dad," I whisper.

"Yeah. He and I were working together. Before his . . . I was very sorry to hear about his accident. How are you and your mom holding up? I thought about getting in touch, but I wasn't sure if it was smart."

"You knew Miriam Appelbaum too, didn't you?"

Jamel nods. "I did. Look, I want to talk, but I can't. . . ." His eyes dart behind me, to the elevator at the end of the hall. "This isn't a good place to have this conversation. You're going to have to trust me—it needs to be in private."

"Absolutely not."

"Please. I want to tell you everything, but I can't do it here. I swear, I'm legit. Will you meet me at the coffee shop on the corner of Main and Barber? Twenty minutes? You leave first. Find a table in the back if you can. Also, if anyone at reception asks if you found me when you're leaving, tell them you didn't."

"Doesn't anyone else work down here?" I can't help but ask. I have to assume the answer is no, since no one appeared when I screamed bloody murder.

He shakes his head. "Just me. Me and all the old filing cabinets. It's . . . I'll explain it all, I promise. Twenty minutes, okay?"

"Fine," I say reluctantly.

Jamel finds me at a table in the back corner of Ground Zero Coffee twenty minutes later, as promised. On the walk here I checked my phone and there was nothing from Ally or Henry, no apology for their behavior earlier. Whatever. I don't need them. I'm doing fine on my own, minus the whole almost-scared-to-death thing back at town hall.

Jamel slides into the seat across from me and starts right in. "How did you find me?" he says quietly. "When I opened the door, I assumed—I assumed you knew who I was. I'm sorry I freaked you out."

"How did you know my dad?" I stuff my hands under my legs so he can't see them shake.

He chews his lower lip, then answers. "I met him about two months before he—before his accident. Through Miriam.

She was working on a freelance piece and came down to town hall to look at some public records. I was still working in that department at the time—"

"Why aren't you now?" I ask. "Why are you in the basement?"

"I'll get to that, I promise. Like I said, I was working in Public Records"—he lowers his voice and I have to lean forward to hear him—"and I was pretty sure something shady was going on at town hall. Ballot measures were being pushed through that were really bad for citizens of Brawner but helped the big businesses in town—all the corporations that had set up shop here, plus commercial real estate developers. When Miriam showed up at the records department, it was like a godsend. A reporter on-site. Someone I could talk to about what I'd been seeing. She jumped on the story immediately—she was hungry. I still can't believe what happened to her. . . ."

He sighs, then starts talking again. "Anyway, after a month or two, she and I were sure someone on the city council was being bribed by an outside party. But we didn't know who. Miriam suggested bringing your dad into it—he had more tools at his disposal, given his job at the newspaper. The three of us figured out that the person was hiding what they were doing behind multiple shell companies with different PO box addresses."

"That's horrible," I say. It sounds like the sort of story my dad would pursue—he always said journalism was at its best when it was used to help expose abuses of power.

Jamel continues. "Yeah. It is. Unfortunately, before we

could figure out who exactly was involved, your dad had his accident."

A lump lodges in my throat, but I nod brusquely.

"After that, Miriam was more determined than ever. She was going to write the article alone, but give your dad credit. She had plans to pitch it to a publication. At least, that's what I thought was going to happen. But one day she just up and quit on me. Told me she wasn't interested in pursuing the story anymore. I told her she was being ridiculous—we were *so* close to figuring out who was involved—but she refused to listen."

"She gave up?" That doesn't sound like her. The Appelbaum I knew always told us to be determined in our pursuit of the truth.

"Yes," Jamel says. "She told me she decided we were wrong about everything, which was absurd and she knew it. . . . Anyway. I got frustrated—told her she'd regret it. We got into a huge argument. That's the last time I saw her."

My entire body tenses. "Wait. You had an argument with her? Was it at her house?"

He nods.

He's the man whose voice I heard. The one in Appelbaum's house that afternoon. "*You!* Oh my God. I heard you that day, at her house. I didn't recognize your voice back at town hall. You told her she'd regret it—" I pale.

She'd regret it.

He must see that I'm starting to freak out because he shakes his head. "No, no, no. I didn't kill her, if that's what you're thinking. We were working together! I was annoyed when she quit, sure, but I would never have hurt her for it. She was a friend! I was with my brother up in Scranton the weekend she died. You're welcome to call him and ask—"

He holds out his phone, so sincere I can't help but believe him. I let out a breath and sit back.

"Here, see?" He pulls his phone back when I don't take it and scrolls, then holds it out again. "Look, this is me and my brother in a bar in Scranton that Friday night. Also, Ally, they already caught the guy who did it—I know it's confusing since he was released from prison, but having your sentence vacated isn't the same as having it overturned."

"He didn't do it," I tell him firmly.

Jamel arches one eyebrow. "Oh yeah? And how do you know that?"

I fill him in on Berkeley and Jake's alibi that no one in a position of power seems willing to believe. As I talk, Jamel's eyes grow wide.

"What?" I finally ask.

"You're . . . you're just so much like your dad."

Him saying that is the best thing that's happened to me in days. "I am?" I ask.

"You are." He smiles.

I clear my throat. "Well, thanks. Did you ever figure out who was involved in what you all were looking into? The outside party? Or the city council member's name?"

"No," Jamel says, clearly disappointed. "After Miriam dropped out, things at work fell apart, too. I can't prove it, but I think someone figured out what we'd been doing. I suddenly got booted down to Archives, in the basement, which is a place *no one* wants to work—it's basically where they put you when they're punishing you. And then Miriam was murdered and . . . I got a little freaked out, to be honest. There was a moment there, after the news of her murder broke, where I wondered . . ." He winces and pushes a hand through his hair. "Maybe I shouldn't say this. . . ."

"What?" I press.

"I wondered if maybe . . . maybe they were connected. Your dad's death and Miriam's. Think of it this way," he says, "they were both working on the story with me, and within a few months, they both end up dead. I started spinning out. The three of us met that day—"

"The twelfth of October," I say. "The day of my dad's accident."

He nods. "That afternoon, a few hours before he died, your dad told us that he thought he might have found a break in the case."

Oh my God. If he thinks my dad figured out something big, and later that day, he wound up dead . . .

"And then he died," I say, hardly able to get the words out. "And then Appelbaum was killed. You're saying you . . . you wondered if my dad . . ." I swallow. "If my dad's accident wasn't actually an accident?"

Jamel nods and my world cracks in two.

He thinks my dad might have been murdered. Just like Ms. Appelbaum.

"Are you okay, Ally?" Jamel's looking at me with concern. "I don't really think that anymore; I was just spiraling after Miriam's death. . . . Shoot, I shouldn't have said anything."

I lick my lips, nod. Struggle to pull myself back together.

I can't fall apart now. Jamel might not think it anymore, but it makes sense. If there's any chance that it's true, I have to keep going. For my dad.

I take a deep breath and plunge forward. "What did he figure out? My dad?"

"He wouldn't say. He told the two of us that if it was true, it was huge and he wanted to be absolutely certain before he said anything."

I reach around for my bag, which is hanging on the back of my chair, and pull out my dad's planner. I flip through the pages until I get to his final day.

I turn the planner so Jamel can see it. "Do you know this address?"

"Twenty-two ninety-five Hydraulic Road?" he reads aloud, then looks up at me. "No."

"Could it have had something to do with what he figured out?" I ask.

"I don't know. It's a possibility." Jamel glances at his phone. "Ally, I'm so sorry to do this right after I dropped that bomb on you, but I have to get back to work soon. I don't want anyone wondering why you were asking about me. I'm probably being overly cautious, but I'd never forgive myself if something happened to you. Can you call a friend? Ask someone to meet you here? I have a few minutes to spare—"

"Um," I say, not wanting to admit that actually I don't have any friends I can call right now. I might not have any friends at all. My hands are shaking in my lap. I know he's trying to be a responsible adult and not leave me alone after blowing up my world, but I don't want him waiting around with me. I want him to leave. I need to go to the address on Hydraulic Road. Whatever's there could hold the key to my dad's death.

"Actually, see the girl over there?" I point to a girl about my age sitting alone by the front window. "We go to school together. I can go hang with her for a little."

The girl looks up and I wave at her. She hesitates, then waves back.

"Great," says Jamel, distracted by something on his phone. "Look, if you want to go check out that address you found, I'm happy to go with you—maybe this weekend? Let me give you my number, okay?" He recites his phone number and I plug it into my phone.

"Great. I'll talk to you soon, Ally," Jamel says. "Have fun with your friend." He hurries out of the coffee shop, smiling at the confused girl by the window as he passes by.

I watch as he exits the shop and then I open Google Maps. I type the address into the search bar and it pulls it up. Street View shows a building on the outskirts of town, in an area that looks sort of familiar—

My breath catches as I realize why. It's only a few streets from where my dad's accident happened.

This had to have been where he was going that night.

But why?

I have to find out.

GRACE

OCTOBER 20

BY THE TIME THE final bell rings, I'm exhausted. Ever since lunch, I've been struggling, weighed down by a heaviness in my gut. Today has been terrible.

I send a text to Ally as I head down the hall, ignoring the curious glances and angry glares of my classmates, only slowing for a moment to wave to Meghan and her girl-friend. She signals for me to stop and talk, and I pretend like I don't see. We still haven't spoken about everything, but I don't have the time or the emotional wherewithal to deal with that conversation right now.

All day, I've been haunted by Lara's words. I can't be-lieve she threatened to kick me out of her wedding party.

I need to talk to her. Clear the air.

I message her.

Are you home?

I know it's a long shot; between her internship and school, she's rarely at her place during the day. I hold my breath, waiting for a reply.

When none comes, I continue.

> I'm so sorry, Lara. For everything.
> I'm done with all that stupid stuff.
> Can we please talk? In person?

At last, three dots appear.

I'll be home shortly, she writes. *You can come over.*

I get to her condo building first. She and Evan moved in early last year, about a month before they got engaged. Lara's never said it outright, but from what I can surmise, they got a sweet deal on rent because Evan's family owns the building.

I pace the parking lot as I wait, and her car turns in after a few minutes.

I head over to greet her as she climbs out. She's wearing a white blouse and pencil skirt and has a briefcase in one hand. She looks grown up. Professional. I smooth the front of my wrinkled hoodie.

"Can you grab that, please?" She gestures to the back seat. She's not being rude, not outright at least, but there's no warmth in her words.

I open the car door and find an overflowing file box sitting on the floor. I point to it. "This?"

"Yeah, it's from the firm. Case stuff I'm working on."

"What's in the briefcase then?"

She frowns. "Schoolwork, obviously."

I grab the box and follow her into the building.

When we get inside her apartment, I set the box down by the front door. Lara is across the room, already pulling her laptop out of her briefcase. She sets it on the desk in the far corner of the room and opens it.

"Isn't dinner with Evan's family in a few hours?" I ask.

"Yes. But I have some stuff I need to do before then," she says.

"Oh, right . . ." I was hoping she'd be the one to bring up our argument, but it's becoming clear that it's up to me. "Um, so. I wanted to come over here and say—"

"Hang on," she interrupts. "Can I go change before we get into everything? This skirt is pinching me in all the wrong places." She tugs at her waistband and makes a face.

Even though the thought of gearing myself up to talk about all of this again makes me more tired, I nod.

She disappears in the direction of the bedroom and I grab my phone from my bag, then head into the kitchen to get some water. There are a bunch of new messages from Henry in the thread with Ally, asking her where she is, if she needs a ride home today, if she's okay. She hasn't responded.

I can't say I'm surprised by her silence; she made her feelings about everything extremely clear at lunch. But I'm glad Henry's trying.

I grab a glass from the cabinet and head to the water

dispenser on the refrigerator to fill it. As I do, I idly scan the wedding invitations, greeting cards, pictures decorating the doors. My eyes land on a small rectangular card from Anny's Florist, the flower shop on Main Street downtown.

It reads *July 2024: Parting is such sweet sorrow, that I shall say good night till it be morrow.*

It's unsigned.

I read it a second time. I've seen that quote before, recently.

But where?

I think hard, struggling to place it, then it clicks. A few days ago, the three of us in Appelbaum's house, going through her office . . . the card Henry found in her keepsake box that Ally mocked. It had this exact quote on it. Shakespeare.

I pull the card off the fridge, snap a picture of it, then stick it back up, trying to make sure to put it in precisely the same spot as before.

I text the thread, *Does this look familiar?* and attach the picture.

Henry responds immediately.

> **That's the card we found at Appelbaum's, right? I thought Ally still had it**

I stare at his response then type back.

> It's not the same card

> **I don't get it. what is it then? That's the same quote, same company**

**Wait. I see it now. The one in your pic is
dated July 2024? The other one was from
August 2022. I'm confused. Where did
you find that?**

I have no idea how to respond.

After several beats of silence, another message arrives:

Grace? Where are you?

Lara's

You got the note from Lara's?

I hesitate. The note might not mean anything. It might be a total coincidence. Although, if it is, it's the biggest coincidence of all time.

I'm trying to figure out how to respond when I'm interrupted.

"What's up?" Lara comes into the kitchen and I spin around, dropping my phone to my side, heart thumping.

"Hey, hi," I say.

I must sound strange, because she frowns and asks, "You okay?" She's changed into more casual clothing.

"Yep!" I say, plastering on a smile. This is all a big misunderstanding; it must be. There's no way what I'm thinking is true. Right?

There's no way.

I pull the card off the fridge. "This is really random, but who, who is this, um . . . who . . ."

This card can't be from Evan. Someone else must have

sent it, someone who also knew Ms. Appelbaum and who had a very logical reason to send both her and Lara flowers from the exact same florist, with the exact same Shakespeare quote on the card.

In the back of my mind, I understand that I'm attempting some serious mental gymnastics.

Lara arches an eyebrow. "You're acting really weird again. Are you trying to ask me who the card is from?"

She comes over and takes the card from my hand, then reads it out loud. *"Parting is such sweet sorrow, that I shall say good night till it be morrow."* She smiles. "Evan loves that quote. It's his go-to whenever he sends me flowers. It's even in his vows."

"Evan?" I squeak, needing even more confirmation. Needing to make sure there's no possibility I misheard.

Lara nods.

Evan sent it.

Which means Evan must have sent the card we found at Appelbaum's.

But Evan and Lara were dating in August 2022. Why would he have sent Appelbaum a note with a romantic quote on it? That's not something you send to a friend.

Plus, he told me he barely knew Ms. Appelbaum.

I reach out for the counter to keep myself upright.

"Hey, for real, are you okay?" Lara is staring at me, concern creasing her face. "You're really pale. Do you want to sit?"

I nod and she takes my elbow and leads me to a chair.

I sit, trying to steady my breath, trying to understand what this means.

When Ally and I talked to Appelbaum's friends, they told

us they heard a man's voice in the background one morning when they called her. She had already broken up with Berkeley by then, so they thought it was some one-night stand.

But what if it wasn't?

What if Evan and Appelbaum were having an affair?

I squeeze my eyes shut, tilting forward.

"Gracie?" Lara sounds worried. "What is going on?"

"I . . ." I force myself to look at her.

She takes the seat next to me. "What's up?"

"Are you sure that Evan . . ." I trail off. I don't know what to say. How do you tell your sister that you think her fiancé might have been cheating on her with a murdered woman?

"The note—" I say, but the buzz of Lara's phone interrupts.

She picks it up and reads the screen. "Sorry. I hate to cut this short, but I have to take this. And it might be a long one. Are you okay?"

I don't know what to say. Am I? No.

"I . . . ," I start, but Lara's staring at her phone. "Yeah. I'm fine."

"Great. We'll talk more later, okay? At the restaurant?"

Before I can reply, the phone is to her ear.

"Hello? Leo? Yeah, it's Lara. Yes, now is fine—"

She disappears out of the room.

I hurry out of her apartment, texting Henry and Ally as I go.

We need to talk ASAP

Are you okay? What's going on?

Have you heard from Ally?

**No. Not since lunch. I went to the
newspaper office after final period to see
if she was there but they hadn't seen her**

I need her to stop being so stubborn.

I pound out a message: *Ally . . . if you're seeing this, you
need to get over what happened earlier and respond to me ASAP*

ALLY!!

Henry sidebars me.

Are you okay??

I don't know. My fingers are shaking. *I need to talk to you.
In person. Where are you?*

At home

Can I come over?

Several seconds go by before he writes back.

Can we meet at yours?

I push through the building doors to the parking lot and
hurry toward my car. Halfway between here and home is

the park where I met Henry and Ally the morning we talked to Mrs. Flowers.

Grant Park. Ten minutes.

Can you tell me what's going on?

just come okay? It'll be easier
to explain in person

All right. See you there

Henry's already waiting when I arrive.

"Grace, hey." He hurries over to me as I step out of my car. "Where did you find that card?"

"My sister's." The words physically pain me as they come out of my mouth. I know what Henry's going to think. The same thing I can't stop thinking.

His face changes as he processes this new information. "You found it at *Lara's*?"

"Yeah," I tell him. "Like you said, it's the exact same note, just with a different date: 2022 on Appelbaum's, 2024 on Lara's."

"Where did you find it?"

"On her fridge."

He stares at me. "Evan sent it to her?"

I nod.

"And to Appelbaum." He immediately arrives at the same conclusion I did.

"That's . . . yeah. I assume that was from him, too. Otherwise, it's way too big of a coincidence, right?"

"I think so."

"But Lara was already dating Evan in August 2022," I say, still struggling to accept the truth. "Plus, he told me he barely knew Ms. Appelbaum in high school. What was he doing sending her a love note?"

Henry's brows pinch together. "He said that? Are you sure?"

"Yeah, why?"

"Appelbaum's yearbook was also in the box I took from her place. Ally and I found Appelbaum in some group pictures of different clubs. And in one of them, she was sitting right next to Evan. They definitely knew each other."

My heart drops. "Just because they were sitting next to each other doesn't mean . . ."

"She was practically sitting in his lap."

"Maybe it was just a one-off? A random thing that they ended up next to each other? Wait, I have an idea." I unlock my phone and find the contact for Mrs. Flowers. "I'm going to ask her sister."

Hi Mrs. Flowers, I text. *This is Grace Topham from Brawner. If it's okay, I have to talk to you about something to do with Miriam. it's personal but it's important so I hope you'll be open to it*

She responds quickly. *Hi Grace, good to hear from you. What is it?*

I hold my breath as I type. *I have a source who tells me she was close with Evan Miller in high school. Is that true?*

The three dots appear and disappear on the screen, then my phone starts to ring.

It's her.

I take a deep breath and answer.

"Hi, Grace. I thought it might be better to speak about this rather than text," Appelbaum's sister says. "Where did you hear that?"

It's so much easier to lie over text. "Um"—I'm thinking fast—"we talked to her friends from high school, Rachael Wu and Lucy Phillips. They told me before they realized Lara is my sister."

She sighs. "Right. Okay. I'm sorry about that. I didn't want to bring it up while you were here because . . . well, it's awkward, isn't it? I was trying to be respectful of your sister's engagement and not bring up more of the past unnecessarily."

"What do you mean, respectful of her engagement?" I hold my breath, waiting for her answer.

She sighs. "Well, my sister and Evan dated on and off for several years, all throughout high school."

"They dated for *years*?" This is even worse than I expected.

"Who dated?" Henry hisses over my shoulder, and I wave him off.

"Yes."

"Were they . . . serious?"

"It was a long time ago. But . . . yes. It was serious for a while, at least on Miriam's end."

She's giving me a lot, but it's not quite enough. Which means I'm going to have to lie again.

"But that wasn't the end of it, was it?" I press, crossing my fingers that I'm on the right track and she doesn't just hang up on me.

There's a silence and then Mrs. Flowers says in a tight voice, "What do you mean?"

"They were seeing each other more recently, too." I say it like it's a fact, not a question.

"Rachael and Lucy always did have big mouths," she mutters, clearly annoyed. "I'm not sure I understand why exactly my sister's dating life is of any concern to your article."

Heart pounding, I say, "I'm just double-checking. We want to make sure we have all our facts straight before we go to print. We need to know if she and Evan were seeing each other again."

When she speaks again, her voice is softer. "Ah. I understand. This isn't about your article at all, is it? It's about your sister."

I cringe. I'm so transparent. I'm scrambling, trying to figure out a way to remedy this, when she speaks.

Her voice is kinder. "You could have just told me that. I understand sisterly bonds better than most, you know. I always tried to protect Miriam, but . . ." Her voice breaks. "Clearly, I didn't do a very good job of it. I admire you, looking out for Lara even though she's older."

The sadness in her voice is tangible. I can't imagine the pain she's gone through. I think about the last few weeks, the ways I've hurt Lara, and vow yet again to be better to her.

"I'll be honest with you, Grace," Mrs. Flowers continues, "because I think you and your sister deserve to know. After she graduated from college, Miriam moved to Philly to write for a newspaper. A year later, she quit and moved back to Brawner. I never asked her outright, but I suspect it was because Evan was here. He'd moved back to work for his dad after graduating from USC. They reconnected. But as far as Miriam would tell me, they only dated for a few months."

"So when did they break up for good?" I hold my breath as I wait for her answer. Lara graduated from college in May 2022, and she and Evan started dating that summer. From what Mrs. Flowers is saying, it sounds like Evan and Appelbaum were already over by then.

Then why was the card dated August 2022? When Evan and Lara were already together and serious?

"They broke up in mid-2021."

"And they didn't get back together after that?"

"Please understand I'm not certain about this, but . . . I have to admit I've questioned whether my sister and Evan were seeing each other again in the months before she died. A few things made me wonder. . . . I really hope there wasn't any overlap, because he was with your sister then, but I can't say for sure. My sister was a good person, but for some reason Evan was always her weak spot. Please don't hold it against her."

It takes me a minute to process what she's saying. "Did you ever tell the cops about this?"

"The cops?" She sounds surprised. "No. Why would I have? It was clear right from the start who killed Miriam. Plus, Evan might not be my favorite person, but I've known him for years. He cared about Miriam. He never would have . . . Anyway, I understand you're probably going to tell Lara about this—I would do the same—but I need you to do me a favor and end it there. Please don't spread it around. I'm only telling you because, well . . . it's been this weight on me since Miriam died, and I do think Lara deserves to know the truth. That said, whatever happened between my sister and Evan is over and done and she . . ." Her voice cracks. "Miriam is gone. No good will come from revisiting this part of her past. It would only hurt her memory, and your sister."

I must respond, because she's saying goodbye and we're hanging up on each other, and I'm shaking. My whole body, shaking. Mrs. Flowers might be convinced that Jake did it, but I am not. In fact, I'm positive someone else is out there who had motive to kill Ms. Appelbaum.

Evan lied. Evan knew Appelbaum. Evan *dated* Appelbaum. That note we found in her closet was from Evan. Evan sent her flowers a few months before she was killed.

Evan was cheating on my sister with my murdered English teacher.

Talk about motive.

I sink down to my knees with Henry standing over me.

"Grace, are you okay? Grace? Grace? *Grace?*"

I barely hear him over my spinning thoughts.

HENRY

OCTOBER 20

I HELP GRACE INTO the passenger seat of my car. She's breathing heavily, face pale.

"Put your head between your knees," I instruct, like I have any idea what I'm talking about. I'm trying my best; I think she might be having a panic attack.

She drops her head into her hands. Her shoulders rise and fall quickly, then slow as we sit together in the quiet. I rub her back. All I want, more than anything, is to take away her pain.

"What happened?" I finally ask.

She looks up at me. Her eyes are glassy and red, but dry.

"You were right. Evan and Appelbaum knew each other. They *dated.*"

"In high school?"

She nods. "Yes. But also more recently. Her sister said . . . she said she thinks it's possible Appelbaum moved back to Brawner because of Evan. Because he was here. Which would mean she left the job she'd landed at that newspaper in Philadelphia to come back, just to be closer to him. It would mean she gave up her *dream* for him. And apparently Mrs. Flowers thinks it's possible they were seeing each other even after he started dating Lara."

Grace presses a hand to her cheek, taking several deep breaths. "I need to slow down. Figure this all out. Mrs. Flowers said she never told the cops about Evan and Appelbaum."

"We don't have to do this right now," I tell her. I reach out and tuck a stray hair behind her ear.

She juts out her jaw, stubborn. "Yes, we do. Evan was cheating on my sister with Appelbaum. That's *motive,* Henry."

"Do you think Appelbaum knew? Do you think *Lara* knows?"

"No way. If Lara knew, she'd dump his ass in a heartbeat. She wouldn't put up with that."

"Do you think Ms. Appelbaum knew about Lara?"

She winces. "I don't know. I hope not, but . . . his relationship with Lara was public; he wasn't hiding *her.* It would have been hard for Appelbaum not to have known. What if she got sick of being the other woman and confronted him about it and . . ."

"But you know Evan," I say, like that means anything at all. As if all of this hasn't proved to me how little we actually know about other people.

Grace's mouth wobbles. "What are we supposed to do?"

She picks her phone up off the dashboard.

"And where is Ally?"

I take my own phone out of my pocket. No new notifications.

Then one arrives.

Where are you????? We need to talk!!! From Grace.

We both watch our screens, but there's no reply.

"I'm going to kill her," Grace says. "I need to tell Lara. She's supposed to marry Evan this weekend! But I need the card that he sent to Appelbaum. She'll never believe me without it—she's already so pissed at me. But Ally has it."

I start the car.

"What are you doing?" Grace asks. "My car is here."

"We'll get it later. We're going to Ally's."

Five minutes later, we pull into Ally's driveway. Mrs. Copeland isn't home, but I sent her a message on the way here and told her I had forgotten something inside.

Here, I text Mrs. Copeland. As promised, the garage begins to open.

"I don't think Ally's home," Grace says. "And she had all the stuff with her at school today, right? The card?"

"She did." I unbuckle my seat belt. "But her mom set up a FindMyKids account after Ally's dad died. I think I can pull it up on her computer."

"So we can see where Ally is! Great idea!" Grace says, impressed. I swell with pride.

We enter the kitchen through the garage. Mrs. Copeland's laptop sits on a small desk in an alcove by the refrigerator.

"There used to be a Post-it with her password in here. . . ." I rummage through the desk drawers and finally find it stuck to the front of a Chinese take-out menu.

I open the computer and type *AllyLamb444* into the password prompt. The computer unlocks. "Okay, here's FindMyKids and . . ." I open the app and click on Ally's name. A map appears, and on it a red dot, moving at a steady clip toward the outskirts of town.

"Where's she going?" Grace asks, leaning over my shoulder to see the screen. "She's almost out of town."

As we watch, the dot slows and then stops. I click it and an address pops up. "Twenty-two ninety-five Hydraulic Road . . . where is that?"

Grace peers over my shoulder at the screen, her hair tickling the side of my face. "That name is really familiar."

"What? Hydraulic?"

"Yeah. I feel like . . . hold on." I twist to look at her. She has her eyes closed, thinking. "I know I've heard it before. Not too long ago . . ."

I wait quietly, watching her.

Her breath catches and her eyes pop open wide.

"What?"

"I figured it out. Evan and Lara were over a couple of months ago and Evan took a work call outside. I went to the bathroom off our family room, and you know how you can hear stuff in there? People talking out back?"

"Yeah?"

"Well, I could hear his end of the conversation. I mean, it wasn't really anything, or at least I didn't think it was at the time, but I remember hearing him say that road name, mostly because it's so weird."

"Are you serious?"

"Unfortunately, yes. But what is Ally doing there?"

"I don't know, but we need to go." I stand, slam Ms. Copeland's laptop shut, and grab my keys from the desk. "Now."

ALLY

OCTOBER 20

BY THE TIME I get to Hydraulic Road, it's almost four-thirty. Several more texts from Grace and Henry have arrived, but I'm not in the mood to respond. I don't feel like listening to a lecture on all the reasons I shouldn't be doing what I'm doing or about why anything that involves my dead father isn't important.

I clutch my book bag tighter, trying to get my brain to shut up as the Uber pulls up along the curb.

I thank the driver and exit the car. Twenty-two ninety-five is a small, generic office building. Why did my dad think this place was important?

A sound in the distance makes me jump, goose bumps popping up along my arms.

Maybe I shouldn't have come here alone.

Maybe I *should* text Henry and Grace.

Except when I look at my phone, it's dead.

My heart sinks. Not only can I not text them, I have absolutely no idea how I'm going to get home.

I take a few huge, deep breaths to calm myself. I don't need Grace and Henry. I'm fine. This is fine. Getting home is an issue for future me.

Right now, I have to figure out what connects this place to my dad.

GRACE

OCTOBER 20

HENRY'S DRIVING US TOWARD Hydraulic Road like a bat out of hell.

The closer we get, the more panicked I am. The drive has given me too much time to think. "Evan was connected to Appelbaum in all sorts of ways we didn't know. All sorts of ways he lied about. That night, the night she died, the person I saw who I thought was Jake. I thought it was Jake because they were Jake's size and wearing his jacket. How tall is Jake?"

Henry scrunches his nose, thinking. "He's as tall as me. Six feet?"

"So is Evan! Six feet. They're the same height. It could have been him. It makes sense. He wouldn't have walked up to her house from the front, not with my house right across the street. Someone could have spotted him. Instead he would have cut through the woods and entered through the back. What if he grabbed the jacket from Jake's car on his way to Appelbaum's? A disguise, in case anyone saw him. Because he already planned to kill her."

I press a hand over my eyes. My breath is coming out in little short gasps. "I can't. This is horrible. My sister is supposed to *marry* him." My voice cracks on the final word.

Henry takes a hand off the wheel and grabs mine, holding it tight. "Grace, breathe."

I nod. I squeeze my eyes shut and take a few deep breaths while I try to pull up a mental image of the person I saw that night walking into Appelbaum's backyard.

It's impossible. Time and stress have blurred the memory beyond repair.

Was it Evan?

Did I play right into his hands? Evan and Lara come over for Sunday dinner every week—at least, they used to, before wedding planning got so intense. I always told Lara about everything at those dinners. Henry, Ally, Jake. Evan would have known Jake's car was always unlocked. He would have known about that stupid jean jacket. He would have known about Appelbaum catching Jake with drugs, their argument, his expulsion.

"You know how we talked about the possibility that Jake was framed?" I say.

"Yeah?"

"Evan knew everything. All the reasons why Jake was the perfect person to pin it on. Because of me. I talked about all of it in front of him." I drop my head into my hands. "This is my fault, Jake's life being ruined."

"Grace—" Henry starts, but I talk over him.

"Now Ally is off, all alone, trying to solve the mess I created. . . ."

"We'll be at the address in three minutes," Henry says. "Has she texted back?"

I look at my phone. "No. I'll call her again."

This time it goes straight to voicemail, which is when I make up my mind.

"I'm calling the cops," I say.

ALLY

OCTOBER 20

I SLOWLY HEAD UP the concrete steps to the front door of the building and examine the directory of businesses inside, none of which I've heard of. I have no idea what any of them are and I can't Google them because my phone's dead.

The only way I'm going to figure anything out is if I go inside.

I push through the door and step into a dingy lobby. Two hallways run off it in either direction, and in the center of the room is a small staircase leading to the second floor. A few feet from where I'm standing I spot a large, wilted houseplant sitting next to an unmanned desk. The air smells faintly of burned coffee.

I'm trying to decide where to go first when there's a burst of noise from the stairwell. A man's voice, loud and angry.

My heart stops. *Hide.*

I dart behind the desk and squat down, trying to quiet my breathing.

"No, Jordan, I told you that's— No, that's not going to work for me. It's *your* district, you should be able to— What? Your *mom*? Jordan, you have got to be kidding me. We talked about this."

The voice is growing louder. He's coming down the stairs. I wrap my arms around my legs, tight, trying to make myself as tiny as possible.

"What the hell am I paying you for, then? You're on the city council, for fuck's sake! You're supposed to be . . . *What?* My dad has nothing to do with it. You know he's never taken me seriously, just like your mom's never taken you— Exactly! Ever since I moved back here, it's been like that. *Evan, you made another mistake. Evan, if you weren't my kid, I'd have fired you a long time ago. Evan—*"

It takes my brain a minute to register what I'm hearing.

Evan. Evan Miller.

Grace's sister's fiancé.

Oh my God.

The Millers own a huge commercial real estate company in town.

Evan's dad runs it. They're the ones behind the redevelopment of Brawner's downtown—the subject of some of the articles Appelbaum had in her folders, written by my dad.

"*Yes.* Jesus Christ. I know we *said* that, but the money is good, isn't it? You tell me it isn't. Better than what they pay you for government work. Better than the pathetic salary my own *father* pays me—"

Jamel said that my dad and Appelbaum had suspected a city council member was being bribed by someone to push ballot measures through. That the outside person must have set up a bunch of shell companies to hide behind.

My dad must have traced those fake companies here . . . to this address.

"—I'm tired of it."

The voice is close now. Too close. I hold my breath.

"Look, I'm done arguing with you about this. Get it done or I'll . . . I'll tell Aunt Betsy about where you really were that summer in college, when you told her you were volunteering for Habitat for Humanity. Does *Ibiza* ring any bells?"

Evan's so close, I can hear the person on the other end of the line squawking in displeasure. So close, I can hear him breathing. So close—

Feet come around the side of the desk.

Stop right in front of me.

"I need a pen! Why can't I find a—"

He falls silent.

"What the fuck—"

I look up and lock eyes with Evan Miller.

His phone drops away from his ear.

ALLY

OCTOBER 20

I'M TRAPPED.

"I know you," Evan says, poking me with the toe of one shoe. "You live near the Tophams."

I point to my chest. "Ally. Ally Copeland."

Something flashes across his face when he hears my name. "Right."

An alert dings on his phone, and he seems to remember he was midcall when he found me. He presses it back against his ear.

"Jordan? Yeah, sorry. I have to go deal with something." He hangs up.

"You were one of the kids with Grace last night, down at the police station, weren't you?" he says. "Lara was really upset about her sister's involvement, so I talked to my cousins who are on the force. They said you were playing detective, trying to help Jake Hanson. I mean, what sort of dumbass *is* Grace, getting involved in that? And now you're here."

He pulls his lower lip between his teeth, sucking. The noise makes my skin crawl.

"So, what are you doing here, Ally Copeland?" he says.

I pull myself out from under the desk. If I'm going to have any chance of making it out of here, I can't be tucked into that cramped space.

Evan moves back, allowing me to climb to my feet.

"I—I was—" I take a step toward the front door. "I made a mistake. Coming here. I actually have to go. . . ."

He steps around me, blocking my path to the exit. "Hang on. I think we need to sort this out first," he says. "I mean, just when I thought things couldn't get worse, you show up. What's up with you kids? Where's your mom? Shouldn't there be some adult in your lives to stop you from running around, making stupid decisions? When *I* was in high school, my parents were strict. They didn't let me roam the streets, doing whatever I wanted."

"Actually, yeah," I say. "My mom's expecting me home soon. . . ."

He presses a hand to his eyes. "God, I'm tired. All I want is to be taken seriously. It's all I've *ever* wanted, dammit. Everyone in this town thinks I'm some . . . some *nepo* baby who only has a job because of his daddy, who can only pay his bills because of his daddy. . . . And you know the worst of it? *He* doesn't even take me seriously! Even now that I'm with Lara, he *still* doesn't take me seriously. Sure, I work for—*with* him, but he doesn't treat me like everyone else. He saves all the good stuff for other people. So *sue* me if

I wanted something for myself for once! I mean, do you think I *wanted* to move back to Brawner after college? Do you think I wanted to work in *real* estate? No! I wanted to be a screenwriter! Work in the movies! Live in LA! But that's not the Miller way, at least not according to my parents. So here I am, in this crappy office building, trying to make my own money so I can get out from under my dad's thumb for the first time in my life. But no one will leave me alone! First your dad—"

"My dad?" I squeak.

Evan ignores me. "—then Miriam, of all people, now a fricking *teenager*? What I'm doing isn't even that illegal! And on top of it all, I'm supposed to get married this weekend! Three hundred people are coming. Three hundred! Isn't that ridiculous? My parents and Lara insisted—you know, sometimes I think they wish she was their child instead of me—I won't even know some of the guests' names and—"

I can't take his ranting anymore. "What did you do to my dad?" I scream at him. "What did you do to Ms. Appelbaum?"

Evan's lips turn down. "I wish you hadn't come here, Ally. Everything that happened was a mistake, don't you see? It wasn't my fault. Your dad—he wouldn't stop poking his nose into things, and then he managed to track this place down. . . . I tried to reason with him, you know. I offered him money! But instead he told me where to shove it and took off in his car. I had to follow him! If he had just *listened* to me. . . . I don't know what happened. It was raining that night. He wouldn't stop, even when I caught up to him, and the next thing I knew . . ."

He moves toward me, but I duck under his arm and take off at a run.

I need to get to the exit.

I'm halfway there, halfway to freedom, when something heavy and hard slams into my back. I go flying face down on the laminate floor.

Pain explodes in my chest and stars dance in my vision.

The world goes black.

GRACE

OCTOBER 20

NIGHT IS FALLING AS Henry screeches to a stop in front of the building.

We're the only car on the street.

"Are you sure the cops are coming?" Henry asks me. "I don't hear sirens."

It's been five minutes since I called. They should be on their way.

"Yes," I say, more confidently than I feel. The person I spoke to when I dialed 911 sounded confused. *You don't know if your friend is in trouble, miss? Is this actually an emergency?* "They'll be here," I add.

Henry and I climb out of the car and meet on the sidewalk.

"Do you think she's in there?" he asks.

"There's only one way to find out," I say, and start jogging toward the brick office building.

I stop at the front door and peer in through the glass. The scene inside makes my heart seize.

Evan stands over Ally, who's splayed out on the ground, unmoving.

"*Ally!*" I scream, pushing the door open.

Evan whirls around. "Grace? What are you—"

"What did you do to her?" Henry cries as he runs to Ally. He squats next to her to check for a pulse.

Evan holds up his hands in front of him like a shield. "I didn't do anything! I swear! It's not my fault."

"Is she okay?" I ask Henry. His face is pale and he looks worried.

"She's breathing," he says.

I turn back to Evan. "You dated Ms. Appelbaum! You told me you didn't know her, but the two of you dated! You sent her flowers with a corny love note the August before she died . . . while you were dating Lara! Did you cheat on my sister with Ms. Appelbaum?"

Evan shakes his head.

"I don't believe you," I say, moving toward him, hands balled into fists by my sides.

"Here's what I think happened," I tell him. "You and Appelbaum were together in high school. When she moved back to Brawner, you started dating again, but broke up a few months later. You met Lara. Started dating *her*. And then, while you were still dating my sister, you started seeing Ms. Appelbaum again. I bet that Ms. Appelbaum didn't know about Lara at first, but when she found out, she confronted you and threatened to tell Lara. But you couldn't have that, so you smashed her head open and stuffed her body into that freezer.

"I was thinking about things on the drive here and I remembered something—the weekend she died, you were in Baltimore for a conference. Except you didn't leave until Saturday morning. You had to go—your dad would have noticed if you didn't—which explains why her body ended up in the freezer. You didn't have time to move her somewhere else before you had to leave. *You* killed Ms. Appelbaum."

"For God's sake," Evan says. "Like I already told your friend over there, none of this is my fault, all right? You have it all wrong. Miriam knew *all* about Lara. You all seem to think she was a saint for some reason, but she absolutely was not. All those nights I had to sit there at Sunday dinner, listening to you babble on about you amazing, awesome journalism teacher. God! It made me sick."

My stomach sinks. I was so sure Ms. Appelbaum didn't know. That she would never have done something like that.

"Miriam knew you were dating Lara when you started seeing her again?" I ask in a small voice.

"Yes! Are you even listening? I just said she did. When it all started again, I hadn't seen Miriam in *months*. I wanted nothing to do with her. We were done. Forever. Plus, no matter what you might think, I love your sister. But then Miriam showed up on my doorstep one night, babbling all about some article she was working on with Michael Copeland. Town hall, corruption, blah, blah, blah. . . . She wouldn't shut up about it!"

What is he talking about? Ally's dad? Town hall? Corruption?

I'm confused, but I'm not about to let him see that.

He continues, "She told me that I owed her for the years of crap—her word, not mine—I'd put her through. Said that if it hadn't been for me, she never would have moved back to Brawner. That it was somehow *my* fault she'd left her job in Philly. I never *asked* her to do that; she moved back here without consulting me! Anyway, she kept insisting that I had to use my family connections to figure out if there was something shady going on down at town hall. So I did what I had to do. I, you know, made her think I was interested in her again. I needed to keep her close, keep an eye on her. Steer her investigation in the right direction. It took literally forever, but I finally managed to get her to drop it. The night she died, I was at her house to break *up* with her!"

My heart's beating in my throat. I'm almost there. He's so close to confessing, I can taste it.

"And what, she got upset?" I ask.

He snorts. "Yeah, you could say that. Miriam's always had a temper. She freaked the fuck out. She knew I was the one bribing the council member, that once she published her article I was going to be in deep shit. One thing led to another. . . . She shoved me; I shoved her back—it was just instinct! I don't normally put my hands on women—I don't! Ask your sister. I'm a good guy. But Miriam fell. Smashed her head against the hearth. . . . It was a whole big mess. Blood everywhere. I freaked out. I didn't know what to do! I didn't mean to hurt her, and there she is, on the ground, babbling about how she's going to turn me in for assault, all this crazy stuff. My dad would have killed me! I didn't know what to do, so I—I, um, I went to the bathroom. To take a break."

"A *break*?"

In the distance, sirens cut through the night, but I barely register them through my horror.

Ally lets out a moan from the floor.

Evan ignores her. "God, will you stop looking at me like that? We're going to be family, and I'd expect *you*, of all people, to understand. You hate conflict! And she was *yelling* at me. Telling me that my life was over . . . What would you have done?"

"I would have called an ambulance!"

"Please," he scoffs. "It was an impossible situation, really. I know what you would have done. You turned your boyfriend's brother in to the cops for murder! You did what you needed to do, just like I did. Anyway, I got back to the room and saw the, um—"

He cuts himself off, shaking his head. "It doesn't matter. By then she was gone. It was too late . . . the decision had been made for me. I'm not saying I was *glad*, but—"

He's interrupted by the long, mournful call of a siren from out front of the building. Flashing blues and reds dance across the lobby's ceiling. Car doors slam and shouts fill the air.

His mouth drops open in horror. "Grace, what did you do? Did you call the police? I thought we were *family*. Lara's going to be so disappointed in you."

My stomach tightens at his words, but I shake my head.

"No," I say. "This time Lara is going to be disappointed in *you*."

OCTOBER 21

THEBRAWNERTIMES.COM

BREAKING NEWS:

New arrest made in murder of Miriam Appelbaum
BY KATE CHAKRAVORTY

News broke late last night that the Brawner Police Department has made a new arrest in the murder of Miriam Appelbaum, one that may prove Jake Hanson's innocence and give him back his freedom. We're still waiting on more information, but what we know so far is this: Yesterday afternoon, police responded to a distress call at 2295 Hydraulic Road, an industrial building on the far edge of town.

When they arrived, they found three minors and one adult in the middle of an altercation. One of the minors was taken to a local hospital for treatment of their injuries. The adult, Evan Miller of Miller Real Estate, was taken into custody for questioning and subsequently arrested on multiple charges, including voluntary manslaughter, perjury, obstruction of justice, and falsifying evidence.

Mr. Miller is awaiting formal arraignment and could face up to thirty years in federal prison if found guilty.

Charges against Miller were filed after he confessed to violently assaulting Miriam Appelbaum on the day she died, an assault that resulted in her fatal wound. Miller subsequently framed Jake Hanson for the murder.

Mr. Miller also appears to have been the brains behind an illegal real estate scheme, which he had set up with his cousin, Jordan Miller, who works in the real estate division of Brawner's Department of Tax Administration and is an alderman.

According to our sources, the Millers were working together, one inside city government and one outside, scamming desperate homeowners by offering to "help" them pay back delinquent real estate taxes, while embedding into their legal agreements the clause that if/when the owner defaulted on their taxes again, Evan Miller would gain control of the property.

More to come as the situation develops.

Kate Chakravorty is a senior news reporter for the Brawner Times. She can be reached via email at katec@brawnertimes.com.

HENRY

OCTOBER 24

ALL THE LIGHTS IN our house are on.

There are people here—people other than the three of us and our team of lawyers—for the first time in two years.

And we're celebrating. A new thing. Jake is back home, for good this time.

Monday night when the cops showed up at that building, I told them what happened. How Evan assaulted Ally, who was still half-unconscious on the floor and bleeding from her head. How he murdered Miriam Appelbaum . . . and how I recorded his entire confession to Grace on my phone.

After the cops took Evan down to the station, he confessed immediately. Almost like telling someone was a relief, after all these years of living with what he had done.

What was most interesting to me about Evan's confession was how he framed my brother. Grace was right: he knew that Jake had been getting into more and more trouble, he knew about Jake and Ms. Appelbaum's confrontation and that if he pointed the cops in Jake's direction, they'd fall for it. Jake was the perfect patsy.

After killing Appelbaum that night, Evan snuck out of her house and grabbed Jake's notebook and jacket from his car.

A risky move, sure, but one I guess he thought was necessary, given the circumstances.

His plan was to leave both the notebook and the jacket at Appelbaum's, where the cops would easily find them; it was just a stroke of luck on his end that Grace saw him as she was cutting through Ally's backyard on her way home from my house and recognized the jacket. Luck that she went to the cops and told them she had seen my brother. Luck that Mr. Berkeley denied being with Jake that night to avoid the cops asking more questions.

"How are you doing?" my mom asks Jake for the four hundredth time this afternoon as she fills a pitcher with lemonade. He was released after Evan's arrest.

She's been hovering around him nonstop, like she expects him to disappear, even though the news broke yesterday that the DA plans to drop all charges against him. I get it, though; after two years of nonstop bad, it's hard to believe it's finally over.

"I'm fine, Mom." Jake rolls his eyes, but gives her a little smile.

That's another new thing—Jake smiling.

"And how are you doing?" my mom asks Grace, who's sitting at the counter, staring into her cup. I walk over to her and wrap my arms around her from behind, trying to remind her that everything's okay.

She twists to smile at me, then looks at Jake, my mom, Ally.

"I'm okay," she says. She clears her throat. "Sorry. I actually have to use the bathroom."

My mom waits until Grace has left the room and asks, "Is she okay?"

"I think she's dealing with a lot of stuff at home," Ally says. She sits on a stool next to the one Grace just abandoned, a bandage still affixed to the side of her head. Her injuries ended up being minor; I think she likes the look of it more than anything.

"And at school," she continues. "A lot of the people she's gotten to be friends with over the past couple of years are being dicks about her involvement in bringing down half the lacrosse team. Stupid, if you ask me. They were the ones dealing drugs, not Grace."

Jake winces, and my mom puts a hand on his arm.

"Plus, Lara isn't taking the Evan stuff well—I mean, who would?—and has temporarily moved back home. . . . I think Grace feels like it's her fault that Lara's wedding was called off and her fiancé is facing prison time. Even though that's clearly ridiculous. Evan's a cheater and a murderer. Lara's *lucky* she didn't marry him before we figured it all out. If anything, she should be thanking us."

"I'm sure she will eventually," my mom says, patting Ally's hand. "But in the meantime, know that *we* thank you. Even though the way you went about it was a little . . . well, the word that comes to mind is *terrifying*, you didn't give up. You saved Jake."

Jake clears his throat. "Yeah . . . I owe you one."

My throat tightens at his words. I can't believe I played a part in his imprisonment, but at least now I've made up for it.

My brother is home.

GRACE

OCTOBER 24

MY STOMACH IS IN knots as I wash my hands in the bathroom sink.

I should be feeling good right now.

Evan's behind bars. Jake is free. Henry and Ally have forgiven me. Henry and I are . . . something. Not quite back together, but on our way.

Everything is how it should be.

Except my sister. She's barely left her bedroom since Evan's arrest, except to go to class and one trip to the jail to see him.

I'm not sad that Evan is behind bars, but I wish Lara hadn't gotten caught in the cross fire.

I turn off the water and take a deep breath, forcing a smile at my reflection in the mirror. This is supposed to be a celebration.

I grab the hand towel from the countertop and dry off my hands, mentally preparing to go back out there. Yes, it sucks that Lara's upset right now, but who can blame her? The man she was supposed to marry not only cheated on her, he literally *murdered* the other woman. And my sister's been living with him for the past two years.

Sleeping in the same bed.

Ugh.

It's going to take time, but she'll be okay in the end. Better, in fact.

I toss the towel back onto the counter, and it hits the framed photos next to the sink, toppling one of them onto its side.

I pick it up. It's a picture of Henry and Jake from a few years ago. Going off Henry's haircut, it was taken shortly before Ms. Appelbaum was murdered.

The boys are standing together, wearing suits and tense smiles.

I start to set the photo back down, but something in it catches my eye.

Jake.

In the photo, he's shorter than Henry. Thinner. I forget that he was so small back then, how much he grew while he was in prison. A late bloomer.

Now he and Henry are the same height.

My heart skips a beat.

The person I saw that night . . . I thought it was Jake because of the jacket, but also because of their height. When I asked Henry how tall Jake is and he said six feet—the same as him, the same as Evan—he must have been thinking about how tall Jake is *now*. Not back then.

But if Jake was so much shorter than Evan . . . would I have confused the two of them?

Moreover, could Evan have even fit into Jake's jacket? Or would it have been too small?

I drop the picture back on the counter. I'm being ridiculous. The stress of everything has been wearing on me.

Evan confessed. He told the cops he stole that jacket. The notebook. That he pushed Appelbaum.

He told them he did it. There's no way he would have admitted that if he hadn't.

I shake my doubts out of my head.

But hours later, as I lie in bed, it's still there. A little nagging voice in the back of my mind, asking me what I really saw that night.

I need to talk to someone, but I don't want to bother Henry with this; I don't want him to think I'm second-guessing what we did. Proving Evan's guilt. Jake's innocence. Because I'm not. I don't think Jake did it, but—

I text Ally.

I have a question

What

I hesitate. Am I sure I want to do this? Knowing Ally, she's going to eviscerate me.

But I have to. I can't go through another day with these questions tumbling around in my head.

Jake was smaller

What??

Back then. Two years ago. Jake was a lot
smaller than he is now. I didn't remember
that until today

And? So?

So . . . would his jacket even have fit Evan?

I hold my breath as I wait for her reply.

Finally, it comes. Exactly how I expected it. Exactly how
I wanted, if I'm being honest.

Oh my god. Evan CONFESSED, Grace.
What more do you want? You're being
ridiculous. What are you trying to say—
that JAKE did it after all??

It's a good question—what *am* I trying to say?

No! God. I don't know. I'm just thinking

I'm sure Evan could have shoved his
way into Jake's clothing if he was
desperate. Which he clearly was. Plus, HE
CONFESSED!!!!

Right. Yeah. You're right

JFC Grace give it a rest

I don't respond or comment on the irony of *Ally*, of all people, telling me to give it a rest. Instead, I grab my diary and flip back through the pages to the weekend of the murder.

When I read these entries a few weeks ago, I didn't really pay attention to what I'd written that night; I was more interested in the aftermath, in what I told the cops I saw.

December 15

Tonight I stayed at Henry's house after Ally left. We made out for hours.

But we still haven't told Ally. I think we're both too nervous?? It'll make it official. What will it mean for our friendship? And then . . . what if something happens? What if we break up? I don't want to lose Henry as my friend, but I really, really like him. I don't know what to do.

Then when I got home tonight, my mom was all pissy because Lara was supposed to bring Evan over for dinner, but they canceled at the last minute.

Sometimes I wonder if she's—

I drop my diary into my lap.

Lara and Evan were supposed to come over for dinner that night, but they canceled?

They *both* canceled?

There's no way. I'm being crazy. Ally's right. I need to let this go.

But I don't.

I send her a text, then leap off my bed and head into the hallway.

I pause at the closed door. I'm home alone. My parents are out at dinner, Lara's at class.

What do I think I'm going to find in there, anyway?

I push the door to Lara's room open. Inside, a few open suitcases are scattered across the floor, their contents bulging out of their insides.

Lara's usually so tidy.

I'm being ridiculous. So what if her room's messy? She's grieving. And here I am . . . what? Sneaking into her room because I suspect something? Something horrible?

And if she did do something—which she did *not*—do I really think she brought evidence here?

Evan *confessed*.

I step into her room.

Head over to the first suitcase I see.

A cough interrupts me before I can even reach inside it.

I whirl around.

"What are you doing?"

My sister stands in the doorway, staring at me.

"N-nothing," I stammer.

"Are you going through my stuff?"

I scramble to my feet and move away from the suitcase. "No."

She raises an eyebrow. "So what exactly are you doing, then?"

"I was . . . nothing. I just wanted to make sure you're okay. With everything."

"I'm fine." She walks over and kicks the lid of the suitcase shut.

I back toward the doorway, away from her. "I'm really sorry again, about everything . . . about Evan. I know this has been hard—"

"Yeah. Thanks."

I was planning to walk away, but her dismissive tone irks me. It's the same voice she's used with me for years, her *Gracie, you're so pretty but not so bright* voice. The one that always makes me feel small.

It's the same one I've heard for years from teachers who had me after Lara, when they realized that just because I was her sister didn't mean I was going to make straight As.

I'm so, so tired of people underestimating me.

"You and Evan were supposed to come to dinner. The night Ms. Appelbaum died."

"What?" Lara's forehead crinkles.

I step forward. "The night Ms. Appelbaum was murdered. I wrote in my diary that Mom was upset because you guys were supposed to come over for dinner but canceled at the last minute. *Both* of you canceled. Why?"

Her eyes narrow. "Excuse me? What are you saying? Are you saying that I was with *Evan* that night? Are you serious? I've had the worst week of my life and this is what I come home to? My little sister accusing me of . . . What are you accusing me of, anyway? Care to share?"

I pull myself up straighter, even though I'm shaking.

"If Evan was at Ms. Appelbaum's that night, where were you?"

She makes a face, and I know.

"It was you."

She rolls her eyes. "What was me?"

"You—*you* told me that I should go to the cops and tell them I saw Jake." The realization washes over me. Lara, assuring me I'd seen Jake. That I needed to do what was right. And I did, because she said it was the right thing to do.

"Every time I started to question it back then, there you were in my ear, telling me to trust myself. Trust my eyes. Except it wasn't my eyes I was listening to, was it? It was your voice."

Lara takes a step toward me. "Gracie, you're being crazy right now. This has been a stressful week for everyone, but even so, I honestly can't believe this. I'm your *sister.*"

I block her words out. "I realized something earlier. Jake was much smaller back then. Now he's Evan's size, but two years ago? Two years ago, he was short. Your height. The person I saw that night was wearing Jake's jean jacket . . . but I don't think Evan would have even *fit* into that jacket. I figured Evan knew about Jake's fight with Appelbaum, and about all the trouble he'd been getting into, and how he always left his stuff in his car because I'd talked about it in front of him. But you knew about all of that, too. What did you do?"

She's staring at me like I've lost it, but I don't care. I knew there was something missing—something that didn't quite fit.

And now I know what it is.

"Did you know about Evan and Ms. Appelbaum?" I ask her.

Her mouth twists.

I'm not stopping now. I don't care that she's looking at me like she hates me. "Did you, Lara? You must have known they dated in high school. Did you know Appelbaum moved back here because of him? That they dated when she moved back, before you started seeing him? That he was *cheating* on you with her? That he—"

"It wasn't like that!" she explodes, taking another step toward me. I force myself to hold my ground.

"Did you know?" My voice breaks. "Did you?"

"He wasn't cheating on me because he still loved her. He was cheating—he was *seeing* her because she was writing a stupid article that would have been really bad for him. He was trying to get her to drop it. Why couldn't she have just *dropped* it?"

"He was cheating on you," I say softly. My heart breaks.

"No! That isn't what happened!" Her mouth trembles. "You don't understand, Gracie. Things are always so black-and-white for you. Getting older . . . it means compromising. Evan was doing what he needed to do—"

"He was defrauding people, Lara! Bribing city officials! What he was doing was totally illegal, not to mention immoral and horrible. As a future lawyer, you of all people should see that. Did you know what he was doing?"

"No! Not until . . . not until that night. He called me freaking out because Miriam had fallen—"

"He pushed her!"

"—and her head was bleeding. He didn't know what do. She was threatening him! But of course, he couldn't handle it on his own. He expected me to go over there and clean up his mess for him, just like he always has, just like you always have."

"I do not!" *Do I?*

"The thing is that, unlike Evan, I plan ahead," Lara continues, ignoring me. "I brought some gloves and a black baseball hat from my apartment. I knew I'd need to cut through Miriam's backyard to get to her house so I wouldn't be seen from the street. But I also knew that you and Ally and Henry were always walking through Ally's backyard, so I grabbed Jake's jacket out of his car. In case I was spotted, you know? While I was getting it, I saw his notebook and did what I needed to do. Jake was always in so much trouble—selling drugs, *doing* drugs—his future was wrecked already. Evan has—had—a bright future. It was a fair trade."

I have stumbled into an actual living nightmare. I'm struggling to breathe, to stay upright. But I manage. "It was you, wasn't it? Wearing Jake's jacket. *You.* God, how convenient for you, that it was *me,* of all people, who saw you. You could manage me, just like you always have. You *told* me to go to the cops—"

"And what, you can't think for yourself, Gracie? All I did was steer you in one direction. I didn't force you to do anything!"

I glare at her. "Appelbaum was dead when you got there, right, Lara? That's why you didn't call 911? Why you didn't try to help her?"

A flash of anger cuts across her face. "She was *sleeping* with my boyfriend! She'd always been up in Evan's face. Like she thought she had some special hold over him because they dated in high school? She needed to get a life.

Move on. It was pathetic. When I got there, she was unconscious, but Evan told me she'd been babbling about how she was going to turn him in to the cops for what he'd done. There was blood *everywhere*, Grace. Everywhere. She wasn't going to make it anyway, even if we had called 911—"

"What did you *do*?" My sister. The person I always counted on when I was little to be there for me, to help me, to give me sage advice. Did I ever see her clearly, until now?

"Evan was freaking out, so he went to the bathroom. I knew he'd never make a decision—it's one of his issues in business too. He's incapable of being decisive and it drives me *crazy*; it's always, *Whatever you want, babe.* What I want is to not always have to be in *charge* all the time. So I made the decision for us."

"What does that mean?" My heart stutters in my chest waiting for her reply.

She blinks, like she just remembered where she is, who she's talking to. Her face crashes shut.

"Nothing."

"She was alive when Evan went to the bathroom and then . . ."

She glares at me.

"And then what, Lara?" I close the gap between us, until I can feel my sister's hot breath on my face. "And then what? *What did you do?*"

"I did what had to be done! I took care of the problem. I grabbed a pillow from Miriam's couch and I held it over her face until her chest stopped moving and I stuffed the bloody pillow into her garbage. Then when Evan got back, he assumed—" She cuts herself off, her breathing ragged.

"He assumed his push had killed her," I finish. "How did the coroner not figure that out?"

She laughs. "The *Brawner* coroner? Please. That guy is a drunk. Everyone at the law firm says so. I knew he'd think the cause of death was the head injury and wouldn't bother to look any closer. Anyway, it basically was. Evan didn't need to know what I had done. It was fine because it was over and we could move on, together. He had to leave early the next morning for a stupid business trip to Baltimore, and we didn't have time to clean the whole place *and* figure out what to do with the body, so we put it in the freezer and then I sent him home. He was no help anyway—he'd fallen totally apart at that point. I did the best I could cleaning up the mess, our fingerprints. Wiping down the place took forever. When I left, I took the trash bag with the pillow in it. I got rid of it. I thought we'd have time to move her body after Evan got back. Who knew her sister would show up the next morning and start asking questions—"

"You killed her," I whisper.

Her lips tighten, disappear, and then—just as quickly—her face relaxes. "I handled it! But it doesn't matter. Evan confessed. He owed me. It's fine, Gracie. It's over; this can stay between us, okay?"

"No—"

Her nostrils flare. "It doesn't matter. I know you're not recording me because I have your phone. I took it from your bedroom before I came in here, just to be sure, because I heard someone rummaging around, and thought maybe . . . maybe, even though I never thought it would happen, Gracie *actually* figured it out—so all of this is just between us. If you tell anyone, I'll say you're lying, and who do you think people will believe? *You?* Or me?"

I stare at my sister. The person I used to admire. The person who I thought I wanted to emulate. The person who used me, manipulated me, who *killed* Ms. Appelbaum.

I'm going to throw up.

"It's over, okay?" Lara says, putting a hand on my arm. "It's done."

I shake her hand off. "I think they'll believe me."

"What?" she says in disbelief. "What are you saying? That you're going to turn me in? Are you serious, Grace? I'm your sister. Not to mention, you don't have it in you to do something like that."

That tone of voice again. Patronizing. Like I'm some dumb child. If I have learned anything in the past few weeks, it's that I'm stronger than I thought I was. "You're wrong," I tell her. "And they will believe me, because it makes perfect sense, Lara. You don't have an alibi for that night, do you? And you have motive—a *huge* motive, in fact. Plus, I bet Evan will be quite interested to hear what you just told me. Once he does, I highly doubt he'll take the fall for you."

She stares at me like she can't quite believe what's happening, and then her eyes narrow and her mouth twists. And I see her. The person who murdered our next-door neighbor. There in front of me.

"Lara—" I start, but a voice from the hallway interrupts me.

"Hello? Grace?"

Ally appears in the bedroom doorway.

ALLY

OCTOBER 24

THE EXPRESSION ON LARA'S face makes my blood run cold. Grace was right.

"Ally!" Grace says. She tries to take a step in my direction, but Lara blocks her. "You got my text?"

I nod. "You okay?" I ask.

"Yeah—" she starts.

"Shut the fuck up, Grace," Lara snarls.

"Do you have your phone?" Grace calls to me.

I hold it up.

"Good," she says. "You have to get out of here. Go. Call the cops—"

Lara lunges forward, pressing a hand over Grace's mouth. Grace thrashes and manages to yell, "Ally! Go!"

I back out of the doorway slowly, like my body hasn't quite caught up with what's happening.

"Go!" Grace screams, jarring me into motion. I run down the hallway, around a sharp corner, to the top of the stairs. I make it down two steps, then I'm flying, feet not connecting with the ground, tumbling down . . . down . . . down. . . .

I land at the bottom with a thud, breath gone. Tears in my eyes, bones jerked out of place.

Everything hurts.

I have to get out of here.

Footsteps on the stairs.

I'm still clutching my phone in my hand. I need to make the call.

More footsteps. Closer.

"Ally, just give it to me," Lara says, her voice calm and detached, like she's talking about the weather. "Give me your phone and we can all forget this ever happened. Okay?"

I shove my phone under my stomach. Try to relax, make myself heavy on top of it. Hard to move. I should have done more than come over here. I should have told Henry I was coming here. I should have called the cops. I should have—

"I don't want to hurt you, Ally, but I need that phone. Okay? You and Grace are overreacting. What happened to Miriam was an accident."

"Liar!" Grace's voice from the top of the stairs. "You suffocated her! You could have called an ambulance."

"She was already dying, Grace!"

I sigh with relief as Lara's feet move away.

"You're not a doctor. She might have made it. You didn't even give her the chance!"

I twist my head, trying to gauge exactly where Lara is. I spot her on the stairs, a few feet away. She's looking up at Grace.

I might be able to . . .

"She was sleeping with my boyfriend! Making a fool of me. Like I said, I had to decide, like I always do. It could have happened to anyone. I would have done the same thing for you."

"You should have called for help!"

I wriggle my hand under my body and slowly pull the phone free. A stab of pain runs down my arm and I suppress a whimper. If Lara sees what I'm doing, she's going to take the phone, and then who knows what she'll do to me and Grace?

Once the phone is in my eyeline, I dial.

"Nine-one-one. What's your emergency?"

"Please . . . please come," I whisper, then shove the phone back under my body, hoping against hope the operator heard me. That they'll trace the call and send a car.

Lara's footsteps retreat farther. I start pulling myself toward the door, an inch at a time, my body screaming in protest every time I move.

"Why are you doing this?" Lara says to Grace. "You're my sister. You're supposed to have my back. You're supposed to—"

"You've been manipulating me for *years*!" Grace interrupts her, loud and angry. "You used me to put Jake in prison!"

In the distance, a siren wails, and hope stirs in my chest. The nearest police station is only a couple of miles away. They could be on their way.

Lara and Grace keep arguing as I inch toward the door slowly. So slowly. Too slowly.

Another siren, this time so close. Sounds like it's on our street.

"What was that?" Lara asks sharply.

"What was what?" Grace says.

There's a pause and then, "*Ally!*" Lara stomps toward me.

I freeze. Do I try to get up? Try to run out of the house? But she's stronger than me and she didn't just fall down an entire flight of stairs.

Lara's on top of me now, clawing at my arms, my torso, trying to roll me over as I thrash against her. But my body is in a massive amount of pain and her nails are digging deep into my skin.

"Lara, leave her alone!" Grace screams from the top of the stairs.

"Ally, please stop fighting. Just give me that phone."

"No!" I curl into a ball, tucking my head into my chest, hugging it to my body.

"If . . . you . . . would . . . just . . ." She's scratching at my arms, trying to unwrap them.

"Get off her!" Grace's voice is closer now.

"Ow!" Lara screams, releasing me. "That's my hair, you bitch!"

"I said get off her!"

Lara stumbles and falls directly onto me.

I try to focus through the pain. The sirens cut off. I think they're outside.

"I thought you were amazing," Grace cries, her voice choked with tears. "I thought you could do anything, but—"

"You never saw me!" The words rip out of Lara. "No one ever sees me. Everyone wants me to help them, to give them advice, to be their shoulder to cry on, but who do *I* have? No one! Everyone thinks, *Oh, Lara, she can take care of herself.* Mom used to make me babysit you all the time when you were little, instead of allowing me to have a life. Just because I was mature, responsible. No one has ever stopped to consider what I want!"

There's a shout from outside the front door.

"Police! Open up!"

"Don't," I hear Lara whisper to Grace. "Please, Gracie. Don't tell them. Help me. We can deal with Ally together, and then you and I—we're the only ones who know. It'll be our secret, our bond. We're *sisters.*"

There's a moment's pause; the sound of Grace crying.

And then:

"In here!" Grace screams. "We're in here."

HENRY

___

OCTOBER 30

IT'S DRIZZLING AS I cross through my yard into Ally's. The news vans are back, parked on her street and mine, outside of the high school, and—from what I've seen on TV—outside Miller Real Estate, too.

I hurry up her back porch and knock on the sliding glass door that leads into the kitchen.

After a moment, Mrs. Copeland answers. "Hey, Henry. How was school?"

"Good," I say as I follow her into the house.

It's not a lie—school has been much more manageable since Jake was officially exonerated and half the lacrosse team was expelled for working for Berkeley. He's behind bars, and Nick Marion is, too, although from what I hear, Nick's lawyers hope to be able to get him a lighter sentence in exchange for information and his testimony against Berkeley and Joe Fontaine.

I've heard a few mean comments about Grace and her family in the halls, but it's nothing like what I dealt with, thankfully. Meghan and her girlfriend, Carmen, have made sure of that.

The one thing that gets me is the fact that no one has apologized to me. I guess it's asking too much to expect it, but it bugs me, how most people are pretending like we've always been cool.

People like Macey Brown have been coming up to me, asking questions about how Grace, Ally, and I figured out who really killed Ms. Appelbaum while also managing to bust up Berkeley's drug ring.

At least once a day, someone yells, *"What's up, Sherlock?"* at me.

One of our classmates started a fan page for the three of us on Instagram.

It's weird.

And with Ally and Grace both temporarily out of school, I've had to deal with it all on my own.

"I saw your brother today," Ally's mom says. She grabs a glass of water off the counter and takes a sip from it.

"At the winery?"

She nods. "He came in to apply for that barback job I told your mom about. My boss really likes him. He has a soft spot for kids who've been through hard stuff. . . . I think he's going to offer Jake the position."

Jake, rejoining the world. My mom is going to be thrilled.

"That's great," I say, but there's a part of me that wonders if he's ready. He's been better since we proved his innocence, but . . . he's still anxious as hell. His first therapy session is next week, and I'm hoping that helps.

"Hey!" Ally hobbles into the kitchen on her crutches. "I taped up another box," she says to her mom. She's been resting at home since being released from the hospital last weekend, and the two of them have started packing up her dad's things.

"Thanks, honey. I'll handle the next couple. You kids have fun." Her mom smiles at me and then heads out of the room.

"Taylor's coming over later," Ally says as she takes a block of cheese out of the fridge. She slices a piece off the side and sticks it in her mouth.

"To help out with research for the article?"

"Yeah."

After the news of Lara's arrest broke and the media descended, Ally decided she wanted to be the one to tell the world what happened. Taylor's helping out with some of the details, fact-checking, stuff like that. Ally asked her in part because she felt guilty about how she'd disappeared and left Taylor with most of the work for the *Boar,* and in part (I think) as a bribe so Taylor wouldn't hold an emergency election and kick Ally out of the editor in chief position.

It was fine by me, and Grace . . . well, Grace has been mostly unreachable. I know she's home; at night, the lights come on inside her house, but she hasn't responded to any of our texts.

"All right. I just wanted to say hi before . . ." I hesitate.

"You're going to Grace's, aren't you?" Ally asks.

It's the one thing I haven't done yet—gone to her house.

"Do you remember after Jake was arrested? How you came over a few days later and forced me to see you?"

Ally nods.

"It was the thing that helped me the most during that time—knowing I had a friend."

"Well, I'm pretty sure her parents are at their lawyer's office right now, so she should be there alone. . . ." She pauses, and I cringe, waiting for her to say something snarky or rude about me ditching her for Grace.

She shifts on her crutches. "You know . . . I've had a lot of time to think recently, because"—she waves one of the crutches in the air—"and . . . I want to apologize."

I blink in surprise.

"I mean," she says with a sigh, "don't get me wrong, after my dad died, you guys were absolutely not great. I felt abandoned."

"Yeah. I know . . . I'm sorry again. We—"

She holds up a hand to stop me. "Hang on, I wasn't finished. Looking back now, though, I sort of see why you didn't tell me about you and Grace. I didn't exactly make it easy for you guys, did I? Even before my dad . . . I was sort of a jerk about you two hanging out without me. I just felt . . . I was worried you wouldn't need me anymore."

"Yeah, but even so, Grace and I should have done a better job."

"Well, yeah. But we all should have done a better job. So here I am, trying to do that now, okay?" She rolls her eyes. "You know I'm bad at this stuff. Basically, I'm trying to say that I'm done being annoyed by it, okay? I get that it's okay for you guys to have a relationship that doesn't necessarily include me—I mean, don't go off ditching me all the time, but if you start dating, I'll deal with it. Better than I did before."

It's the most Ally-like apology ever, but I wouldn't expect anything less from her.

"Thank you," I say.

"So are you? Like, getting together again?"

I wince. "I don't know. I can only speak for myself, and . . . I would be into that, yeah. I still really like her, Ally."

She pulls a face. "Gross. But I'm happy for you. And I'm pretty sure she feels the same way, dummy."

"I hope so." I glance at the clock on the microwave. "I'm going to go, okay?"

"Do you want me to come?" she says, and then immediately backtracks. "Actually, no. You go. You guys deserve to have some time together, alone."

My eyebrows jump. "Really?"

She nods firmly.

I give her a big hug. "I'll let you know how she's doing, okay?"

"You better," she says. "Also, Henry?"

"Yeah?"

"Tell her thank you. For, you know, saving my life."

I have to go the long way around to avoid the reporters in front of Grace's house, arriving in her backyard a few minutes after I leave Ally's.

The house is dark, but I knock on the back door once, twice.

Finally, a light goes on upstairs.

Grace's room.

"Grace!" I call softly. I text her, *It's me.*

The light switches back off and my stomach drops.

She hates me. How could I think she'd possibly feel otherwise? Exchanging my brother for her sister—it can't feel like a fair trade.

It's not.

Nothing about this is fair.

I knock again.

My phone's still silent. The house still dark.

My heart splinters. She's not coming. It's over.

I'm about to walk away when a light comes on in the living room and I spot Grace.

She stops in the middle of the room and stares at me through the glass door. Her hair is long and loose around her shoulders and she's wearing joggers and an oversized hoodie and she's the most beautiful person I've ever seen.

I pull a piece of paper out of my back pocket and hold it up against the door.

Grace reads it once, twice, and then her face collapses and tears start streaming down her cheeks.

She walks toward me, then stops on the other side of the glass.

There's a click as she unlocks the door.

"I love you, too," she says.

ACKNOWLEDGMENTS

Some books are easy to write. This, my friends, was not one of those books. This book was hard as hell. In fact, at times I wondered if this book was ever going to happen at all. The fact that it did and that it's now in your hands is a testament to the faith and hard work of several people, first and foremost my fantastic and *very* patient editor, Krista Marino.

Thank you, Krista, for your enduiring faith in me over the last six years, for your keen editorial eye, and just, for everything. I'm incredibly grateful for all the hours (and hours) (and even more hours) you poured into this story and for your enabling me to cowrite two other books along the way. You're amazing. And to Lydia Gregovic, a fantastic editor in her own right, who provided invaluable feedback and support throughout: Thank you so very much.

I'm very, very lucky to work with a wonderful team at Delacorte Press and Random House Children's Books, which includes RHCB President Barbara Marcus, Delacorte Press Publisher Wendy Loggia, Judith Haut, Gillian Levinson, Emma Leynse, Tamar Schwartz, Shameiza Ally,

Colleen Fellingham, and Ken Crossland. Thank you all so much.

The cover of this book is absolutely incredible (I mean, right? It's goreous), so I have to do a special shout-out to cover designer Liz Dresner and cover artist Sasha Vinogradova! I literally gasped the first time I saw it. I love it so much.

To Andrea Morrison, my agent, whose advice and encouragement is always on point. I'm so grateful to have you in my corner and for all your support along the way.

And to Hayley Burdett Wilmot at Writers House, and to Olivia Burgher and Hilary Zaitz Michael at WME: Thank you.

To my family: Joel and Mary Ann Lawson. Tori and Nick. James, Millie, and Ella. (Ella: I WILL name a character after you someday, I promise!!) Joel and Kate. Harper and Smith. Joanne and Joel. Ida. Shannon and JC. Ryan and Syd. Kristen and Levi. Bode, Logan, Cori, and Casey. I love you!

To my friends who let me steal various parts of their names for this book: Meghan O'Hair, Stephanie Cheng, Taylor Billingsley, Avantika Chakravorty, Elle Patout (who also read this early and was oh so encouraging!), and Kathleen Glasgow (you made me write a book without you—rude—so of course I had to get you in there somehow). I also have to shout out Jeff Bishop (where in the world are you right now!?) or he'll be mad at me. And to all my other friends in various parts of the world: I love you all.

My sister's tennis team, who were all so enthusiastic and supportive of *The Agathas* and its sequel, need a paragraph unto themselves. Thank you all so much for spreading the word about my books.

To Nicole Musgrove & family: I hope you enjoy seeing Jamal Gallant in print!

Asking other authors to blurb your book is always . . . anxiety inducing (to say the least), and so I appreciate those who took the time out of their busy schedules to say nice things about *Murder Between Friends.* I am happy to return the favor at any time.

To the exclamation point: I am sorry for overusing you and then having to go back and delete you from whatever I'm writing. You deserve better from me. From us all, really. To the phrase "I mean" and the word "muttered" (which I still can't spell correctly even though I write it at least once a day)—I'm overly dependent on you both and I want you to know that I'm trying to do better.

I must acknowledge the laziest assistants in the world (aka my cats), who are so cute and distracting and sleep all day long and step on my computer and . . . wait a second. You're fired!!

On a less joyful note, while I was writing these acknowledgments, someone very special to my family passed away, and I would be remiss if I didn't mention him here. Bobby Kowit, we will miss your humor, your laugh, your encouragement, your brilliance, and . . . well. You.

And last but not least, as always, to Reed & Jackson. I love you times a billion trillion (infinity plus one).

ABOUT THE AUTHOR

Liz Lawson is the *New York Times* bestselling coauthor of *The Agathas* and its sequel, *The Night in Question* (with Kathleen Glasgow), and *The Lucky Ones*. Liz lives with her family and two *very* bratty cats.

lizlawsonauthor.com